To Myrtle—
thanks for reading!
Robin Carrig
2007

A
Place To Call
Home

Robin Carrig

PublishAmerica

Baltimore

First printing

ISBN: 1-4137-0410-7
PUBLISHED BY PUBLISHAMERICA, LLLP
www.publishamerica.com
Baltimore

Printed in the United States of America

This book is dedicated to my father, who passed along a love for history and reading; and to my mother, who always told me to finish what I start.

Special thanks to Jeri Newman for her encouragement and to all my friends at the Mary Lou Johnson/Hardin County District Library in Kenton, Ohio, for their help in finding materials I needed for research.

Chapter One

October, 1893

Maura heard it before she saw it and it startled her.

Pacing in front of the school where she had lived half her life and where she had taught for the last six years, she was afraid the sound she had heard was her new traveling skirt catching and ripping on one of the many rusty nails poking out of the plank board sidewalk. But when she stood still, the noise continued and drew her attention a few feet away to a collection of dry maple leaves skittering down the length of the walkway toward her.

She watched one noisily bounce end over end along with the others, then finally break away and shoot across the walk, coming to an abrupt stop against the carpetbag by her feet. It had been quite some time since even a drop of rain had fallen in western Ohio. Not unusual, really, and Maura recalled the old saying that if one didn't like the weather in Ohio they should just wait a moment and it would change.

Maura bent to take a closer look at the leaf and instinctively knew that when she touched it, the leaf could disintegrate in a hundred, dry brown shards. She took it gingerly into her fingers and appreciated the veins that reached out like so many branches of the tree the leaf had fallen from. Then in a moment of frustration, she slowly closed her hand around the leaf, crushing it without mercy. Maura reversed the motion and watched the brittle fragments pour out of her palm like grains of sand and disappear with the autumn wind. "That's how I feel," she said to herself. "As if I am being torn to pieces."

Maura looked again at the school building. It was the smallest structure on the old Allen County infirmary property - the place she had been brought to when she was 11 years old, after her parents and younger brother had succumbed to an outbreak of malaria. Even as a young child, Maura had thought the disease had too exotic a name to have been rampant in the plain, simple towns of western Ohio, but the sad fact of the matter was, hundreds of nameless people had died before it had touched her little family.

A painfully shy girl, Maura Cieran O'Brien had been unceremoniously deposited on the doorstep of the infirmary by the landlord of the apartment building her family had lived in. Coming from a close-knit, loving family, her memories were filled with hugs, the scents of cinnamon and vanilla from her mother, and pipe tobacco and coal from her father who worked in the nearby railroad yard. Those memories were faded by years of disinfectant and cold winter days spent alone on her bunk, no family to distract her from the reality of the bitter west winds.

It was during those youthful days of innocence before her family was taken that her own life characteristics were formed. "Organization," her mother would say, "Is the key to a happy life." Living in a small apartment, Maura's mother, Shannon, had insisted upon cleanliness and order in her home, including not only her two children in the work, but her hardworking husband as well. Maura's father, Sean, hadn't minded that the rules applied to him, even though his fellow workers at the shop teased him for his "henpecked" ways. They rarely lifted a finger around their homes and Maura knew that their homes had shown that. She also knew that her proud Papa had enjoyed coming home to orderly rooms, free from clutter and the dust of dry summer days.

Memory can play tricks, cause pain, or it can comfort, and for Maura, her memories of those days lived in her heart in the same way she had lived in her parents' home - tucked lovingly and securely in their own spot. At times, it had been painful to remember, but Maura found a sweet comfort in the pain - knowing that, at least one time in her life, she had been loved.

Maura could count on one hand the number of friends she had made during her stay at the infirmary's children's home. She had preferred her own company and the companionship of the few books that lined one wall in the administrator's office. Too many children had come to the home as orphans and gone on to other families and she had remained in her solitude rather than lose someone close again. "People come and go, but a story will always stay with you," her father had told her one night, as he put her to bed.

He had just told the tale of a sailor who loved a mermaid so much he would rather die than give her up. It was Maura's favorite and she had made him tell it again and again as she grew up. Later, she had been surprised when she recalled each and every word after her father was gone - and she could almost smell the sea salt and hear her father's voice again as she remembered the story.

Maura didn't know why she had never been chosen by another family. Perhaps younger children had been wanted but she had not fit the mold. Perhaps girls were considered too frail for farm work. Or perhaps, she thought unhappily, "They just didn't want me". She preferred not to think about that and in any event, she had early on accepted her lot and filled her days with reading and helping the other children. The home's administrator, Homer Wallace, had taken an interest in Maura and gave her encouragement when he found that not only could she read and write well and had a talent with numbers, but she also had a gift for passing her knowledge on to others.

One of those orphans she had spent many hours tutoring was the reason she stood on the sidewalk today. Although she was at least seven years younger than he, Maura had helped a boy named James Cole get enough education to join the U.S. Army, where he made his way quickly through the ranks to a captaincy. She remembered James as a handsome young man, though perhaps, a bit self-centered and troubled by his lot in life. His choice of career had surprised everyone, including Maura, due to the fact that, while he lived at the home, James had seemed at war with the world and had been labeled a discipline problem, not caring to listen to teachers or authority figures who would try to tell him what to do.

At the time, Mr. Wallace had assigned James to Maura as a last resort, warning her that should James give her any trouble she was to report it immediately and their tutoring sessions would cease. But Maura's quiet assurance had proven to be a calming influence on him instead, and he had soon buckled down to learn his letters and sums and before he left, had even thanked her for her aid.

Her success with James had led to her ultimate choice to make education her career and she was rewarded with the teaching position when the former instructor had taken a post elsewhere, just shy of Maura's 18th birthday. At that time she was one of the oldest children at the home, all others usually leaving for work or homes of their own, well before her age.

The crumpled letter from James was in the right pocket of Maura's heavy wool coat and as she fingered the smooth envelope and thought about its contents, she wondered for the umpteenth time whether she was doing the right thing by agreeing to James' request in the letter. Unexpectedly, and rather eloquently, he had placed pen to paper and outlined reasons why Maura should leave the school and head to the turbulent west to become his wife.

Current events had always been a part of her classroom, so Maura had read the sensational reports about the warring Indians and the attacks on white people - male and female - but she had also heard about the Army's massacre of innocents not so long ago at a place called Wounded Knee - all combining for another point of confusion. These people had been fighting for years for their way of life, for their land. It was something she could understand, even if others could not. But the thoughts of war continued to nag her - Would she be safe, not only on her journey, but once she arrived? And if so, at what cost to others?

Maura had looked into her past and recalled the ill treatment her own people, the Irish, had endured since coming to America. Taunts about her red hair had been prevalent and the heavy accents of her parents who had come from the homeland hoping to make a new beginning had rubbed off on Maura. Her accent was not so thick as theirs, but the jeers from others hurt her tender young heart. She knew from experience that being different was cause enough for some to make fun or even to kill.

One of her father's friends who had made the trip with him had been severely beaten and left for dead - only because of his heritage. Protecting her own was something Maura could relate to as well. But she disliked the killing from either side of the issue and was, perhaps rather selfishly, afraid for her own safety in the midst of the fray. But, as if to anticipate her concerns and allay her fears, she recalled that James had written confidently, "Most of the Indians are contained on their reservations anyway, although I will not lie to you - there is a band of renegades on the loose in our area, attacking innocent travelers, but I have no doubt we will apprehend them long before your arrival. And after all, Maura, you will be with soldiers of the United States Army. There are none better. You will be safe. You have my word."

Maura felt inside the pocket and pulled the letter from its resting place. The first several pages of the missive were devoted to James' descriptions of his life in the new state of South Dakota - a life that he was inviting her to join. His descriptions of sunsets over the grassy plains, the wildlife that Maura could never hope to see otherwise, and the clear water at the place where the Missouri and Cheyenne rivers met, made her yearn to touch the colors of the sky and place her toes in the icy waters.

Picking her way through the letter (she could almost picture him, head bent, an unruly lock of dark brown hair falling over his forehead, his left hand holding the pen at an odd angle as he wrote), she found the one particular section she had read over and over.

"You know, dearest Maura," James wrote, "that I always thought highly of you during our time together at the home. You have remained in my thoughts because you were ever the only person to make my dreary life bearable. You took my ranting with a grain of salt and gave me back tenfold. I wish you were here to do the same now – only, as my wife. You, my dear, must be quite aware that you have no one to hold you there. Be an adventurer! Join me out in the Dakotas and help me again, why don't you? We will work together, so that I may move even higher in rank. A grand opportunity will be arising for me soon. Our fort is scheduled for abandonment. No, my dear, we won't leave you here. That just means we will move on to another fort, possibly further west in Wyoming, but I have every reason to believe that I will be chosen to lead the detachment that will remain behind to oversee things until the fort is handed over to a school teacher for the nearby reservation. This will be my chance to show my mettle and leadership skills. I won't lie to you - in the Army, we move around a great deal and you will be left to your own devices from time to time while I am assigned to outside duty, but I have no doubt in my mind that you, my dear, would make the perfect Army wife - you are organized, intelligent and, I'm sure, will prove to be a wonderful hostess. Everything that would aid me to attain my desire."

He had continued with other pleas, but concluded the missive with his final request. "Please say yes, won't you? Give yourself some time to think about it, but write back, as soon as you possibly can and let me know what you decide. We can make arrangements for your travel at that time, but don't take too long, as the Dakota winters can be too harsh for traveling.

"I look forward to hearing from you with a positive answer to my request. Your fervent admirer, James."

Maura held on fast to the letter as a sudden gust of wind threatened to pull it from her fingers. She had been holding it tightly anyway as she read it for what seemed to be the hundredth time. It was a less than romantic way to obtain a husband, but then, Maura had never experienced romance in her life, though she did faintly recall the little things her parents would do for each other and their loving manner toward each other before they were taken from her.

"Romance isn't everything," she reminded herself with a sigh, "and besides, James does compliment me in his letter and I'm sure I'll find that as we spend time together and get to know each other again, some affection will grow between us. I hope so, anyway."

The picture of a loving family formed in her mind and gave her hope for a life, which did not include the incessant loneliness that had been hers for quite some time now.

"Besides, my dear," James had written, "As my commander's wife said, at your age and under the circumstances, you have few choices open to you for a future. You must grasp life while you may."

"Humpf," Maura sighed, remembering. "I really don't think I'm going to like that woman."

But the opinions of others had never really weighed heavily in any of the decisions Maura had made during her life and so it was that the adventurous side of her had eventually won out. And, she admitted to herself, it did sound exciting to help settle the new state. Maura felt certain that putting her trust and her life in James' hands was the best thing she could do.

Besides, she had even gone through a wedding by proxy of sorts. James had insisted that Maura do so, and though he had given no reason for it, she felt it was a way for him to protect her. She had felt silly, though, with Mr. Wallace standing in James' place, as the home's chaplain read the vows and she answered. It was hard to even picture the man who should be standing there, but James had assured her that they would have a real wedding soon after her arrival. She did not feel married, and though she had gone along with his request, she did not wish to call herself James's wife. Not yet, at least.

Maura sighed and turned toward the street, searching through the growing number of passing conveyances for Mr. Kettler's milk wagon, which would take her to the railroad station and the first leg of her journey to her new life in the west. Her train would take her to Fort Wayne, Indiana, and on to Chicago, then west to Omaha, Nebraska. From there she would travel by stage and freight wagon to her final destination.

In a moment of vanity, she reached into her reticule and pulled out a small, engraved silver compact (a going-away gift from Mr. Wallace). Opening it, she used the mirror to check the status of her hairpins, which she found to be firmly in place in her thick, shiny hair despite the wind.

Then still thinking about the reason for her journey, she used a critical eye to judge the face reflected back at her. It wasn't the prettiest one she had ever seen, but it did have some nice qualities. Her emerald green eyes were bright and framed by long lashes that feathered and softened her face. "It's a good face," she admitted to herself, but it wasn't one that any man would clamor toward. Despite that, she felt that with a little work, she could do James proud. He wouldn't be sorry that he had chosen her for his bride.

Maura was about to return the mirror to its place when a blurred reflection of movement caught her eye. Looking closer, she saw a small face pressed tight against the schoolhouse window glass behind her.

As she turned toward the building, a small patch of fog appeared on the pane as the child's warm breath met the cool glass. Then another patch formed, as another and yet another child's face peered out at her. Maura's heart clenched as she watched the Miller triplets appear. A tear parted the window fog and slid to the bottom of the glass in front of Hattie Miller. Bobby Miller eyed her, as little Victoria waved excitedly by his side.

The two Patterson boys, young Evan Tremain and his friend Dan Bardo, caught her eye as they stood in the next window, looking older and more in control.

"What a rainbow of emotions," Maura thought to herself. Each of the seven children before her exhibited his or her own personality variations and each and every one were her children. Not children of her body, but children of her heart. Her students. The one thing that was crushing her, just as surely as she had crushed the dry leaf. It was this she was having trouble dealing with in this move.

Goodbyes had always been hard for Maura and when she had said goodbye to her class the day before, she had placed a smile on her face and asked them to join in the excitement of her trip. She had promised to write and describe her journey step by step. She had asked them to pray for her and to work with their new teacher to follow her travels on the large wall map of the United States, which was located in the classroom. Surprisingly, Maura had managed to retain her composure throughout the ordeal. The children, however, had made no attempt to hide their feelings.

Some, like Hattie now, cried; others sat in stunned silence. Maura O'Brien was the only teacher some of them had known, and in several cases, was the only person who had ever offered a hug in comfort, a laugh for a joke they had made up, or a sympathetic ear when the loneliness proved too much for them to bear. She was the closest thing to love they had found in their young lives.

Parting from these children was the hardest thing that Maura had ever done, next to watching her parents and then her younger brother, end their suffering and pass on to the next world. The only thing that saved her was the other offer from James – that there was a possibility she could teach at a fort school for the children of the soldiers. The schools out west were desperately in need of teachers with her qualifications, he had explained. Maura felt certain that if she could continue in the field she loved, she would be able to make this move. Explaining that to these children, though, was impossible. So was saying goodbye.

Shaking her head, as if to clear the thoughts away, Maura acknowledged her fears about leaving, but she knew right now that if she didn't get moving soon, she'd miss the train to Fort Wayne and beyond. "Where are you Mr. Kettler?" she asked aloud, thinking that do so would conjure him before her to take her away.

But before that happened, she knew that she had to say goodbye one more time to those seven natural wonders in the windows.

To the Miller triplets, three kisses pressed against each nose. To the Pattersons, a look that stopped their crying and made them laugh. To Dan Bardo, a tip of her prim, laced hat, and finally, to Evan, a hand placed to mirror his own on the glass.

In each case, no words were exchanged; none were needed.

Maura likened pulling her hand away from the window to trying to separate a magnet from steel. Finally, she wrenched it away, placed her fisted hands against her heart, and then raised them open toward the children, signaling her love for them. As she did so, she heard the wooden wheels of Mr. Kettler's wagon scrape against the walk and his friendly shout of greeting. "Maura girl, are ye ready?" Maura quickly turned, grabbed her carpetbag and ran toward the street, hopping into the wagon before it even came to a complete stop.

"Please go, Mr. Kettler," she begged, and could not force herself to look back through her blinding tears.

Chapter Two

The trip by rail was a little less than the thrilling ride she had envisioned, Maura decided. Having grown up watching her father at work on the great engines in need of repair, she was familiar with, and unafraid of, the travel time she would be spending on the Chicago & Erie line. However, she had had insufficient funds to purchase a space in the more elite private car, and was forced to endure the thundering snores and less than hygienic personages of her railcar seat mates from Lima to Fort Wayne.

Suffering an irritating first few hours on her journey, Maura happily noted that many of those taking up space in her car were departing at the station in Indiana. But her glee was soon replaced by dismay as after the short stop, more than twice as many people embarked on the journey to Chicago, thereby increasing the approaching nighttime decibels to those of battlefield cannon proportions. That, compounded with seats less comfortable than those she had ever endured in her schoolroom, and cool night air sneaking between the wooden floor boards; Maura could only wonder what conditions she would face during the next leg of her journey.

"Chi-ca-go! Approaching, Chi-ca-go!" the conductor cried, as the train rumbled closer to the Lake Michigan shore. After spending the last few hours crushed between the side of the railcar and the bony side of an elderly woman, who seemed to take every opportunity to jab her elbow into her companion's side, Maura's outlook was revived by the words of the conductor. She was enthralled by the sights that met her eyes after she used her sleeve to wipe the glass and craned her neck to see out the window of her car. She would have almost 24 hours to explore the largest city she had ever seen, as her train to Omaha would not depart until the next day.

Gathering her things as the train slowed, Maura rummaged through her bag for the name of the rooming house James had suggested that she stay in. Finding the address, she stopped the conductor and asked if he was familiar with the city. "Quite so, miss," he said. "This be my hometown, it is. Grew up here and when I leave, I always come back." He checked her paper and found, to Maura's delight, that the street was not far from his own home. "A right nice establishment you'll be in, Miss. If you'll wait just a bit while I get me gear and finish up me work, I'll be happy to escort you there meself, medear. Wouldn't want anythin' happenin' to a fine Irish gel such as yerself, when yer not used ta bein' in the big city."

Maura beamed as she collected her bag and made her way off the train. She found an empty spot on one of the benches in the station where she patiently waited for the conductor, who had introduced himself as Jedidiah Jewell. She recognized this as a good time for people-watching, which was one of her favorite pastimes. She watched as the ladies in fine hats, gloves and beautiful, frilly, traveling outfits clung to the arms of their gentlemen, as they left the station for places throughout the city. Maura thought, "One day quite soon, I will be on James' arm as we travel. I will never have to go anywhere alone again."

Her thoughts were suddenly disrupted by the arrival of her escort. "Well, are ya ready to see the sights?" Mr. Jewell asked, as he stepped toward her. "Oh, yes!" Maura answered, jumping up to retrieve her things and the pair set off for the rooming house.

Maura's eyes widened and shone brightly, as she stepped briskly through the streets of Chicago. To her utter delight, the conductor suggested taking the "scenic route" and began pointing out some highlights of the city. The streets were so crowded with morning traffic – horses and buggies, freight wagons and pedestrians crossing in between, that the sight caused Maura's stomach to jump. "My goodness, Mr. Jewell," Maura said, "Never have I seen so many people! Where do they all come from, and where could they all be going?"

"Well, Maura, some could be goin' ter work in the Union Stock Yards, tradin' in that fancy stock market or workin' the rails just like me. And some of 'em might be visitors what come to town, just to see the wonders at what they're callin' the Columbian Exposition. Now that's somethin' yer ought to be seein' while yer here. It's right eye-poppin', with electrical lights that light up the outdoors at night like it was noon!"

"My goodness!" Maura exclaimed. Electricity had been something that other people had – the school and infirmary couldn't afford such luxuries, so she had studied by the light of her solitary hurricane lamp.

After arriving at the rooming house, which Maura was pleased to see, was quite clean and neat as a pin, she settled in, removing her traveling suit and sponging off, using the water in the pitcher on the dresser. Then finding she was a bit tired after her adventures, Maura lay down on the feather mattress for what she planned to be a short nap. She was to dine with the Jewell family that evening, and then later, they were to take a walk to look at the lights.

Maura was surprised when she saw that the room was turning dark by the time she awakened. "Oh my goodness, I'll be late!" she cried, and quickly donned her suit and headed out the door.

Following the conductor's careful directions, Maura arrived at their doorstep, but before she could grab the knocker, the door was opened and she was pulled inside. Though a stranger to the entire family, Maura found the Jewell home to be a welcoming place, with Mrs. Jewell a fantastic cook and the children, Maurice, Ross and Amelia, a delight. After dinner, the little entourage took off on foot, so Maura could see even more of the city.

As they neared the exposition, the night sky glowed brightly over the city's tall buildings. Finally, the exposition's administration building came into view, as did what seemed to be, a million lightning bugs gathered around to show off the display. "Oh, Mr. Jewell," Maura exclaimed, and then finding she was holding her breath, she exhaled slowly. "It's the most beautiful sight I've ever seen." And it was one she would remember for a very long time. The lights drew the small party toward the displays like a moth to a flame and they stopped here and there to see all there was to see. Caught up in the excitement of the evening, Maura could not believe that their time together was gone so soon, when Mr. Jewell announced it was time to return home and get the children back in bed. At the doorstep, he sent his family inside after hugs all around and offered to escort Maura back to her night's lodging.

Gratefully accepting his arm, the pair made their way, in what seemed now to be, relative darkness and when it came time to say goodbye, Maura was suddenly struck with anxiety and was loathe to part from the comfort of a familiar face.

After what seemed a sleepless night, Maura headed back to the station and boarded a train for the trip to Omaha, Nebraska. Though the trip was long, it was never boring and if her seat was uncomfortable, she didn't notice, as she enjoyed speaking with her seat mate, a middle-aged gentleman, also heading to the Dakotas.

"Of course, I've been there before, you know," William Shakley explained. "It's a beautiful place – God's country, really, with the land so different from one end to the other. There's the grass prairies and what they call the Badlands and then there's the Black Hills." After a while, Mr. Shakley reached into one of his bags and pulled out a strange-looking, black leather-covered box with several holes in it. Maura eyed it curiously, and then searched her companion's face for an explanation.

"I've a photographic studio of my own back home," he explained, "but I'm planning to use this new box camera to record my journeys in the west from start to finish. Going to share the beauty I've seen with my friends in the east." Shakley was quiet for a moment, and then asked, "Have you ever been somewhere, miss, and felt a deep connection with the land – such as you'd been there before, maybe even lived there before in another life? That's how I feel about the Dakotas. Right in here, it's my home," he said, laying his fist on his heart.

"That's how I hope to feel about it," Maura answered. "After all, I'll be living there for quite some time." Fascinated by the box camera Mr. Shakley held, she asked if she could take a closer look. "I've seen cameras before, but never one this small. And where is the stand and the black hood?"

"You don't need either one anymore, miss, thanks to Mr. Eastman in New York. He made this camera so that people such as yourself could take pictures of their everyday life and sights they see without any trouble at all. Why, you can take 100 photographs on a roll of film, send the camera back to the company and get the photographs returned to you in no time, along with a fresh roll of film loaded into your camera for you. I have a studio back home containing the large equipment you're thinking of, but on this trip I decided I wanted to try out this newfangled piece of machinery."

"Amazing," Maura said. "I would be pleased to see your photographs some day, Mr. Shakley."

"I hope you shall, my dear. I hope you shall."

The pair continued their conversation well into the first evening of the trip and were surprised to find that they had both opted to take a stagecoach north into South Dakota rather than risk the approaching winter waters of the Missouri River.

They traveled in companionable silence or commented excitedly about some passing scenery, until upon arriving in Omaha several days later, the pair headed to the stage office where they would board the coach that would take them to their destination. As luck would have it, their timing could not have been much better, as a stage would be picking up passengers for the northern climes the next day.

Though quite tired, Maura preferred to use the reprieve from travel to take a relaxing bath in a hotel room. She vigorously brushed out her thick red hair until it gleamed, then took a quiet stroll along neighboring streets, while her friend took advantage of the local barber for a quick shave and haircut. They came together again that evening to enjoy a hearty meal, then separated to rest up for the next part of their trip. As the sun broke free of the horizon the next day, Maura and her new friend greeted their four fellow passengers, and the coach pulled away with a jolt and a cloud of dust, to bear them away from the Nebraska city.

The combined weight of the passengers and traveling gear didn't seem to faze the animals pulling the stage in the least, and for each mile the horses propelled the coach along, Maura swore she could feel every stone and every crack in the trail. "My bottom will never be the same," she thought to herself, and immediately raised an eyebrow and grinned, thinking what the others would think of her, had she said that aloud.

"Well, it's true," she added, and consoled herself by repeating, "It will be over before I know it. It will be over before I know it. I should feel lucky I don't have to walk."

She was hard pressed, however, to consider the coach as a modern convenience and a true blessing on her journey, with its horsehair seats disguising springs that lurked none too far from the surface. Maura couldn't help herself and occasionally found an excuse to wiggle around to try to find a more comfortable location, as the wires hit her wrong with every bounce of the wheels.

"Dagnabbit!" howled old Mr. Jenkins, seated across from the photographer. His fuzzy head had taken another hit, as he bounced high off the seat and was stopped by the ceiling of the coach. "Damn stage driver is tryin' to knock me senseless. A'course, that might not be such a bad idea. I'd miss the rest of this gol' darn ride!"

Maura giggled as she listened, and her reaction made the other passenger smile despite his sore head.

"Here we go agin!" Mr. Jenkins yelled, as he flew high in the air for the umpteenth time when a wheel hit a sizeable rock, but this time, instead of plopping back in his seat, he landed across the aisle in the lap of the rather rotund woman sitting next to Maura.

"Land's sakes! Get off me you oaf! Keep to your side of the stage! You did that on purpose, just so you could put your hands on my person, didn't you? Didn't you?"

As Mr. Jenkins attempted to right himself and deny the accusation, the woman held up her hand and as she did so, the sunlight caught on one of the many diamond rings that Maura believed had to have been placed on her fingers long before, when they were slimmer.

"No use denyin' it. I won't believe it anyway."

Mr. Jenkins settled back into his seat as best he could, and sighed.

"I don't know why they have to go so fast, anyway," the woman said. "It seems to me that they could slow this down a little and still make good time."

"I hear tell they're trying to avoid Injuns," the man sitting to the right of Mr. Jenkins said. "The stage master told me at the last stop that there's been some trouble from here on north lately. Seems a band of renegades that belong on the reservation have been attacking innocent people."

"Oh, my Lord," Maura said, only half as an epithet, but more as a prayer. She was within several hundred miles of her new life. Nothing could happen now, could it?

No one seemed to want to comment further after that, perhaps believing that to speak aloud would make the attackers materialize.

To keep her mind on other things, Maura helped Mr. Shakley keep watch out the small windows, to catch a glimpse of interesting people at the stations and native flora and fauna nearby, to add to his growing collection of photographs on the roll.

As the pair conversed and spied likely subjects, one of the other passengers, who had been conspicuously quiet the entire trip thus far, unobtrusively eyed Maura and her friend.

Lounging as best he could in a corner of the coach, the man, dressed in a dark suit, crisp white shirt and polished black boots, drew no notice from the pair, as they continued to talk and laugh. He appeared at first glance to be an average, though fashionably dressed traveler by current standards. A closer look, however, revealed that his jet-black, shiny hair was quite long and tied at the back of his neck in a cord. If anyone had cared to examine him closer, they would have realized that his darker skin was not the result of time spent in the sun, but of heritage. And had they dared to ask about the bone and bead choker around his neck, he would have told them it was none of their business.

Joseph Walks Alone believed he had probably not even earned a second look from the red-haired woman and her friend, and he envied their camaraderie and closeness. He envisioned the two as lifelong friends or even as lovers, never dreaming they had only just met days before. He did eventually rate second, third, and even fourth glances and finally sneers from the largest of the coach's passengers, however, and he waited for what was to come.

Finally, having his fill of the looks of disdain from the portly woman, squeezed into a food-stained wrinkled satin dress in the seat opposite him, and tired of biting his tongue, as he listened to her critical comments she did not even attempt to disguise, Joseph raised an eyebrow and leaned forward. The time had come. "You heap big squaw," he said. "Make fine second wife," and he almost choked on the words.

"Oh! How dare you! I knew you was one of them ungrateful dirty Indians. Why they let your kind on the stage with good folks like us is beyond me. Look at you, dressed in some poor white man's clothes. I'm going to complain to the stationmaster when we arrive, that's what I'm going to do. Why my husband is in the Army and I know for a fact that your kind is being fed and clothed by the United States government for free. If it weren't for us, you'd starve and freeze to death. You can obviously pretty yourselves up, but civilized you are not!"

Joseph looked directly into her small, bloodshot eyes and calmly said, "Oh, I beg to differ, madam. I believe 'my kind' fed and clothed themselves very well, thank you, for generations before 'your kind' was even brave enough to make the journey across the Atlantic. Now 'your kind' are killing my people by taking away their way of life."

Continuing in an even tone, Joseph pointed out, "Just so that you are aware, I purchased my suit from one of the finest clothiers in Washington, D.C. But one look at you tells me that no food was taken from your mouth in order to give an Indian child a mealy sack of flour, and though 'my kind' wear ill-fitting clothing forced upon them by the government, I think if the same people clothed you, you would probably look much better in Army issue than you do in that unsightly frock."

"Oh! How dare you! Speak to me again and I will report you to the nearest authorities," the woman screamed, fanning herself wildly and turning sideways in her seat, much to the chagrin of the cramped pair sitting with her.

The initial exchange between the two had been enough to pull Maura's attention away from the window and after the final comment, she was able to catch Joseph's eye. Her own eyes twinkled and she unsuccessfully attempted to suppress a wide grin. Joseph winked at her, settled back into his seat, crossed his arms, stretched his legs, and closed his eyes.

Maura smiled to herself and returned her gaze out the window as the Nebraska countryside flew by. She hadn't really thought much about the man in the opposite corner before, but his speech had intrigued her. He was unlike anyone she had ever met in her sheltered life. Not only was he the first Indian she had ever seen, but also he was not at all as she had pictured one, having read many newspaper accounts of western life and warfare and several old dime novels she had borrowed from Mr. Wallace. He was very witty, and bore handsome features that showed great strength.

It was his eyes, however, that told a story without need of words. They were very dark, and there was a sadness about them. But when he had been chastising the woman, those same orbs revealed a spark of mischief.

"Perhaps it's just that he's so different. I'm sure I shall see many more natives as I make my way across this land," she thought, returning her attention to Mr. Shakley, who was pointing out a herd of antelope.

All in all, she thought, the journey so far had proven pleasant, the landscapes ever-changing and the people they met so friendly that Maura could not believe when they arrived at the Army outpost that the time had gone by so quickly. James had arranged for a military supply wagon to await Maura's arrival, before setting out with its load of goods for the soldiers at Fort Sully. Just this last leg of her journey and she would be with James, a thought that both pleased and frightened her.

"What if I've made the wrong decision, Mr. Shakley?" she asked, while nervously waiting for the corporal to load the wagon. "How could I have ever considered this to be a good idea?" After a thoughtful moment, the photographer took Maura's hands in his and looked into her eyes. "My dear, as we've spoken this past week, I feel as if I've known you for years and so I feel comfortable saying this to you. I believe you never would have begun your journey had you not felt deep in your heart that it was the right thing for you to do. You are a woman who does not make decisions lightly and I know you considered this long and hard. Your future is in South Dakota, Maura, where love awaits. After all, who could not possibly adore you?"

"Oh, Mr. Shakley, what will I do without you? I've so enjoyed your friendship. I'm not sure that I can bear to lose you."

"I am happy to hear you say that Maura, as you will have to continue to endure my presence, my dear," he announced. "I've just come from purchasing a fine piece of horseflesh that I intend to ride alongside your wagon. Dangers abound so there's safety in numbers, you know. But if you don't see me now and again, you'll know I've stopped to photograph something that's caught my eye!"

Maura's smile would have rivaled the bright lights of Chicago. "I'll keep watch for you along the way!" she said, then thinking to herself, realized that Mr. Shakley was the first person she had claimed friendship with since she was a young girl. "I'm so glad he will continue to be in my life, if only for a few days more," she said, hugging herself and looking straight ahead as the wagon began the final miles toward her new life.

At the same time, Joseph led his own newly purchased horse from the corral. He'd had a hard time convincing the young stable master that he should not be arrested for being off the reservation. Finally, he'd been forced to pull out the letter of introduction from his benefactor, something he had hoped he would not have to do. The letter, with its official seal, was ultimately sufficient to complete the sale – that, and an additional shiny new dollar thrown at the proprietor.

"Hey, mister!" the young man cried, as he ran after Joseph. "Don't you wanna buy a saddle, too? I got a right nice tooled leather one here, what came with a dead cowpoke stropped to it. Just has a little bloodstain on it, that's all. It'll clean up just fine."

"Thank you," Joseph replied, "but I don't think I'll be needing it." He smiled at the young man's quizzical look, turned, and took a deep breath. "It is time to remember," he said to himself, exhaling slowly and pulling his body easily onto the animal's bare back.

Letting the smooth leather of the reins slide through his fingers, Joseph decided that it felt good, and savoring the warmth of the horse's flesh between his legs and the breeze blowing his face, he gave the animal's neck a rub and spoke softly into its ear. "I will know your name later. For now, we will just learn from each other." With a loud "Heya!" Joseph nudged the sides of his horse and gripped them tightly with his thighs, as they raced through the tall grasses of the rolling prairie. He did not even notice when the wind took the leather thong from his hair and allowed it to blow free.

Chapter Three

"How long have you been in the Army, Corporal Wyatt?"

"About five months, Miss Maura. Right now, with the Indians quiet on the reservations, I have the most important job there is – bringing supplies to the men at the fort. Everybody misses me and everybody is always happy to see me when I come back."

"I'm looking forward to seeing Fort Sully, corporal," Maura said. "And, I must admit, I'm a little afraid as well."

"Oh, shucks, you ain't got nuthin' to be ascared of, Miss Maura. Why Captain Cole is right excited to see you agin. He even made special sure that I come here a couple days ago so I'd be here waitin' to bring you straight to him when you arrived at the post. I think that's a right thoughtful thing to do, and best you know it – it's not somethin' he'd do for just any ol' body."

"I know you're right, sir, and my next question will sound rather strange coming from the woman who is to marry him, but what is James, er, Captain Cole really like? Like you said, he seems very thoughtful but it has been many years since we have seen one another," she admitted.

"You'll get along fine with him, miss," the corporal said. "He's very serious about keeping his men safe and doing his duty and I know he's gonna look out for you right fine."

"I understand there are other women at the fort," Maura continued.

"Yes'm, that's right. Let's see, there's the commander's wife, and, well, I probably ought'n be tellin' you this, but her nose couldn't get any higher in the air than if'n it was the dang sun itself. Then, lessee, oh, yeh, there's Sgt.

Anderson's wife, she's right nice, and a couple others I don't know too well.

"There's even some kids too, miss. Maybe someday you'll have one of your own. Oh, sorry. That's kinda personal like. Well, to get back to Captain Cole, the past few months he's been trying his damndest, oh, sorry, Miss, he's been trying his best to catch ahold of a group of renegadin' Injuns that have been attacking stagecoaches and settlers out on their own. But they be slipperier than shit on ice, oh, sorry. They either got a good hidey-hole to lay low in or they can get back to the reservation and melt right in, miss – quicker than you can say buffalo chips."

Maura looked around nervously, as the wagon lumbered on the trail. "They wouldn't attack us, would they, Corporal Wyatt?"

"Oh, no, Miss. They know better'n to attack a U.S. Army wagon. Why the entire fort would swoop down on 'em and end their thievin', killin' ways. If'n they can catch 'em, a course. Ah, which they surely would do, Miss, no doubt about it. Yessiree. We're safer than a turtle in his shell in this here Army wagon."

"That is a relief to my mind, corporal," Maura noted, taking another look around, not only to reassure herself that there were no "renegadin' Injuns" but to try to locate the whereabouts of Mr. Shakley. "I haven't seen my friend for quite some time, Corporal Wyatt. I'm becoming a bit concerned." Earlier, they had made a precarious, but safe crossing of the White River and continued to head north with no sign of the photographer.

"Now don't you worry about a thing, Miss. Mr. Shakley seemed to me to know his ass from his head, oh, sorry, Miss. I just mean he seems to be wise to the ways of the land. I heard tell he's been in these parts before so he knows not to stray too far from us. Why, when we stop for some grub, I bet he'll be here lickety-split to partake of the victuals with us."

"I'm certain you're right, Corporal," Maura said.

The sun faded behind the clouds and the winds picked up to the point that Maura felt the need to take the buffalo robe out from under the seat of the wagon and wrap up tightly inside. "My goodness, the temperatures surely do change quickly around here, don't they?"

"Oh, Miss Maura, you ain't seen nothin'. Just you wait 'til summertime. Why I remember last June, when it was warm as hell during one afternoon and there was snow on the ground the next morning and we all froze our asses off, if'n you'll pardon the expression, Miss."

Maura brought the robe up closer around her face to block the chill. Her eyes scanned the horizon to watch the soft oranges and reds in the western sky. "Don't you think we should be stopping soon, Corporal Wyatt?"

"Yes'm. Just as soon as I spot a safe place for us to be. Hopefully, your friend, Mr. Shakley will be meetin' up with us. I'd hate ta think of him out on the prairie on his own at night."

"Yes, I was just thinking the same thing," Maura agreed. Enough light was left in the sky for her to observe what appeared to be a small cloud of dust. "Perhaps this is him heading our way," she observed. Corporal Wyatt turned his gaze toward the direction she faced. He slowed the wagon and pulled the reins toward his chest.

"Well, I suppose this is as good a place as any to stop," he said, jumping from the wagon near an outcropping of rock. "Let me unhitch the team and I'll help you unload the provisions. If you want, you could get some kindling out of that box of wood in the back, and I'll start a fire as soon as I'm done and maybe he'll be here by then."

Maura went around to the rear of the wagon, lifted the canvas top and peered into the darkness beneath. She pushed her carpetbag aside and looked for the spot where Corporal Wyatt had placed the kindling box after breaking camp earlier that day. Her eyes traveled over the large barrel of salt, several 100-pound bags of flour, several crates of canned goods and a large, bulky tarp. After eyeing the tarp the past several days, Maura could no longer contain her curiosity as to what was inside. She loosened the knots and pulled on the cords securing the ends. Carefully lifting the edge she saw the smooth, gleaming barrels of about two-dozen rifles. A cold chill settled in the back of her neck as she touched the steel. Quickly, she replaced the tarp, looked further and finally found the wood box, selected some kindling and several logs and carried them to a clear spot for a fire.

When Corporal Wyatt reached the area, a curious Maura asked, "Corporal, don't all of the soldiers at the fort already have their own weapons?"

"Well, yes'm," he replied. "Why do ya ask?"

"I saw rifles in the back of the wagon, and I wondered why they were there, that's all. Has there been trouble? Are more weapons necessary?"

"Don't you worry about a thing, Miss. The rifles was on the commander's list and they probably just need a few more to replace some old ones or some such."

"Oh, I see. Thank you, corporal."

Hoof beats made both of them turn their heads in the direction of the sound. Maura breathed a sigh of relief when she recognized Mr. Shakley on the back of the panting animal. "William! How glad I am to see you," Maura said. "Wherever have you been? I've been concerned for your safety."

"I'm so sorry, my dear. I was having such a wonderful time that I never noticed how late it was getting. I'm happy to report that I've spent the entire day with an Indian family in an encampment nearby. Apparently, we are either on or quite near the reservation lands. Which is it, Corporal?"

"Well, we're actually a bit south of the nearest one, sir. It starts over that ridge there. Hope them Injuns you saw was on the right side of it."

"Quite so, sir. I was scouting about when all of a sudden I spotted a few antelope. Hoping to be able to photograph them, I followed them for a time until what did I see but a congregation of tepees. I carefully approached them, and found that they were delightful families of what we call the Sioux people. We communicated by hand signals – sign language, some call it, as well as using some well-chosen words. We got on quite well, actually. They offered me a meal and even allowed me to take a number of fine photographs of their life. It wasn't until about an hour ago that I realized the day was coming to an end and I'd better take my leave and find the two of you. I was just about at the end of my roll of film anyway. I'll find a few things to photograph near camp in the morning, and then get out my other camera before we continue on our way. Oh, this has been a glorious adventure!"

Maura was pleased to see the happiness and excitement radiating from her friend and was now sorry that she had chastised him for his lateness. If she had the sense of adventure that he possessed, she, too could enjoy the sights of things she'd never before experienced. As it was, she was finding herself with an almost overpowering anxiousness – seeing all those rifles had started that, she knew, and although Corporal Wyatt had offered her a perfectly plausible explanation of their presence, she could not remove them from her thoughts.

The three enjoyed a pot of coffee and though Mr. Shakley declined a portion of the meal, since he had dined with the natives, the time spent in the fresh air had apparently caused Maura to work up a rather unladylike appetite and she dove into her plate of beans and biscuits, as if it were a meal from the finest of restaurants. After cleaning the dishes in a nearby creek and stacking them for the morning, Maura carefully removed her dress on the side of the wagon opposite the fire, draped it over a wheel and bedded down underneath the buffalo robe. She had found during the previous nights that that cover alone was quite sufficient to keep the night chills away. The two men stayed up watching the fire die and regaled each other with tales of the territory.

Maura thought she was dreaming of being back in Ohio when she heard what sounded to her like a large flock of Canadian geese communicating with each other as they flew across the sky. She sat up, disoriented, striking her head on the bottom of the wagon. Watching the sun just beginning to peek over the ridge, she was startled to see a group, not of geese, but of Indians whooping and riding hell bent for leather toward their camp.

"Corporal Wyatt! Mr. Shakley! Quickly!" she called and ran over to shake the men awake but their slumber was deep after their long night of talking.

The corporal grabbed his gun and threw another at the photographer, yelling "Hold your fire 'til we see what's happening, but from here it don't look good. When I fire, you fire."

"My thoughts exactly, my boy. I await your lead," Mr. Shakley said. It was hard to see what was happening in the shadowed lights of dawn but Maura could make out the lathering horses, flying jet-black hair and what she believed to be some sort of long sticks in the outstretched hands of the six or seven riders. "Git under that wagon, Miss Maura!" Corporal Wyatt ordered. "And don't you dare come out 'til it's me atellin' ya to!"

Maura scrambled underneath the wagon, and grabbing onto the spokes of a wheel, watched the scene unfold before her horrified eyes. What she had taken for long sticks were rifles and the Indians were now raising them toward the small camp.

"Fire!" The order came from Corporal Wyatt and the two men commenced a hale of bullets toward the approaching group. Maura could see that several had been hit, but not severely enough for them to drop from their horses and they continued to bear down on the trio, continually firing, until one of the deadly missiles hit Corporal Wyatt full in the chest. "No," Maura said, quietly to herself, then screamed, "No! No! No!" over and over, as Mr. Shakley's lifeless body fell sideways into the dust, blood and brain matter streaming from a massive wound to the head.

Shaking uncontrollably, Maura tried to crouch smaller and smaller, her mind not allowing her to fully comprehend the scene before her. As the Indians jumped from their horses, she attempted to quickly crawl behind a nearby outcropping, but the men easily spotted her movements. "Make sure they're dead," the one who appeared to be the leader ordered another. "I'll get the woman."

"No, no, no," Maura could not stop herself from crying or saying that one word over and over, as she watched the half-dressed man coming toward her. The light in the sky was still insufficient for her to make out many details of his face, as she backed away on her buttocks, using her arms to push herself away, as if she were rowing a boat across the sea. The man said nothing as he came up beside her and grabbed her by her hair and at the same time pulling out the largest knife that Maura had ever seen. She had heard tales of scalping and now imagined this fate for herself. Instead, he used her long hair as a rope, pulling her entire body weight along by it. As the rest of the Indians went through the wagon, the man yanked Maura toward the bodies of her friends.

Maura felt detached from the events taking place and was unable to utter a sound. She was actually afraid that if she did speak, it would come out as a scream that would not stop and that was something she could not allow to happen. The man looked down upon her with piercing blue eyes but still said nothing. Continuing to hold her hair with his right hand, he grabbed the front of her sleeping garment and ripped the bodice down the front, pushing her to the ground. The action finally woke Maura from her stupor. "No," she said again, but this time, more forcibly than before, and at the same time, began to fight back, hitting, scratching and biting as hard as she could. Finally, the man slammed his fist into her face, sending Maura backward into the outcropping of rock, where she struck the side of her head. As her world darkened, she heard a tearing sound, which reminded her of a dry leaf skittering across a wood plank walk. Then she heard no more.

Maura awoke minutes later with a sharp pain intensely piercing her temple and a stickiness between her legs but she was aware enough to know that the Indians were still in the camp. Trying to turn her head slowly, so as not to draw attention to herself, she witnessed them placing the last of the rifles on a packhorse.

As she turned the other way, she came face to face with what remained of Mr. Shakley. Controlling her emotions, she noticed his box camera lying on its side, very close to her right hand. Slowly, gliding her hand along the ground, she was able to move the apparatus slightly with her fingertips. Remembering that the photographer had mentioned there were only two, maybe three, frames left on the roll, she carefully maneuvered the equipment so that it faced the group of Indians. Unable to lift it in any manner, there was no way she could know what would appear in the frame, but she knew in her heart that she had to try.

Whispering the prayer, "Dear God, this is for Mr. Shakley," Maura did as she had seen the photographer do many times, pulling up on the beaded end of the pull on top of the camera to cock the shutter, then pushed the shutter button on the side. It seemed to her that it made a great deal of noise, but the men were too busy concentrating on what they were doing, to notice. Maura took one more photograph before the roll would no longer advance and she dropped her hand to the dirt, as the men mounted their horses and without a glance in her direction, rode off with their prizes. During her remaining moments of consciousness, Maura smoothed the dust back and forth with her hand, finally grabbing a handful and lifting it, until she could watch as she let it filter through the slits between her fingers, much like shards of crushed dry leaves on a sidewalk in Ohio.

Chapter Four

Joseph Walks Alone had not expected the homecoming he had received on the reservation, when he rode in several days before. He had not even been certain that there would be anyone to greet him upon his arrival, but word had spread quickly and his grandparents had been waiting for him. Joseph's parents had been killed at Wounded Knee Creek after participating in the Ghost Dances and now Joseph was here now to pay his respects to his grandparents, who had thankfully not made the long trip with Big Foot at that fateful time.

His grandparents were his only living relatives – relations that he had not seen since he had been forcibly removed from his family some 15 years before to "voluntarily" attend a school for Indians in the East. His departure then had been the last time he had seen his parents alive. On one hand, Joseph did not like to remember those days, but on the other, he felt he must keep those days with him and in his own way try to do something so that other young people did not have to experience the horrors that he had been forced to see.

Now, he was on top of a high ridge on the reservation land, respecting his heritage and at the same time, remembering the positive things that had come to him despite things over which he had not had control.

Joseph had spent the past day and a half with no food, deep in prayer and staring into the steel gray sky. He had thought himself in a dream when he saw two snakes sliding across the dirt before him. The larger reptile was ahead of the other smaller snake. Suddenly the second snake surprised Joseph by speeding forward and attacking the first, then coiled backward, and raising its head, struck the other one and held fast until it was dead. The Indian wondered at the significance of what he had seen, and knew he would have to seek out and question his grandmother about it.

It was at that moment his ears caught the faint sound of gun blasts in the distance. Knowing his own people would not be firing so frequently, he was curious to know what was going on. He did not want someone bringing danger to his family and friends and felt compelled to investigate. He had made the trip up the ridge on foot and so was forced to set out in the same manner.

He knew that the shots could be coming from several miles away and aimed his feet in the direction of the sounds, which by this time had faded away to silence. He continued, breaking into a run to make his way quickly. Crouching, he slowed his pace and knelt in the prairie grass as he came close to where he believed the shots had originated. He observed a small band of men riding at breakneck speed away from a camp where a large wagon could be seen. One horse within the group appeared to be rider-less and either carried its passenger over its back or was loaded with other cargo. He could not determine much more about the men from his distance.

When they were safely out of the way, Joseph straightened and made his way toward the wagon, keeping an eye on the band that left a swath of trampled prairie grass in its wake. He approached the camp warily, and called out, "Hello, the camp!" But no answer was returned. An eerie silence pervaded and Joseph stealthily circumnavigated the area. No sound, not even the song of a bird or the chatter of a prairie dog, could be heard. As he moved with the sun at his back, Joseph caught sight of a stockinged foot on the ground, and as he came closer, he could see that it belonged to a young man wearing military trousers. It was quite evident that the young man would not be serving his country ever again. Quite nearby, an older man lay on his left side, a large pool of blood soaking into the ground around his head. He, too, had breathed his last. There was something about the man that seemed familiar to Joseph, but with only a portion of his face remaining, his features were, for the most part, indistinguishable.

Then he saw it. The black box camera. Joseph had admired one like it on the stagecoach and it seemed incongruous to find such equipment dumped in the dirt in this camp. And lying right beside it, a woman's hand. Joseph knelt quickly among the rocks, grabbed the hand and was relieved to note that it was still warm and pink. Following the arm to the torso, neck and head, he found what he had been dreading. The two had been inseparable on the stage ride – it stood to reason that they had been together here. Blood seeped from a wound on the side of her head and her face showed black and blue. Her clothing was torn to shreds and blood was smeared between her legs, but the woman was alive. Since he had witnessed the exodus of the marauders, Joseph knew she had not lain here long, and he realized that he could not allow her to lie in the dirt much longer or she might join her two friends in their new heavenly home.

Looking around for anything that might come to his aid, he went to the rear of the wagon where the contents had been ransacked. A carpetbag lay on its side, and its contents, including women's clothing, was strewn about on the ground. Joseph found what he was looking for and after bending down to pick it up, he straightened, facing the interior of the wagon. He had no clear idea of what, if anything, may have been in the tarp inside, which now lay twisted on the wagon floor and he noted that there was a great deal of foodstuffs, some tools, and other items within. Heading back to the woman, Joseph ripped two large sections from the petticoat he had found and folded them into haphazard squares. He tore the remainder of the garment into strips and used those to hold the squares in place where they were needed most.

Returning to the wagon, Joseph pushed aside the barrels and rearranged the tarp, then reached under the wagon where he had spied a buffalo robe. Spreading it on top of the tarp, he returned to the woman. He lifted her gently, but the action was enough to elicit a small cry from her lips and he knew not whether it was one of physical or emotional pain, but he did not stop.

Placing her on the blankets, he jumped into the wagon to arrange them around her for the trip they must make. As he worked, her eyelids fluttered and opened wide, revealing what Joseph remembered would be a brilliant green, when it was not clouded by pain. The woman stared, took a tortured breath, and uttered one word, "No."

"Yes," Joseph replied.

Chapter Five

"He has brought another white into our camp. What will he do next? First the white man with the box comes, now Joseph brings this woman. Next time it may be more men. More white men who will tell us what to eat, what to wear, where to lay our head at night. He has only returned for two days and already he has endangered us, not only bringing the woman, but also, bringing her in an Army wagon! A wagon filled with food that would fill our children's bellies for weeks! But he will not allow us to touch it. He guards it with one eye, while he guards the woman with the other. There will come a time that his eyes will close, then we will see what happens."

"You talk too much, Two Hawks. Our Joseph knows what he does. The woman needs help quickly. She does not need your lips flapping. Go work in your field. Maybe getting behind the white man's plow will take some of that hate from you. You did not like Joseph when he was young. You do not like him still. That is what is behind all of this." Joseph's grandmother had never been afraid to speak her mind and she did not save her words from Two Hawks, who, unfortunately, was not through.

"Joseph!" Two Hawks spat the name from between his lips. "He holds a white man's name dear when he says he is here to remember the old ways. He should return to the name that was given to him long ago, not use the name given to him by the whites."

"Go, Two Hawks. My ears are tired of listening to you. Besides, you know he still holds 'Walks Alone' as part of his name. They did not take that away from him. There are many things they could not take away from him. He will show you, but in his own time. Now leave."

Two Hawks looked upon the woman with hatred in his eyes. He turned quickly and, lifting the flap of the tepee, entered the sunlight. "Joseph will regret the day he returned to our camp," he vowed. "I know not what will happen, but he will not like it."

Having ignored the exchange between his grandmother and Two Hawks, who had entered uninvited directly behind him, Joseph concentrated on the women who were administering to the red-haired woman. Ordinarily, he would have been told to leave as well, but he had insisted upon staying. He did not know what drew him to this woman, she was nothing to him, but something inside him would not let him leave her side. He had said nothing to his grandmother when he had brought the white woman into his grandparents' tepee. She had understood the moment she had seen his face, and after examining the woman, she had called in the others and deferred to their skill. If the woman could be saved, they would have the means to do so. If not, it was written long before.

Joseph felt the light touch of a hand on his elbow, as he stood within the structure. Knowing it was the wisest woman remaining in the camp, he leaned into her strength and felt it enter his own body. "My grandson, we must let them do their work. The woman will live without us here to watch, and if it is willed, she does not need us to die, either. Our presence does not guarantee her survival."

"I know, grandmother," Joseph admitted. "I wish to stay because I feel a need I do not understand."

"I understand," his grandmother said. "I have lived many years and I understand many things. This feeling will not leave, but we must."

"Yes, grandmother," Joseph said, and followed her from the tepee.

His grandfather sat outside on a hand-hewn bench, using a sharp stick to draw in the dust. "The woman?" he questioned.

"She is being taken care of," the older woman said.

"It is so," her husband said.

Joseph looked into the sky and noted dark clouds gathering. Soon, the sun would be no more. "We will soon have snow," his grandfather said. "The air grows colder and my bones grow more stiff, day by day."

"You will be dancing around us for many years yet, grandfather," Joseph said. "Of this I am sure, and because of this, I am happy. I have missed you these many years. We have lost much time."

"We have lost nothing, grandson. We have been together in spirit. Have you not felt our presence? Did you not think of our words and our family over the years?"

"Yes, grandfather," said Joseph, thinking back on his life. "I thought of you many times. Some days, no, but most days I called upon our talks to gain wisdom for the experiences I faced. I leaned upon you most heavily, grandfather."

"So that is why I am so bent," the older man exclaimed. "I thought it my age, but it was you."

Joseph's mouth curved upward at his grandfather's humor. "'Walks Alone' is not a name that suggests togetherness, is it?"

"My grandson, you know."

"Yes, but I need to hear the memories from someone else's lips, grandfather. Sometimes I wondered if what I remembered was real at all."

"The whites gave you the name Joseph. It is a good name. It is from their holy book. It is comes from a boy who is separated from his family, but grows into a great man who will help his people and return to his family. In many ways, you and that Joseph of old are much alike."

At this point, the grandfather grew quiet and appeared to watch the clouds. "You know you did not walk alone, my grandson."

"Yes, grandfather. This I know. Wakan Tanka was with me always, as were my beloved parents, as were you and my grandmother."

"What the whites who took you could not do was to translate your name as it should be. Our language is a mystery to them that they do not wish to solve. They use what they understand and discard the rest. Your name, He Who Walks Alone With Wild Horses, came to you when you were young and captured two wild horses with help from no one. You put a rope around the neck of each, then, being too small to mount, led them back to camp holding the ropes, one on either side. It was a great deed for such a young boy, and your father gave you the name to remember your skill. We all remember."

"I remember, grandfather, but it was good to hear the story again. Thank you. I owe you much."

"You owe me nothing, my grandson."

Joseph walked away from the bench where his grandfather sat and stared out across the prairie. "I know our people need the flour and other things in the Army wagon, but I cannot allow them to take it. If I did, the Army would say that we attacked those people to get the food and they will use it as yet another weapon against us. This cannot happen. I must take the wagon back to the camp and leave it, and when the whites find it, it will be as it was."

"I understand, grandson, but there are some in this camp who do not."

"Two Hawks, you mean," Joseph said.

"Yes. Two Hawks. He has much hate inside and he would be happy to use the food meant for the Army." A pause filled the air and if it were any other man, Joseph would have assumed he was hesitating. But his grandfather never hesitated. His moments of silence had purpose.

"What will you do about the woman?" Grandfather asked.

"That is something I must think about," Joseph replied.

"Do not think too long, grandson."

Maura woke with the scent of wood smoke in her nostrils. Believing herself still in the camp in the midst of battle, she tried to roll to one side planning to crawl from under the wagon but as she did, she rolled onto the wound on the side of her head. The resulting pain almost sent her back into oblivion but she was able to retain consciousness by holding her breath and closing her eyes.

When the worst had past, she slowly lifted her eyelids and tried to ascertain her surroundings. What was this place? "This is definitely not the underside of the wagon," she said to herself. That thought brought back all the horrors of the preceding hours and Maura began to shake her head back and forth, as tears ran in rivers from the outer corners of her eyes and trailed into the whorls of her ears.

A few moments later, calmed after the storm, she realized that she still did not know where she was. It appeared she was in a cone-shaped dwelling, perhaps one of the tepees that William Shakley had been describing only the night before. "Oh, he was so happy last night." Now things had deteriorated far beyond Maura's comprehension.

Her thoughts were interrupted by the sound of voices, and although

Maura was unable to understand what they were saying, she could tell by their tone that they were arguing. Fear struck a cord, but attempting to remain calm, she closed her eyes just as the flap was being lifted to allow entry into the structure.

"Do not hide from me in the tepee like a woman, Joseph. Hear what I have to say. I am telling you that you must return the woman to the whites. She cannot stay here. You do not care about us. You endanger us by bringing her here and letting her stay."

"That is enough, Two Hawks," Joseph countered. "As soon as I know the woman is all right, I will take her away from here. But in the meantime, even you should have enough heart to let her rest and not lie out in the open to die."

"Bah, she is just another white. When have they had any feelings for us? Our people will starve or freeze waiting for their sympathy. You should have left her where you found her."

"I could not, and I did not. She is here now; let the matter die. She will be gone soon enough".

"Not soon enough for me," Two Hawks said, adding in a lower tone but one still loud enough for Joseph to hear, "and neither will you." Giving Joseph a look sharper than a lance, the tall man walked away from the tepee entrance and joined several others who had been standing close by. The foursome was soon in deep conversation and Joseph shook his head, bent to enter the tepee and closed the flap. He allowed his eyes to adjust to the darkness of the interior, which had only the light from a small cooking fire to illuminate it. Finally, he could see the woman lying on the opposite side of the flames. Her eyes were closed, but Joseph intuitively felt that she was aware of what was going on.

"Your color is looking better," he said aloud. The woman did not move, and so he advanced toward her to check the bandages. As his hand reached down, Maura's eyes flew open and her own hand grabbed his wrist. "No," she said. "Yes," Joseph answered, and he brought his other hand up to gently touch the side of her head. As his fingers lightly smoothed the bandage over that wound, Maura slowly exhaled, not realizing that she had been holding her breath since the man had entered the tepee.

"Are you one of them?" she asked, and searched Joseph's eyes for the truth.

"If you speak of those who attacked your camp, no," he replied. "I heard the shots and came too late to help. They had already gone and left you for dead."

"My friends... They are dead, and I should be too," she said. "I did what the corporal said and stayed under the wagon. I should have fought with him and William. Maybe they would be alive right now, too."

"Most probably, you would be dead as well, instead," Joseph answered.

"Maybe, after what happened, that would have been better," Maura said quietly.

"You should not say such things," Joseph chastised. "You are young and still have much to live for."

"You don't know, you don't know," Maura chanted. "He grabbed my hair and pulled me away. He did something... I could not stop him. I scratched him and hit him and still he kept doing it."

Joseph did not stop her description of the rape. He knew it was better for her to speak of what happened. It was a way to help the healing. And so he listened, continuing to stroke the side of her head with his fingertips as she continued.

"What will I tell my fiancé? I was traveling to Fort Sully to be with him, and now he will never want me." She had not considered that before saying it out loud, and a sour feeling crept into her stomach.

"Your fiancé? This William was not your husband or lover?" Joseph asked. "I saw you both on the stage and I thought you were together." Maura was shocked, and took a closer look at the man squatting at her side. This time there was no tailored suit, no shiny boots, just a man in buckskin shirt, pants and ornately beaded moccasins. But his eyes were the same as the man on the coach, and when he smiled from the corner of his mouth, she exclaimed, "It was you on the stage! The man who dressed down that foul woman. But I never heard your name."

"Joseph," he said simply.

"Joseph," she repeatedly to herself, appearing to think about the name for a few seconds, then offered, "My name is Maura."

As if speaking released her, a litany of questions followed. "Where are your other clothes? Why are you here?" And as she considered other things, she asked, "Where IS here? He looked like you, you know. Not exactly, but he was one of you – an Indian I mean. They all were."

As if she had not interspersed her questions with descriptions of her attackers, Joseph began answering her first question. "My other clothes are packed away. I have no use for them here. The clothing I have on is more suited to my life while I am visiting my family. 'Here', as you say it, is the tepee of my grandparents. We are together now for a while until my work begins. Then I will unpack my suits once more, but until then, I will remain as I am.

"But, where is this tepee? Is this the reservation that William was telling me about? He said he visited here yesterday. Anyway, I think it was yesterday. He said he'd had a most enjoyable day with the Indians, and now he lies dead because of the same people." Joseph knew that her emotions were ruling her tongue right now and let her comments slide. He did, however, want to dispel any fear she had of her surroundings at this point.

"The men who attacked you did not come from our village," he assured her. "No one from my people would commit such an act. They are only trying to live together in whatever peace we can make for ourselves."

Maura looked suspiciously at Joseph, but said nothing more until posing the question, "What will you do with me?"

"I have considered that," Joseph answered. "I brought you here in the Army wagon and I must take that back to your camp or my people will be accused of what happened. You, I will take on to Pierre." When Maura looked confused, he explained, "It is the nearest city. There, we will find someone to take you on to the place you must go.

"We will begin traveling as soon as you are able, and although we should go slowly because of your condition, I'm afraid we must not take a chance with the weather. My grandfather says there will be snow soon, and I believe he is correct. His bones have never lied before," he explained, with a grin.

Despite herself, Maura also found herself smiling, but she soon remembered the point of the conversation. "I wish to leave as soon as possible," she said. "I do not relish my meeting with my husband-to-be, but we must get this out in the open, so that decisions can be made. I realize with winter arriving, if I am to return to my home, I may have to wait until spring. I would rather not do that, however, so the sooner we move, the better."

Joseph could sense a change in the woman, a decision within herself, perhaps, that was slowly making her stronger. It was strength she would need to draw heavily upon in the near future when she returned to her own people, he thought. They would not be happy to learn of what happened to her and he knew she was unaware of the reception she might receive once the word was out. She might have no choice but to leave before spring. His thoughts in this direction made him sad, for he knew from experience what it was to be considered a pariah.

He looked down to speak with her more, but as he did, he noticed that she had fallen asleep once again. "That is good," he thought to himself. "She will need to sleep much to regain the strength it will take for her to face what will come." Rising to his feet, he quietly walked around the fire and made his way outside once again. His grandmother was nowhere to be found, but like the sun that each day travels from east to west in the sky, his grandfather predictably sat on his bench near the door.

"She has awakened, my grandson?"

"Yes, grandfather."

"Good. Come sit here with me." Joseph picked up a small bag of corn that his grandfather had been using to feed the young chickens running free and sat down in its place on the bench. "You wish to speak to me of the woman," he said simply.

"And now you are a mind reader," his grandfather countered. "You are so certain of what you speak."

"Yes, I am certain," said Joseph. "I know what the others are saying and I know you will speak to me of the good of our people. I, too, want only good, you know this, but would you have had me leave her to die? She regains her strength already and will be leaving as soon as possible. She wants that, too. We have spoken of it just now. Tell me, what else will you bother me about?"

"It seems you are doing all of the talking, my grandson," the older man noted. "I have yet to say a word. Perhaps you would care to tell me what I want to talk about next?"

"You want to know when I will be returning the wagon to the camp.

This I will do the moment you stop talking my ear off. Does this please you?"

"There has never been a time when you did not please me, grandson." Joseph lifted an eyebrow at that statement, but his grandfather lifted his hand. "Do not think that I was pleased with all situations you created, such as the time you put the lizard in your mother's cooking pot and when she lifted the lid, her supper stuck out its tongue!" The old man could not help chuckling at the memory. "Or the time you..."

"All right, Grandfather, I understand. I had forgotten about the lizard though. Now, I must get going before night falls again. I want this wagon far away from here. Do not wait up for me, grandfather."

"I am an old man, grandson. I wait for no one. Do not worry."

Joseph hitched the horses to the wagon under the watchful eyes of Two Hawks and his friends. He drove the team slowly away, keeping it on a straight path despite the chickens and dogs that ran alongside and through the legs of the larger animals. Two Hawks muttered an oath and fixed his gaze upon Joseph and the team, continuing to watch until the wagon was nothing but a speck moving along the horizon.

It took over an hour to reach the small camp, but Joseph had had no doubt about its whereabouts. Five buzzards circled in the sky above the location and it was then that he deeply regretted leaving the bodies of the two men lying where they had fallen. At the time, his mind had centered only on getting aid for the one surviving member of the little group and had not given a second thought to the two men who would live no more. Now, however, he knew he must do something, even though it would have to be very little, to make the scene look as if it remained untouched since the raid.

Pulling the wagon into what he recalled as its former location, he jumped down and shooed the large birds away from their unmoving prey. Looking in the back of the wagon, Joseph grabbed the large tarp lying inside and spread it over the bodies of the two men. It seemed somewhat plausible that the attackers might have done the same, if only in an attempt to hide what they'd done. Unhitching the horses, he led them to the nearby stream for a well-deserved drink, and then returned them to the place where they had been staked out the night before.

He decided that he would not attempt to hide his footprints or the second set of wagon tracks, believing that with the amount of other prints from the attackers and the confusion that reigned at the camp, those who investigated would probably not even take a second look.

Ready to head back to his grandparents, Joseph took one more look around in the fading light of the evening. His eyes fell upon the black box camera lying near the woman's friend. Knowing that the object might bring some comfort to her, and believing that it really would not be missed, he moved over to the camera, picked it up, tucked it under his arm, and walked away.

Chapter Six

Maura closed her eyes and let the winter sun's rays caress her cheeks. She felt much better today, so Joseph had helped her walk outside and let her sit on the bench with his grandfather. He seemed as if he did not want to get too far away from her, however, and even now, while he worked with the horses, she caught him stealing a glance her way.

"He watches you." The old man had been silent for so long that Maura had thought he just did not speak English.

"Yes, I see that," she answered. "I don't know why. I'm not going anywhere."

"Yet," said the old man.

"Yes," said Maura. She looked to her right and noticed Two Hawks standing outside his tepee with his arms crossed and his eyes pointed directly at her. "He is not the only one who watches," she observed.

The old man barely lifted his head but looked in the direction she faced. "Two Hawks. Yes, it does not surprise me that he keeps an eye on you as well. And because he does, you should take care. He hates the whites and will see that you leave here. He does not care how."

Maura shivered and looked over to where a group of children were happily playing with a large hoop. They ran and laughed, seemingly without a care in the world. "They look so happy," she observed quietly. "They remind me of my younger brother and myself. We used to play together." She smiled thoughtfully at the memory. "We loved to make up our own games."

"This *sunkaku*, younger brother. Where is he now? He is back where you came from?"

"No, I'm afraid he died when we were young. Both my parents passed away at the same time. They were all ill and did not recover."

"So you went to grandparents?" the old man wondered.

"No, there was no one else. I went to an orphanage. My parents had come to this country before I was born. They were looking for a better life than the one they had in Ireland."

"Did they find it?"

Maura smiled. "I believe they did. We were very happy in Ohio. My father had a good job and my mother took care of us. We always had food on the table and clothes on our back." A few seconds went by before she added, "And, of course, we had each other. That was the most important thing. I only wish I had realized that then."

"You were a child, were you not? Children do not always see what is right in front of them. Even as adults, the same is true. But when you are young, you believe things will always remain as they are. It is unfortunate that that is not always so."

Maura was quiet for a time, and then began to search for a way to change the subject. Finally, she said, "I am sorry I am so ignorant of your people. I had no idea that you spoke English so well. Before I came here, I had read only what was in the newspapers about Indians, and that was not always good."

"No, I believe the white newspapers write only what the Army men would have you know and believe. It is not surprising. As for knowing your language, it was passed to me from my father who learned it many years ago from the traveling holy fathers. The knowledge has been very useful. Many of us know your words, but the whites do not care to know ours. I am happy, though, to know that you appreciate our knowledge. Many people would not. I can see in your eyes that what you say is the truth."

The old man thought for a moment, and then continued, "You and our Joseph have much in common, I think."

"Why is that, sir?"

"You both have had people who are important to you taken away from you. This, you two have known. Joseph's mother and father were taken from him only recently."

"What happened to them?" Maura asked.

"Ah, my son and his wife were very quiet people. But they could not accept that the only way of life they had known was going away. They participated in what was called 'Ghost Dances', believing that the past could be returned to us and we could once again live in freedom and the buffalo would return to the land that Wakan Takan had given to us to care for. They followed Chief Big Foot, who was a great leader, but in trying to save their way of life, they lost their own. At a place not far away they call Wounded Knee Creek, my son and his wife, and many of their friends, were killed and left lying in the snow as they died by the white bullets."

"Why did you and your wife not join them?" Maura asked. "In the Ghost Dances, I mean."

The old man looked beyond the horizon and let his mind drift through his life. "I have seen many things and one thing that I know – in life, one must accept the past as the past and move on. Learn from it, but do not live it again. We did not like what was happening, my wife and I, but to call upon the past was not the answer, we knew. Younger people are not so accepting. They listen to others who talk too much and they want things to happen now. They do not wait until the time is right."

Maura waited in silence a few moments, and then asked, "You do not believe that changes can be made in your life?"

"My ancestors were driven from their lands in the east and came to this place, wishing only to live in peace with the buffalo, the antelope and the coyote. They did so for many years before the white man came again. Since that time, there have been too many changes in our lives and none of them have been good. I will see no changes for the good in my life," the old man said. "Sometimes the answers lie far beyond us and we must accept this and hope that our grandchildren or great-grandchildren will reap the harvest of what others have sown.

"Do not think wrongly of me. I am old, but I am not stupid. I see what goes on, but I cannot stop it myself. I have seen much death and destruction and I have had enough. I look to Joseph and his sons and their sons after them, as ones who will see that our heritage will be salvaged. Someday, there will be better times for my people. But I will not see them. My time will come soon when I meet my son and his wife again in the land beyond the hills."

Her eyes burning, Maura could not help but reach out her left hand and use it to cover the old man's right hand. He did not look at her, but allowed her hand to remain as it was. They sat together in silence for quite some time before Joseph appeared before her.

"You should lie down again," he announced.

"No," she said.

"Yes," he answered, pulling her up and, placing an arm around her waist, he led her back inside the tepee and laid her on the pallet. "Rest," he said. "You must leave soon."

"I know," she said sadly, and turned her head to the side, letting the tears slide and fall where they may.

Chapter Seven

As they rode into Pierre, Joseph looked toward Maura to try to gauge her temperament. She had been very quiet on the trip from the reservation, but now that they had reached civilization, he was hoping she would become more animated. After all, she was far away from the tragic scene that was no doubt etched into her mind, and, perhaps, she would begin to see the logic in the suggestion he had made to her on the way here.

"I am curious to know what you have been thinking about this day," he said. "You have been very quiet. I know I have dominated the conversation, but you could have interrupted me at any time."

Maura smiled at his wit, as she knew that he was well aware that neither had said more than one or two words during the entire journey. "I was thinking that I will miss your grandparents very much," Maura said, regretfully. "Your grandfather, especially, is a very wise man and I will miss his advice and counsel."

"I should not tell you this, but my grandfather rather enjoyed his conversations with you. He would not tell me what they were about, but I got the feeling that they were not just about the mundane things such as the weather."

"We spoke of many things," Maura said. "And our talks will be among the things that I will treasure much during the remainder of my life. You are very lucky, Joseph, to have two such people in your life. I never did."

Joseph remained quiet as he maneuvered his horse through the streets and at the same time kept an eye on Maura. She was still quite weak but would not admit it for the world, he knew. He admired her greatly for her strength, but he did not think she realized how much she would have to draw upon it during the days to come – days that she would spend alone, as he could not stay with her. He had much work to do that he had put off already, in order to spend time with his people.

Stopping his horse beside a wagon, Joseph leaned over to ask the vehicle's driver where the sheriff's office would be located. A spray of tobacco juice landed on the rider's boot, as the driver shifted the wad of chew from one side of his mouth to the other.

"What does he want?" whispered the woman in the wagon to the driver.

"Who? Ain't nobody talkin' ta me," the driver said, snapping the reins to send his team on its way. In doing so, the wagon bumped Joseph's horse, spooking the animal and causing it to sway into Maura's horse. Holding on for dear life, Maura instinctively reached out for Joseph's arm and as she expected, her hand was clasped tightly by his and she suddenly found herself in his lap on top of his horse.

"Are you all right?" he asked, concern evident in his tone.

"Yes, I was just jarred a bit. It was nothing. You can put me down now."

Joseph looked her in the eye and seeing that she was telling the truth, allowed her to slide off his lap and onto the dirt street below. She pulled her horse nearer, using her reins, then easily stepped into the stirrup and swung around into the saddle.

"Why did he do that, Joseph? That man did that deliberately! This is an abomination! How can he treat you like that?"

Joseph's lopsided grin at her tirade faded slowly, as he began to answer her questions. "You are new here, are you not? This is something that we have lived with all our lives. I am no more than a spider to these people. Something to scream at and stomp with the heel of their boot. It will not get better, so we smile bitterly and go on our way. It is the way of things, Maura."

"I'm so sorry, Joseph," she said sincerely. "I had no idea. If I could change it, I would, you know."

"I know. And in knowing, I am grateful. Now, let us see if we can find the sheriff on our own. I have only one boot left for someone to spit upon. I'd like to save it for a while," he joked.

Maura tried to smile, but inside, her stomach knotted and her heart felt heavy. She took a deep breath and followed Joseph down the street, looking straight ahead, not wishing to look at these people just yet.

A few yards down the street, Joseph motioned Maura to the side and stopped. In front of them was a dress shop and Maura admired the frock on a dress form in the window. She looked down at the fringed dress she wore, which Joseph's grandmother had given her. She thought the dress beautiful, but knew that it would not be appropriate for meeting her intended, even if he would not be her intended much longer.

As she did so, she felt a nudge to her arm and looked toward the man beside her. He was holding out a small leather drawstring bag that appeared to have some weight to it. "You will need this to buy several new dresses. I do not know what will have happened to those you had brought with you from Ohio, but I want you to hold your head high and make a fine impression when you arrive at the fort."

A tear slid down the side of Maura's face and she turned quickly, hoping that Joseph would not see it. Her heart felt as if it could explode at that moment and she smoothed back her hair, at the same time wiping the tear away from her face. She turned back and looked at him; studied his hair, his eyes, his smile, the way he carried himself, then took a deep breath. "You are a good man, Joseph. I don't know how I can repay you, but if there is a way, I want you to know that I will do it. I am not ashamed to wear the clothing I now wear, but I think James will not appreciate the work and care that have gone into them. I will never, never forget what your family has done for me and I will carry them all in my heart forever."

"What about me?" Joseph said, with a twinkle in his eyes and a lopsided grin.

"You! I save an entire corner of my heart for you, Joseph. If not for you, I would be lying dead on the prairie. I know that. I hope that we will see each other again, and that we can remain friends. Perhaps I would be able to visit your family again, sometime."

"I do not think that your James would like that, Maura," he answered. "But I appreciate your thoughts and hope, too, that we will be friends. I have some work to do, but then I will be coming to Fort Sully. I have not told you this, but I will be starting a school for native children as soon as I can, after the fort is abandoned. I will have to come prior to that, so I may be able to see you."

"I would like that very much, Joseph."

"Now, you had better get inside the shop and pick a few things. I know how women work. It may take you a while, and dusk is approaching."

"Oh, you!" Maura gave him a stern look, but she knew he was just teasing her. She also knew he would not accompany her into the shop.

The young woman entered the establishment wearing, of all things, a leather dress. The two store clerks eyed one another knowingly and moved about the store, pretending to rearrange merchandise. They'd seen this kind before and were ready to stop her before she tried to leave the store without paying. The fact that her skin was lighter than most and her hair was red, really didn't matter.

Maura walked between the aisles, lifting this piece and then that, to check on the sizes. As she held a calico blue dress up against her chest, one of the clerks ran over and grabbed it away. "What do you think you are doing, holding this dress up to that dirty animal skin you're wearing? And a white woman wearing such a piece of filth! Land's sakes, I don't know what this world is coming to. Respectable folk can't make a living without trash coming in."

During the woman's tirade, Maura's mouth slowly opened wider and wider. When the woman was finished, Maura's temper took over.

"Of all the low, inconsiderate, foul-mouthed things I have heard during my lifetime, you, miss, have topped my list. I have been through hell and back in the last two weeks and I do not need to hear your opinions while I am attempting to make a purchase in your shop. If you want to see filthy," she said, "I'll show you filthy," and shoved the clerk to the wooden floor of the business. "Filthy is what your rear end is right now on that floor. I swear you must not have swept or mopped in the last six months. Now, I have the money, I have the dresses and undergarments picked out that I need and I will buy them. Not because I want to do you any favors, but because I need them and I lack the time to seek out a more favorable atmosphere."

Maura proceeded to the cash register, laid down the items she wanted to buy, and figuring the amount in her head, counted out the money and left it on the counter. Throwing the clothes over her arm, she lifted her head as high as it would go, straightened her shoulders, and left the store, slamming the door on her way out. "Humph!" she said to herself. "People are so irritating."

"What took you so long?" Joseph asked. He had been allowing his horse a drink at the nearby water trough but walked over to Maura's horse when he saw her leave the store.

"Oh, you know us women," she said, tossing the garments over her horse's neck. "We always have to gab a little."

The two reined in their animals outside the sheriff's office. Maura had finally been able to obtain its location from a passer-by and the two had made it to the office without further mishap.

"Do you want me to go in with you?" Joseph asked. "I will."

"I know, and I appreciate it. But I think it would be best if I went in alone. I will explain that I made my way to a home several miles from the attack and that it is only now that I have been able to come here. Now that I've changed my clothes, please return this dress to your grandmother. I don't want to involve your tribe at all, Joseph. I do not want them to get into trouble because of me."

"They would gladly pay the price."

"I know. That is what I am afraid of. I would rather do this on my own."

Maura dismounted and stepped onto the sidewalk. "Goodbye, Joseph. I hope we will meet again."

"I know we will," he answered and waited until she had gone through the office door. Pulling on the reins of his horse, he directed the animal toward the outskirts of the city. "She is a brave one. And she will not give up. Just like you did not give up when I brought you and your brother to our camp so long ago, Wild One."

Chapter Eight

Maura stood in front of the sheriff's desk while she related what had happened to Corporal Wyatt and William Shakley.

"They had to have come from the reservation, miss. There's nowhere else they could be from," the sheriff said.

"I don't believe that, sir," Maura said. "They could have come from anywhere."

"I don't know, Miss. We don't just have bands of Injuns roamin' around. They got to come from some place and the most likely place is the reservation."

"Well, I believe it's a little late now to speculate, Sheriff. But I do ask that you or your men go out to the site and at least bury my friends and retrieve the items for the Army. I'm sure the men at Fort Sully would be very grateful to you for that."

"Why, yes, I'm sure you're right, Miss. I'll send a couple of my deputies out right now – see what they can find. They'll be able to tell what happened right away, I just know it. Anything we find of your'n we'll give back, too, Miss."

"I'm not too worried about that, Sheriff. I didn't bring much of any worth from Ohio. The only thing I valued on my trip was killed that day on the prairie. Right now, I would appreciate it if you would be so kind as to find someone who could take me to Fort Sully. My arrival is quite overdue, I'm afraid.

"Yes, Miss. I'll get a man on that right away."

"Thank you, Sheriff. When the gentleman comes to take me to the fort, let me know."

"She's waitin' in the back, Matt. You wouldn't believe it. She was a'holdin one of them Injun dresses when she got off her horse. But I saw her hand it to the piece of trash who she come with. She rode up with this Injun and he just done left her here to explain what happened. I bet he had somethin' to do with it. An' if'n he didn't he gol darn knows who did. She knows 'xactly what went down."

"Is your man ready to take me to the fort?" Maura asked as she came into the room.

"Oh, yeah, lemme check. Are you ready, Matt?"

"Yessir," said the younger man, as he stood up so fast he knocked his ladder back chair onto its side.

"Slow down, now, boy. She ain't in that bigga hurry, are ya, miss?"

"Well, Sheriff, I am ready and I'd just leave as soon as possible if I may. What do you say, Matt, is it?"

"Yes'm. I'm ready anyway. Let's git goin'."

"Yes. Let's get this over with," Maura stated.

The wagon lumbered slowly along the roadway and Maura was only half listening to what Deputy Matt was saying. Apparently, he was new to the job and was eager to do exactly what the sheriff had asked him to do, no ifs, ands or buts.

The low log and stone walls of Fort Sully contrasted sharply with the bright blue, sparkling waters of the Missouri River. Maura couldn't help but compare the smooth, still river with the bumpy brown roadway and the dark, rough structures that stood side by side just a stone's throw from the water.

The wagon they rode in passed through the gates of the fort and a sea of blue wool greeted them in the evening light as the troops stood attention for evening taps. Maura had heard the song before, but its melancholy notes seemed to hit home in her current state of mind. She had a feeling that more than just the day was over.

Chapter Nine

June, 1894

Joseph halted his horse on the hill overlooking Fort Sully and the Missouri River. He felt very good. Despite the bad weather that had held him up several times during the past seven months, he had ridden from camp to camp within the reservation, explaining his mission and for the most part, had received favorable comments.

He believed that when it was time to begin his school, he would have good attendance. In October of this year, Fort Sully would be no more. Its walls would no longer echo with the sounds of gunfire and commands of soldiers but would ring with the shouts and laughter of children – children who would not be forcibly torn from their homes and families.

Long ago he had envisioned a place where native children would come freely, receive an education equal to, or better than the white population, and be allowed to speak about their own heritage, not be beaten down because of it. Joseph had spoken of his plan to his benefactor, who had started the wheels turning and in the end, had made his dream possible. He had official permission to take over the fort once it was abandoned by the Army, and to make of it what he would.

He had made contact with Indian families, now it was time to make his final arrangements for the school. Supplies had to be ordered and additional teachers found in the remaining months.

Joseph gently nudged the sides of his horse and let him maneuver slowly down the hill. They passed several structures that appeared to be houses, but to Joseph, it was hard to tell. Due to the lack of wood in the area, people used castoff boards and planks taken from older structures to construct other buildings. Even the Army had had to resort to this. Many a fort had been dismantled and its wood taken elsewhere to build another. Fort Sully was one of these, but judging by its exterior facades, it appeared to be in good shape and would stand for many years, Joseph decided.

He led his horse through the gap in the low wall of stone and logs that surrounded the fort perimeter, walking the animal slowly to make sure that his arrival would not raise an alarm. Eyes turned toward him as he passed, trying to locate the commanding officer's quarters. When he saw a soldier running in the direction of the only whitewashed building on the premises, Joseph knew he'd found what he was looking for and word of his presence would spread within minutes. That fact satisfied Joseph's plans, as he wanted to meet with the officer in charge, present his papers and find a location where he could set up his own offices.

Joseph never got the chance to enter the commanding officer's quarters. He had tied his horse at the rail in front, just as the young soldier he had seen earlier burst back through the door, followed by the sound of heavy footsteps. Three seconds later, the sound was accompanied by an imposing figure of a man dressed in Army blue with stripes, medals, and tassels, "probably bells and whistles somewhere, too," Joseph thought. The man was holding a half-eaten chicken leg in his right hand and a grease-stained cloth in his left.

"This better be good. I'm eating my lunch and if there's one thing I hate, it's cold chicken. Damned stuff'll get caught in yer gullet and never come out." The officer stopped in his tracks as soon as he spied the Indian who had stopped with one foot resting on the nearby water trough.

"Well, what the hell have we got here? Looky boys!" he called to the soldiers beginning to gather around them. "It's a Injun in a Sunday-go-ta-meetin' suit. You sure are gussied-up, boy. Who'd ya steal that from, anyway?" he asked, while picking his brown teeth with his equally brown fingernail.

Joseph picked an imaginary piece of lint from his coat, looked up and eyed the officer squarely. "Might I inquire as to your name, sir? I prefer to know the name of those who would call me 'thief'."

Eyebrows raised and glances were exchanged until all bluecoat eyes were directed at their commanding officer, waiting for his reply. The remnants of the chicken leg dropped to the dirt and the officer, glaring at Joseph with his squinty dull eyes, wiped his mouth, first with his sleeve, then as if remembering his manners, used the cloth in his hand.

"Well, well, well. Men!" he called. "Seems like we got us an edjacated Injun here who thinks he's better'n us. Son, you might know some fancy speakin', but you're talking to an officer in the United States Army, here, and you're surrounded by soldiers, loyal to what the United States stands for. Since you're such a high falutin' know-it-all, state yer business in as few words as you can and get out."

"You haven't answered my question."

"What?"

"You haven't answered my question. Remember? I asked for your name, sir."

"My name ain't really any of your concern, boy, but just soz we kin speed things up, I am Colonel Ezra Coffey. Now, state your business!"

Joseph's right hand moved toward the opening of his coat, a gesture that was met by the sound of several dozen guns being raised and cocked, ready to fire. The soldiers who were not otherwise occupied had spent the last several hours on the parade yard in rigid drills and so were armed and ready for anything. The noise did not deter Joseph from his intent. His hand snaked into the interior pocket where it retrieved an envelope addressed to one "Colonel Ezra Coffey". The native brought it slowly out of his coat, allowing plenty of opportunity for the soldiers at hand to get a good look at what he was doing.

"I believe this is for you, sir."

"For me? What is it?"

"Once you read the document inside, I'm sure you'll understand," Joseph stated, adding for his own amusement even though he knew he would make a bigger enemy of this man, "You can read, can't you sir? If not, I would be happy to assist you."

The colonel's face turned a mottled shade of bright red as he snatched the envelope from Joseph's hand. "Give me that, you insolent Injun! I just may put you in the stockade to teach your smart mouth a lesson!"

"Oh, I don't believe you'll want to do that once you see this letter," Joseph said confidently. "Don't mind me. Just take your time."

Joseph walked over to his horse and used his fingers separated like a comb to groom the animal's mane. He spoke a number of words to the beast, but they were said so softly that none standing there could overhear. In the meantime, Colonel Coffey tore open the envelope and began to read its contents, mouthing the words as he did so. Joseph gave the horse a final pat and returned his attention to the matter at hand.

Reaching the end of the missive, Coffey took a deep breath and dropped the hand that still held the letter. Looking intently at the man standing expectantly before him, the officer announced quietly, "Put yer guns down boys." A few seconds later when the men were slow to respond, he repeated more forcefully, "Put 'em down, boys. I mean it."

Whispers were passed from one man to another, as in unison the company of men lowered their weapons and waited to hear what their commander had to say.

"It says here in this letter, that this Injun - Joseph Walks Alone - will be taking over our fair fort at the end of October, to turn it into some newfangled Injun school. In the meantime, we are to treat him with the utmost respect and courtesy and help him in any way we can." Grumbles filtered through the crowd but the officer raised his right hand in a gesture meant to stop the noise. "I know, boys. I don't like it any more than you. But the Injun standin' here seems to have a friend in high places. What I'm sayin' is, the man that signed this letter is to be obeyed and so am I."

Rifles and handguns dropped.

"Thank you, Colonel Coffey. I appreciate your consideration. Now, if you would be so kind as to direct me toward my quarters..." The officer motioned a non-commissioned soldier toward a line of structures built side by side, as if to support each other. As Joseph untied his horse and followed the man, Coffey rubbed his hand over his thigh. A low-pitched growl drew his attention to the ground where a mongrel camp dog had chewed the forgotten chicken bone down to one knobbed end. "I hope you choke," Coffey said, his eyes returning upward. But it wasn't clear whether he was talking to the dog, or to someone else.

Chapter Ten

After settling his few things into his quarters, Joseph decided to take a walk around the fort. He was curious to see whether he might catch sight of Maura. He realized that after six months away, she was very likely married. He hoped so, anyway. The alternative would be that she had returned to Ohio and he would never see her again.

He searched the parade ground of the inner fort, ignoring the blue stares and the muffled cries of outrage from several women walking past him, huddled together to keep out a pre-summer chill. After about twenty minutes, Joseph was ready to give up and take a look outside the boundaries of the fort when he spied a patch of red hair peeping from beneath the scarf of a woman walking slowly toward him. He checked himself, however, when he realized that the hair could never belong to the woman he was looking for. This woman was about the right height, but she was struggling to carry what appeared to be a large basket of wet clothing. Her eyes were dull and her complexion wan. If that were not enough to convince him, when she turned to the side, even through her cape, it was more than obvious that she was quite pregnant. Nonetheless, Joseph was aware that she was heading for the line of rope tied around two upright poles near the fort's western side and he increased his speed, in order to take the cumbersome basket from her.

"Here, here. You should not be carrying such a load in your condition, madam," he said, grabbing one of the basket handles. As he did so, he found himself staring into familiar green eyes; but they were eyes that held none of the brilliance and awareness he had once seen them possess.

"Maura." The name was a whisper that was almost lost in the passing breeze.

Suddenly, the eyes showed terror, and then turned to outright hatred. "You," she said, as she pulled the basket away from him and began to walk away. "Go away."

Joseph chased after her, trying to understand. "What happened, Maura? How did you come to be...like this?"

"Oh, come now, Mr. Walks Alone. You of all people should know the answer to that question but if you really don't know, I'll be happy to fill you in. It's because of you, you know. If it hadn't been for you, I would have died in the company of friends and my bones would be picked clean by buzzards by now. And to tell you the truth, that sounds infinitely better than what my life has become since you 'saved' me."

Maura walked toward the clothesline and began to hang the articles over it with her back toward Joseph. He felt that he needed time and knew that this was not the right moment to pursue the matter with her, so he turned quickly, walking back to his quarters. At one point, he stopped to let the cooling breeze blow on his face, and then turned to take one more look. She was looking at him, and did not make any attempt to hide the fact after she was caught. Turning away, Joseph used the heel of his palm to hit the door to his quarters, and as it slammed against the wall, the sound reverberated in his ears, much like her hatred echoed in his heart.

Chapter Eleven

Joseph saw Maura here and there over the next several days, but did not approach her again. Instead, he set out to learn what had happened to her after her arrival, and where her supposed husband was. "Of course, if I find him, I'll probably kill him," Joseph said to himself.

His first inclination was to ask his questions of the commanding officer, but thought better of it later. He knew he had made an enemy of the man when he arrived, but when an idea formed, he realized he really didn't need the officer's help to accomplish his plans anyway.

"Is there a doctor serving the fort?" Joseph questioned one of the enlisted men sitting outside the mess, peeling rather rotten-looking potatoes.

"My food ain't that bad, mister," the soldier said defensively, pointing at Joseph with his paring knife as he said it.

"Hold on, that's not what I meant," Joseph said. "I need to see the doctor, if there is one, for other reasons."

"Yeah, you'll find him in his office, a couple doors down."

"Thanks," Joseph said, and headed off in that direction. It took no more than a few seconds to find the door that identified the office of Dr. Henry W. Pierce. The visitor took another second to straighten the doctor's shingle, and then knocked loudly on the door before entering.

He was greeted by the sight of a pair of spectacles pointed in his direction, but balanced on a shock of gray hair that had obviously not been intimidated by a comb for quite some time. Suddenly, the spectacles stared at the ceiling and an equally hairy face met Joseph's gaze. The eyes squinted, looked left and right, then down to the disarray on the desk. Taking a wild guess, Joseph pointed to the top of his own head to give the man a clue. Pushing his fingers through his hair, the gentleman finally came upon his glasses and gently brought them down to rest on the bridge of his nose.

"That's better," he said. "Now, what can I do for you, son? Pull a tooth? Give you some bicarbonate of soda?" He studied Joseph from head to foot and noted, "Don't see any blood. Must not be an emergency." He looked back down at the book lying open on his desk and smoothed its pages with his gnarled left hand. "Ever read Alexandre Dumas?"

A smile slowly spread from Joseph's lips reaching all the way to the crinkles in the corners of his eyes. "*The Man in the Iron Mask* was always my favorite."

"I'm in the middle of *The Count of Monte Cristo* for the umpteenth time. How that man survived the Chateau d'If, I'll never know. And his ideas for revenge! Makes me hope there's nobody out there planning to get me back for one of the many atrocities I've committed during my lifetime." The physician pushed aside a plate containing the remnants of his lunch, searched around several piles of books and moved a collection of bottles containing different levels of substances known only to their owner. Finally, he lifted the fork from his plate, wiped it quickly on his shirtsleeve, and secured it between the pages of the book to mark his place.

"Well, you probably didn't come here to talk literature with me. What is it you want, son?"

Joseph's smile quickly disappeared. "I'm here to inquire about a friend," he began. "A friend who means very much to me and I hope that you will help me."

"Hmm, a friend, eh? What's wrong with this 'friend'? Can't do what he wants to do? Been with the wrong kind of girl? Tell me about it, son. Don't be embarrassed. It happens to the best of us."

Joseph's left eyebrow shot up, as he considered the physician's words. Finally, it registered. "Oh, no, no, no. That's not what I meant at all! I'm here to find out what happened to a woman friend of mine, I discovered is working here as a laundress. I hope that you know her and perhaps have been caring for her. You see, she's, well...quite...pregnant. And I don't believe she's married."

"Ah, Maura."

Joseph was taken aback by the quick response from the doctor. "Exactly," was all he said.

"Son, was it you who was responsible?"

"No, sir. Though Maura thinks I am." At the doctor's quizzical look, Joseph continued. "I found her after it...the rape...occurred. I took her to my family where she was treated for her injuries. If I had not done that, she would most assuredly have died. And that is why Maura believes me to be responsible for her life now."

"Responsible?"

"Yes, sir, you see, she's still alive. But I don't believe she wants to be."

Dr. Pierce sat back hard in his wooden desk chair and pushed his spectacles back to their perch on the top of his head. He began to rub the corners of his eyes, and then the tips of all 10 fingers started a slow massage of his brow, moving to his temples. He then lifted his head, pushed himself forward and brought his fingers together to meet tip to tip before him, with his elbows placed firmly on the desk.

Joseph kept silent as he waited. He knew the physician was wrestling with the weight of the decision he had to make. Should he violate the oath he had undoubtedly taken to keep his patients' affairs to himself? Or should he reveal anything he knew to this stranger who had only just now walked into his office claiming to be a friend? It would not be an easy judgment call and Joseph knew that he was asking too much of the doctor as it was, to push the issue further.

After what seemed an eternity, Joseph finally heard the words, spoken so quietly that none but he could possibly have heard. "What do you want to know?"

"Everything," Joseph said simply. "Everything."

Chapter Twelve

"The first time I saw her, she rode in a wagon with a young deputy from Pierre. He had stopped in front of the commanding officer's quarters, went inside leaving her waiting in the wagon, then returned to ask her to wait where she was." The doctor paused for a moment to gather his thoughts, then continued, "I remember I was standing in front of my door. A young sergeant had just come to me with severe pain from a nasty bite from his horse, and I was examining the wound to determine whether any bones had been broken. It was her hair that had caught my attention first," and to this comment, Joseph could only nod in agreement.

"The flame burst free when the wind caught the dark blue shawl she wore over her head and sent it flying into the air. The pins were next, and soon her head was one tongue of fire leaping and dancing in midair. What could anyone do but admire it? I have never considered myself to be elderly, but I realize I am beyond setting any young woman's head aflutter. However, on this particular day, I forgot who I was and who she might be. I simply watched.

"Unfortunately, and I say this hoping you will repeat none of this, an officer – Captain James Cole – was called to the wagon. He walked slowly from his spot on the parade ground, pulling on the fingers of his white gloves – traveling from pinky to index finger and finally pulling the gloves from each hand. He held both in his right hand, as if they were trying to escape and slapped them repeatedly against his thigh. The deputy said something to him, and for a short while, the officer said nothing. Then he reached up and in a gentlemanly manner, took the woman's hand and assisted her from the wagon. He seemed to greet her with some familiarity, and then led her into the officer's quarters. It was quite some time before he exited that building, leaving the woman inside. About 10 more minutes went by until she was seen coming out, with the shawl wrapped tightly about her head and her eyes glistening with unshed tears. She walked back to the wagon and spoke with the deputy. He argued with her a bit, then climbed into the conveyance and returned the way he had come, leaving her standing alone. She looked from here to there, from left to right, but no one came to her rescue. Finally, I could stand it no longer, the Southern blood flowing inside me being too much to ignore, and, asking no questions, I led her to my office. Later, I was summoned to Coffey's office where I was told that the young lady had been assigned one of the structures outside the fort and would be taken there as soon as possible. I was not to follow or attempt to give comfort in any form or manner.

"Are you certain you want to hear the rest of this?"

"Yes, sir," Joseph answered.

"Well, when I returned here, she was gone. I did not go out looking for her that day, but the next morning, I went outside the fort gates, as I have many a time in the early morning hours, to take a constitutional along the river. The sounds of the rushing waters calm my soul and give me strength to face yet another day. On this day, however, I felt empty. I didn't know this woman, but I felt a connection to her and I knew that something bad had happened to her. As I walked, my eyes searched the banks before me and moved over the lands beyond. I had gone as far as I felt I dared to be safe, and turned to walk back the way I had come when I spied a figure standing as close to the rushing waters of the river as it dared go without being swept away. I shouted a warning and began to walk faster. My knees are arthritic, you see, and will not allow me the privilege of quick movements.

"In any event, she appeared to have not heard me and so I called once more before coming up on her left side, as she stared at the gray waters churning at her feet. I began to speak, 'I say, you must be careful here. The banks have been known to collapse under foot. We don't want you swept away, now. Not when you've only just arrived.'"

The physician hesitated, and then continued. "She just kept staring at the water until finally, she turned her face toward me and I saw that the entire right side of it was bruised – from blue to deep purple and her eye had swollen shut. 'I desperately wish to be swept away,' she told me. 'But I find that I am too much of a coward.'

"What could I say to that? What could I say? We just stood together, then, silently. Two lonely people, wondering whether there was something better someplace else and knowing we may never see it."

Joseph felt his stomach tightening and his hands and teeth began to clench in uncontrollable rage, as he listened to the doctor's narrative.

But all Dr. Pierce saw as he looked at his visitor was a tear sliding down from the outside corner of the Indian's eye. "He loves her," the elder gentleman thought, realizing that he and the man sitting before him had much more in common than he would have realized 15 minutes before.

Chapter Thirteen

"Where do I find him?"

The question was posed in a clipped fashion and the doctor didn't immediately answer.

"Where do I find him?" Joseph repeated, this time much louder.

"I heard you the first time," Dr. Pierce answered. "First of all, I don't know. I hear that he has some troops out on a reconnaissance mission right now and I don't know when he'll be back. Second of all, you've got to calm down before you confront him. You don't know him, Joseph. I do. Believe me, you need all of your wits about you to go head to head with that one."

Joseph did a double take. "How do you know my name? I never told you what it was."

Dr. Pierce chuckled and sat back in his chair, putting his feet on his desk. "Word travels fast, Joseph. I knew you were here the moment you came through those gates, and I not only know your name, but what label is inside your suit coat and that your boots were made in London."

Joseph raised himself from his chair and walked slowly over to the room's lone window. He appeared to be studying something very interesting in the parade yard, but the doctor could tell that his new friend wasn't really looking at anything at all.

"I never should have left her." The words were uttered as their speaker leaned his head against the cool pane of glass and closed his eyelids to look far beyond the fort walls.

"It wouldn't have mattered," the doctor said firmly. "We have had quite a few conversations since that time. We've become friends, Maura and I – more than that really, but friends nonetheless. She tells me she knew that coming here would be risky, but it was something she felt she had to do. She had to carry her trip through to its end, no matter how ugly it became. She's a strong woman, that one. Whether she realizes it or not, she has far more intestinal fortitude than I could ever hope to possess."

"But the laundry," was all that Joseph said. "Why must she do the laundry? Where does she live, who takes care of her? What will become of her?"

"Whoa, whoa, boy! Your questions are going to outnumber my answers."

Dr. Pierce considered his replies for a moment, and then began. "It was obvious to everyone that he would have nothing to do with her, which left her completely on her own. She found no sympathy from any of the other women here, especially Mrs. Coffey, the commanding officer's wife. All the other women follow her lead. They have turned up their pointy little noses and continue to whisper behind their dirty little hands. She is considered a whore here, Joseph. I mean no disrespect to you and yours but when it got out that she had been violated by a band of Indians, – that was the judgment. Any sympathy extended went to him. 'The poor captain. His affiancéd sullied by Injuns,' or 'The poor man, that woman is carryin' an Injun bastard' was pretty much everyone's sentiment around here for quite a while. Now, most people just ignore her.

"She was went to the laundry to ask for work to earn enough money to go back home, but she is paid very little for the back-breaking work she must do and she soon discovered that they charge her to rent the hovel she lives in near the river and she must pay twice as much for the food that she buys in the fort. If I had the money, I would help her, but I don't get paid that much the way it is and the Army's pretty notorious for keeping people waiting for their pay. I try to do for her though. Nailed a few boards for her and helped her chink up the holes before winter set in, so she wouldn't freeze to death. I don't think she would've minded though."

When the good physician stopped speaking, the room's silence echoed off the walls.

"I'm sorry I can't give you a happier story, Joseph. Perhaps, after the Army leaves this place, she will find peace here. This is just a suggestion to you, but I have discovered that she is a very intelligent woman. She could help you with the school you're planning, you know. I know she says she hates you now, but perhaps in time, when she sees she could be useful and treated with respect, well, it's something you should think about."

Joseph filled his lungs with the stale office air and wished he were far away on the long grass prairie where the wind would help to clear his head of the words he had heard today. Ones that he prayed he could erase, not only from his mind, but eventually, from Maura's life.

He shook his head and thanked the doctor for his time. "I know I asked much of you today, but you will not regret the telling," Joseph vowed, moving toward the door. He had just opened the portal and had begun to step through when the physician said, "She needs you. Don't let her drive you away. If I can help, please allow me to do so. Next to you, I am an old man, but I want you to know that I would try to move the mountains for her."

Joseph nodded and closed the door quietly behind him.

Maura had seen Joseph entering Dr. Pierce's office and though she had been back and forth from the river several times, she had not seen him leave.

Several days later, as she worked with the other laundresses, setting up their washtubs near the river, so that water would not have to be hauled far, she continued to wonder at his purpose in visiting the good doctor. And as she carried the clothing back to the fort to hang and dry, her thoughts still centered on the Indian. She had caught glimpses of him now and again since that day, but he had not attempted to speak to her again. She couldn't blame him, really, after the way she had spoken to him, but it was for the best, she decided. She would be nothing but trouble for him now.

Maura was busy adjusting the position of a pair of long johns on the line, when she heard the thundering sound of many horses. She looked toward the fort entrance, just as the first rider passed through, slowing his animal to a walk. The familiar, dark-haired figure jumped from his horse and Maura took a deep breath, attempting to hide behind the clothing on the line as she worked. She knew what Captain James Cole would do should he catch sight of her, and she did not feel up to a confrontation today.

Unfortunately, however, that seemed to be exactly what he wanted. His eyes searched the compound until he saw that someone was at the wash line. A lopsided smile crept to his face and he began to remove his gloves, one finger at a time, as he walked toward her.

"There you are, my dear. How I've missed speaking to you these many days I've been away." The insincerity oozed from his lips, as his eyes made a slow slide down her body. "And my, how you've grown since I've been gone. Your little bastard isn't so little anymore, is it, my dear? You never were a petite woman, Maura, but now you are, shall I say, rather, hmmm. Well, there's just no getting around it, is there? You are fat. You see what your fun has resulted in, now, don't you?" Unconsciously, Maura had begun moving away, but the low fort wall stopped her retreat and he leaned toward her, so close that she could smell one of the hand-rolled cigars that he preferred to keep with him at all times. "Have I already told you? Yes, probably, but I'll say it again. You're such a..."

At the precise moment he would have uttered the expletive, a dark hand clamped James' shoulder. "What the...?" the captain said, surprised at the touch of another. "Unhand me this instant!" he ordered, turning to see who had dared to lay a hand upon his person.

James' face contorted into a sneer when he came face to face with one who stared impassively into the captain's eyes.

"You will not speak to her that way." The native uttered the sentence slowly, evenly, and, if the officer had been listening he would have realized, with just a hint of menace.

"Well, well, well, Maura," the officer said. "Is this one of your boyfriends, come to save your 'honor'? Doesn't he know that your honor went out the window with your virginity? Oh, wait!" Laughter bubbled up from his chest and escaped from his lips. "Or perhaps," he said at last, after catching his breath, "perhaps this is the creator of your bastard! Could it be? Oh, ho! This is rich. What fun!"

Maura's eyes grew wide with fear and anticipation. No one had ever interfered with James' tirades toward her. No one had ever dared. His temperament was widely known to be controlling, demanding and vengeful. Surely, Joseph would not continue. But then, Joseph did not know James, and suddenly, Maura knew fear for one other than herself.

"A wise man once told me, if you discover you are riding a dead horse, the best thing to do is to dismount." The officer looked at Joseph curiously. "Do not beat this dead horse, captain," Joseph warned. "I believe Maura has heard your words before and she will not hear them again, am I correct?"

Capt. James Cole stared at Joseph Walks Alone with lips parted and eyes narrowing. "Who are you?" he asked, each word enunciated separately and pointedly. "And what are you doing in my fort, all dressed up like a dandy? You have no right to speak to me this way. I will have you drawn and quartered like the piece of meat you are!" James' face squeezed into a distorted version of itself, as he continued to vent his rage.

Feeling herself shrinking backward with every word, Maura finally broke free of the spell James' words were weaving upon her. Normally striking cold fear within her soul, a spark fired deep inside her and its warmth began to strengthen her.

"Let him alone," she said, softly at first, and when that produced no response from either man, then louder. "Let him alone!" And she pushed against James' back with both hands. His reaction was to blindly backhand her, missing her face, but striking her rounded belly. Thankfully, her wool cape softened the blow, which only produced a sting.

In his mind's eye, Joseph pictured himself choking the last breath from the man facing him, but he controlled his emotions and instead walked around the captain. Using those same hands that seconds ago were capable of taking a life, he took Maura's in a gentle but firm grip. "She has had enough for today," he said simply. "I, too, have had enough. I believe you are through, captain."

The pair began to walk away, when the officer called after them. "I don't know who you are, but you are a dead man."

"Your commanding officer will tell you who I am," Joseph said, nodding his head toward the portly man standing just outside his office, who had obviously witnessed the entire scene. "And, by the way, I think he may have been surprised to find out that this is 'your' fort, as you described it. You might want to consider an explanation for that on your way over to greet him."

Joseph turned Maura and guided her outside the fort walls, leaving James fuming where he stood, the once pristine white gloves now a sweaty, crumpled mass in his right hand.

Chapter Fourteen

"I tell you, Joseph, I was mesmerized! And admittedly, more than a bit frightened for you as well. I still don't believe you realize what you have done."

Joseph was only half listening to Dr. Pierce as the physician recalled the entire scenario aloud, even though all three present in Maura's home needed no reminding. He was squatting in front of the fireplace, where he watched the infant flames grow larger as Maura filled her teakettle with water from a bucket the doctor had brought in earlier.

"I don't know why he did it," she said, only half to herself, as she busied herself with her task. The words caused Joseph to look to the side and shake his head.

"I'd have done it myself, had I more guts," the doctor admitted. "One of these days, it will be my turn. But I have yet to muster enough gumption. You, though, my boy, have gumption to spare."

"Cole is not worth our time. Let us speak of something else," Joseph suggested, raising himself to stand before the fireplace to watch, as Maura placed the kettle on a small iron rod suspended horizontally over the heat. She returned the few steps to a rickety table shoved against the wall, which she considered to be her kitchen area. Bringing out a loaf of bread, she began slicing it. Joseph walked over and placed his hand over the one that held the knife. "I need nothing to eat. And the doctor has leftovers in his office. Cut only enough for yourself."

Maura looked him in the eye, then slowly lowered the blade and laid it on the counter. As he watched, she placed a towel over what was left, and with her eyes asking for forgiveness, she bit hungrily into the section she had severed and ate every crumb. Joseph smiled and nodded, then turned to the doctor. "We must go so that Maura may rest."

"No, I'm fine," she assured him, but he raised his right hand in a gesture to stop.

"I must return to the fort. I have much work to do and I wish to keep an eye on your captain. I do not trust him as far as the ant can crawl."

"Yes, I have some reading to do as well," Dr. Pierce said. "I'll walk beside you, son."

"That would be most welcome," said Joseph, sincerely, and, opening the door, allowed the doctor to exit first, then gave Maura a long, hard look. "Rest," he said.

"No," she answered.

"Yes."

"You're a son of a bitch, Cole." Colonel Coffey was pacing back and forth behind his desk as his subordinate lounged in the wooden chair opposite. The younger man had been called in just after the confrontation in the yard.

"Captain Cole, sir," Cole corrected. "And my mother was a whore, so she had to be nice to someone. Bitches don't make good whores."

"How did you get this far in rank, Captain Cole? Your mouth should have gotten you in trouble long ago."

"I'm good at what I do. The Army doesn't care about one's mouth, they care about getting the job done and they know that I can do it."

"Well, this time, I'm telling you to stop shooting off your mouth. That Indian you took on this afternoon will be taking over this fort...my fort, by the way...once we've moved on. He has friends in high places, Cole. Higher than you could hope to have, so let him alone. Ignore him. Do what you have to do, but I don't want to hear about any more conflicts with him. He and his little girl friend are off limits, do you hear me?"

"I listen and obey, sir," Capt. Cole said, squeezing the words out between clenched teeth. "I'll let them alone until they force me to do otherwise."

"Cole..." the commanding officer strung the name out in a warning tone.

"Is that all, sir? I'd really rather give you a report on what we discovered on our foray out in the wilds."

"Go ahead, Cole."

"Captain Cole, sir."

Col. Coffey sat down and rolled his eyes. "Just give me the report, captain."

"Sir, we rode out to where our men found the remnants of the latest attack. Starting from the point the bodies of the two families were found, we split into several search parties and lifted every rock, and looked into every crevice but turned up nothing. With nothing more than two piles of rather smelly ashes left, it is difficult to determine what, if anything was missing. This... mess... looked rather similar to the attack on my...former fiancée and her friends, and it is still my belief that that renegade band is coming off the reservation. The attacks occur just miles from that land and if you would only give me permission, I believe the men and I could go in and flush them out."

"No. That is not an option and you know it, captain."

"It will become an option when they begin to use the guns they took from the Army's wagon. Quite possibly, by now they could have sold the weapons or traded them for something even deadlier. Will we have to wait until more of our men are killed? Is that what it's going to take, sir? If you'd let me search the reservation, I know I'd find the guns and the filthy Indians who stole them – from us, I might point out. Not to mention that they killed one of our own. Let's not wait for more."

"Do not question me, captain," Coffey said slowly. "I have my own orders to follow and I'm not asking you to follow mine. I am ordering you to follow them. Stay off the reservation. I can't say it plainer than that."

Cole rose from his chair and took his gloves from where he had tucked them into his belt. "I believe you're going to regret this, sir. I could find them for you and give you all the glory. That band has been a thorn in the Army's side for quite some time. And if you will not allow me to go into the rat's hole, then I believe we should postpone the abandonment of the fort. We will be needed if they are still on the loose."

"The abandonment will move as scheduled, Cole. And with what we've talked about today, now I'm beginning to think it might be a mistake to leave you in charge of the detachment that will remain for the month after the rest of us have moved on. I don't believe I can trust you."

"Oh you can trust me, Colonel. Trust me to do what is best."
"For the Army, or for yourself?" Coffey questioned.
Cole's answer was a smile that did not reach his eyes.

Chapter Fifteen

Joseph rode into Pierre, dressed in his best attire. He had been notified that many of his supplies for the school had arrived from Washington, D.C. and he had to make arrangements for their storage over the next few months until the Army removed itself from the fort.

He was actually rather relieved to be away for a while. He had been hard pressed to avoid James Cole over the last few days and it seemed he could feel the officer's eyes boring into him whenever he walked across the yard.

Maura had kept to herself since the day Cole had returned but when he had seen her, Joseph could sense a difference in her demeanor toward him. She had actually smiled at him yesterday and it gave his heart a lift. She had been accompanied by the young man Joseph had hired to carry the wet laundry for her from the river to the fort. The mother-to-be had balked at the idea at first, but apparently had acquiesced when she realized that she was getting to the point in her pregnancy where she could no longer carry the heavy baskets.

Joseph knew it would not be long before Maura's baby was born. He worried about her reaction to it, once it was here, as in his few conversations with her, she did not talk about the baby or what she would do after it was born. Joseph feared she would reject the child because of its association with what had happened to her. He considered asking his grandmother if she knew of anyone in the village who would want a child of mixed blood to raise, should the worst happen.

He had ridden to the train station where his supplies, packaged in large crates, had been stacked in a tower on the wooden walkway. There was more than he had anticipated, but he managed to talk the owner of a nearby warehouse into renting space to him on a monthly basis. Then he headed to the nearest livery to hire a wagon so that he could move the equipment.

Once that was done, he left the wagon and his horse at the livery and took off on foot to find a restaurant. He had had a piece of hardtack before he left the fort, but had been too busy for a noon meal and now with dusk settling, he was ready for some food. He planned to stay the night, pick up several other items the next day, and then head back to the fort.

He walked into the Pierre Hotel, but didn't bother to register. He would spend the night outside the city limits, under the stars. Joseph found his way to the dining room. After producing a silver dollar for the maitre 'd, he was led to a table by the kitchen door, where the aroma of steaks and chicken frying made his stomach rumble. He gave his order to the waitress, sipped his black coffee and began to peruse the room. One of his favorite occupations had been people watching, and this room, packed with visitors to the city, was the perfect place to take up his hobby.

His eyes moved to a young couple in the corner ignoring everyone else. "Definitely honeymooners," he thought to himself, watching them eat and hold hands without letting go. He felt a twinge of jealousy at that moment, as he sat alone, and his thoughts flew to Maura. He pictured her sitting opposite him at the table, her smile aimed in his direction, but was brought back to reality when the waitress set the plateful of fried chicken, mashed potatoes and gravy, beans and cornbread in front of him.

Joseph continued to watch the other diners, including two middle-aged businessmen creating a cloud of cigar smoke, a table of young women talking animatedly back and forth, and finally, his eyes fell on one particular table located behind a large fern. It was the blue uniform that had drawn his attention at first and he struggled to see who wore it. The officer's back and dark brown head were toward Joseph, but the blonde woman with him was giggling at something that was said and she looked at her companion with adoration shining in her eyes.

Finally, his own dinner finished, Joseph ordered a slice of apple pie, as the waitress cleared the dirty dishes. As he waited, he noticed that the couple was preparing to leave. The officer reached for the young woman's hand, kissed it, and assisted her to rise from her seat. As he turned and tucked her arm beneath his, the face was revealed and for some reason, Joseph was not surprised to see that it was Captain James Cole. The officer did not see Joseph, as he was too occupied in keeping his eyes on the plentiful bosom of his dinner partner. He made a comment to her and she reacted with a sigh, leaning closer to whisper into his ear.

The pair walked from the room and Joseph saw the officer leave the young woman at the desk where they parted company, rather reluctantly on the part of the lady.

"He wasted no time finding someone to decorate his arm," thought Joseph. "I wonder if the young lady knows what she is getting into." At that point, Maura came to his mind once again, and Joseph realized that had circumstances been different, it would have been Maura accompanying the officer. While he would have spared her her recent experiences, he was quite glad that it wasn't.

The following day, Joseph walked through the streets of Pierre on his way to the stage office. He remembered the night before that a package should have arrived some time ago for him and he wanted to check whether it was waiting for him.

He gave his name to the clerk who went to the back room to search among the many boxes and letters awaiting their prairie owners. The clerk came back out carrying a wooden box bearing Joseph's name. "Really, sir, it only just arrived about a week ago. It don't look in too good a shape. Guess it had a rough trip back and I apologize for that, sir. That might be why it was later than you expected. Hope nothin' bad happened to what's inside. That'd be a big disappointment, after all this time and all."

Joseph's stomach did a flop as he listened to the clerk's words. He hadn't told Maura that he had William Shakley's camera. He had sent it back to the company after he had dropped her off at the sheriff's office. He had hoped to surprise her with the photographs, so that they could be something that she could use to remember her friend. Now, he was almost afraid to open the box, thinking he may find only damaged goods inside.

He decided not to prolong the inevitable. Joseph pried the lid off and immediately saw only broken bits of wood lying on top of the camera. "Oh, no," he thought, lifting the black box from the package. It was only then that he saw that not only was the camera intact, but there was something wrapped in brown paper at the bottom of the box. Carefully reaching in, Joseph pulled it out, removed the protective covering, and was relieved to find a stack of photographs. Quickly looking through the round images on paperboard, he saw antelope, flowers and even some sites he recognized, including several from his grandfather's camp. There was also a photograph of Maura with her back against a large boulder, her eyes closed. He hesitated when he saw it, and then slipped it into his jacket pocket.

As he came to the bottom of the stack, the hands holding the photographs began to shake. The final two were slightly blurred, but Joseph could see that they depicted a wagon and several men standing around some horses. The men had long black hair and were carrying what appeared to be rifles. The impact of the images knocked Joseph backward and he grabbed at the counter for support. He could see a portion of Shakley's body at the bottom of the photograph, so he knew that gentleman could not have captured these moments of the attack.

"Maura, what did you do?"

Riding back into the fort, Joseph went directly to his quarters, after tying his horse to the hitching post outside. He carried the box with its treasure inside and sat down at his table and dug out the two photographs he was most interested in. Sitting in his room, Joseph ignored the sounds of life going on outside its walls and concentrated on the images. He was having a difficult time with portions of them and wished that he had the means to see them closer. A thought suddenly struck him and, taking the images with him, he ran out his door and to the office of Dr. Pierce.

Not bothering to knock, Joseph opened the office door in a rush, causing it to slam the wall inside. The resulting noise woke the doctor from a nap over his ledger and his jerky movement sent one of his medicine bottles flying to the floor. Luckily, it had been empty so the crash only destroyed the glass.

"What the...?" the doctor's glasses were perched on his head again but Joseph rushed over and taking the matter into his own hands, pushed the spectacles back to their owner's nose.

"Take a look at these!" he ordered, shoving the photographs in front of Dr. Pierce's face.

"What?" The doctor was still a bit disoriented after being awakened in such a manner and could not quite focus on what Joseph was referring to.

"These photographs. You must look at these. And if you have something that will magnify them, we have to look even closer!"

"My boy, give me just a second to get my wits about me. You've sent me into a tizzy."

Joseph took a deep breath and counted to ten. He was trying his hardest to be patient but the doctor wasn't making it easy. Finally, Dr. Pierce took the two images in hand and held them close to his eyes, first one then the other.

"What are they, and where did you get them?" he asked. "What do they have to do with me?"

"I think Maura took them."

"Maura? Why would she take these photographs? She doesn't even have a camera. She would never be able to afford one."

"It wasn't her camera. Has she ever spoken to you about her friend, William Shakley? He was killed in the attack."

"Oh, yes! He was a photographer. She told me how close they had become and how much she had looked forward to seeing the photographs he had taken, but apparently his camera was never found at the camp. The men buried the bodies where they lay because they were too far gone to transport, and they brought back the wagon and the supplies and personal effects that were in it, but the camera wasn't there."

"That's because I took it," Joseph admitted.

"You took it?"

"Yes. After I found Maura, I used the wagon to take her to my village. When I took it back to what had been their camp, I saw the camera lying next to Shakley and I picked it up. I never told Maura. I sent it back to the company so that the photographs could be developed and she could have them. I thought she might like that. I just picked up the package today and when I saw these two, I rushed back here. Look at them. I believe Maura took them during the attack."

"Oh, my God!" the doctor exclaimed. "You mean to tell me that these are the men who...?"

"Yes, I believe they are. But something is wrong and I'm not quite sure what it is. I need to see them closer. Do you have something that would help me do that?"

Dr. Pierce was quiet for a moment, then leapt from his seat and went over to his bookshelf. "I've been using this to prop my books up, but I think it would better serve you in this case," he told Joseph, clearing a space on his desk and setting a microscope there.

"That should do it," Joseph said, and inserted the photograph between the base and the glass. He looked through the eyepiece and focused, moving the photograph until he found the spot he was looking for.

"There it is."

"What is it, Joseph?" the doctor asked. "What did you find?

"Take a look for yourself," Joseph said, straightening and backing away from the equipment.

The doctor stepped forward, leaned over and studied the photograph. "Joseph, that man..."

"Yes, I thought that's what it was when I looked at it before, but with the microscope, now I'm sure."

What both men saw shot Maura's account of the attack all to hell. She had told them she was attacked by a band of Indians, but, according to the magnifier, one of the "Indians" was holding a long black wig in his hand while his blonde head testified to something totally different.

"She had never seen Indians before. And while being shot at and watching her friends die, it's understandable that she wouldn't notice that something was wrong," Joseph said, and the doctor nodded his agreement. "If there's one white man among them, who's to say that there aren't more?"

"What should we do?" Dr. Pierce asked. "We have to tell someone."

"Not yet. First, I think we should talk to Maura. We need to know how these photographs came about, and, I'm just not sure right now who we can trust. We don't know who these men are or where they came from."

"I never thought about that, but you're right. We have to keep quiet about these. No sense taking any chances. Let's go. I think we need to talk to Maura now."

Joseph agreed and pocketed the two photographs. While the doctor waited, he went to his quarters and retrieved Shakley's photographs to take to Maura as well. He didn't know what her reaction would be, but he was glad that the doctor would be with him when he showed them to her. In her condition, he had no idea what she would do.

The pair headed out of the fort. They both felt, rather than witnessed, many pairs of eyes following them, but Joseph reasoned that no one other than themselves could possibly know about the photographs and the true meaning behind their visit to Maura.

They walked in silence toward the river village of homes that could be described as no more than a slum.

One series of knocks brought the occupant to the door. "Henry! Joseph! What a surprise! What are you doing here?"

"We need to speak with you, Maura. May we come in?"

The look on both men's face made Maura pause. "What's wrong?"

"I have something for you. And we must ask you some questions." Joseph's calm answers helped to allay any fear that Maura had.

"Come in, please."

There was only one chair in the house and Joseph led the woman to it and motioned for her to sit down. Dr. Pierce stood before the fireplace, but at this time of day there were no flames by which to warm himself. Joseph had been carrying the package he had received and now he set it on Maura's lap.

"What is it?" she wondered, looking first at the package, then to Joseph, and Dr. Pierce.

"Open it," Joseph ordered.

Carefully, Maura removed the lid and handed it to Joseph. She looked within the box and inhaled sharply. Her hands shaking, she brought out the familiar black box camera and rubbed its crinkled surface. As she lifted her face to look questioningly at him, Joseph saw a tear begin its slide to her chin and, her voice only a whisper, she said, "Where did you find it?"

Joseph knelt before her and placed his hands over hers, as she gripped the camera. "I picked it up at your camp and when I brought you to Pierre, I sent it back to the company, thinking that looking at the photographs would give you some comfort. I picked up the package this morning, and when I saw it, I knew that I had to see you right away."

Tears streamed down Maura's face as she replied, "I don't know what to say. You just don't know what this means to me. He was my friend."

Joseph's right hand reached out slowly and cupped the left side of Maura's face, his thumb wiping away the tears. "There is more, Maura," Joseph said. "I looked at the photographs. There are two..." He hesitated, and then continued. "There are two that I...that we must talk to you about. Do you feel up to answering some questions?"

"Two...I don't know what you mean. What are you saying?"

Joseph pulled the stack of photographs from the bottom of the box and shuffled through them until he found the ones he needed. Returning the rest to the box, he held the two in front of him with their backs to Maura.

"You must look at these, and you must tell me about them. I have every reason to believe that it was you who took them."

"Me? No, William took all the photographs. I never..." Maura's eyes grew wide and she began to shake her head. "No, not those. Not those. I don't want to!"

Dr. Pierce rushed to Maura's side from where he had stood while Joseph stood and leaned over her, placing his forehead against hers while placing his hands on her shoulders. "I know, I know. I would not ask you to unless it was very, very important." He looked to the doctor with a silent question.

"Go on, son. This will have to be done sooner or later. It is best while we are both here to help her."

"Maura."

"No."

"Yes."

Her eyes closed, Maura began to relate how she had come to take the photographs in question. When she was done, both Joseph and Dr. Pierce exhaled audibly. Relief shone on Maura's face and she was noticeably calmer.

"There is more, Maura. I want you to look much closer at this portion of the photograph. Will you do that for me?" Joseph asked.

"Yes, let me see."

Her eyes followed where Joseph's index finger pointed. "What...I don't understand. That man right there...He looks like he has blonde hair! And he is holding...is that black hair? A wig? How could this be? I never saw him."

"We believe he was wearing the wig when the attack occurred, Maura. And your photograph is the only proof we have that things were not as they seemed," Dr. Pierce explained. "You did a great thing, girl, whether you realize it or not. I don't know how you kept your head about you long enough to do it, with the wound you had and all."

"Is it possible, Maura, that these men thought you were dead?" It was Joseph speaking.

"I almost believed myself dead," she answered, "so, yes, I guess they did, or they believed that I would be soon. There was no one left to help me, until you came, that is."

Joseph rose to his full height and walked toward the door. He opened it, and then stood in the doorway with his back against the jamb for what seemed to be a very long time. Finally, Dr. Pierce came to him and said in a low voice, "What are you thinking?"

"I'm thinking that when we find out who these people are, I may not be responsible for my actions. How could they do this? Especially a white man? How could he condone the killing of his own people and leave a woman to die? I don't understand."

"You are making one mistake, Joseph, that is why you don't understand."

"A mistake? What is that?"

"You believe that all people value life the same way you do. You are what...close to 30 years old?" Joseph nodded. "Have you not, in all those years, met anyone who only valued himself, or, in the greatest stretch, valued others only for what he could gain from them? Think, Joseph."

"A snake."

"Pardon?" asked the doctor.

"A human snake. One who pretends to be one way, but acts another and has no regret for his actions. Beautiful on the outside, but deadly on the inside."

"You've hit the nail on the head, son. That wasn't the description I had been thinking of, but it fits exactly. We are dealing with a snake, and we must use caution, for we do not know when he will strike again."

"Will you work with me on this?" Joseph asked the doctor. "I know it could be dangerous and we don't even know where these men are or who they are. We have to begin our investigation with the attack against Maura and these photographs are better than her memory would be. But this will take some time and we must not reveal these to anyone."

"I agree, and yes, I will help you son. You will not walk alone in this."

Joseph smiled. "I did not think I would."

Chapter Sixteen

It had been several days since Joseph and Dr. Pierce had come to her with the photographs. Since then, Maura had taken every moment she could spare to look at each and every one of them. Some she did not recognize and believed those to have been taken before she had met Mr. Shakley. But others were quite familiar, and although it made her heart ache to know that he would never see them, she found comfort in being able to hold them, and vowed to share them in some way with others.

She was relieved that Joseph had kept the two she had taken, saying that he and Dr. Pierce wished to keep studying them.

Now, as she looked at the wildflowers and animals once more, she began to realize she was running out of daylight. Even though the days were longer, she still did not seem to have enough time to accomplish everything she wished to. She had to admit that part of the reason was that she moved slower these days than she had before. The weight of the baby bore down on her and she found herself huffing and puffing, doing tasks that she had previously accomplished with ease only months before.

Having no money with which to buy lamp oil even if she did own a lamp, which she didn't, Maura decided to spare her eyes and put the photographs back into their box. She was rather tired anyway and was ready to crawl onto her pallet and find peace in sleep.

More and more, lately, her sleep had included visions of Joseph. He had been very kind to her in the last few weeks and she reasoned this to be why she had not only seen him in her dreams, but had found herself thinking about him during the day as well. She had even caught herself looking for him today, and feeling more than a little disappointed when she had not spied him around the fort.

"He has been busy getting ready for his school," she told herself. "He does not have time to spend with me. And why would he anyway? What man in his right mind would want to be with a pregnant, unmarried woman like me? I should stop thinking of him and get down to my own business. I need to find a way to get away from here and find a home of my own. I will never be able to count on anyone to make a place for me. Those days were over long ago."

Placing her hand over her mouth to stifle a yawn, Maura put her other hand in the small of her back and began to rub. When her ache had eased a bit, she took her nightgown from the peg near her pallet and replaced it with her clothing from that day. Slowly she lowered herself to her bed and used her thin quilt in a futile effort to ward off the night chill that surfaced when the sun sank below the horizon.

An hour later, Maura was trying to open her eyes. Her subconscious had caught a sound, one that it could not pin down, and the feeling of unease was forcing her to awaken. She lay in the dark, listening. There were always noises along the river: animals, nocturnal birds, the occupants of the other shacks, and sometimes, the changing of the guard at the fort. But right at this moment, she knew she was hearing something out of the ordinary.

Her first thought was that it was a bird. Perhaps an owl speaking in a low, plaintive manner to the moon. But then the night music became louder and began to reach in to fill Maura's heart as no sound had ever done before until she felt compelled to follow it to its source.

Throwing back her quilt and padding barefoot on the dirt floor, Maura moved as quickly as she could toward the door. The music, really music now because she recognized it as such, drew her outward and it was beyond her control that she reached for the doorknob and turned it, stepped through the open portal and entered the night. The brightness of the moon and the myriad stars caused her to blink and momentarily distracted her, but were soon forgotten.

The soft prairie breeze carried the fragrance of wildflowers and grasses and mixed with a fresh water scent, as it passed over the river to bring its perfume to Maura's nose. That gift combined with the lilting music beckoned her even further from her door and she allowed the night to enfold her, as her ears strained for every note on the wind.

This was no bird and no animal. It was human. A human with a heavenly instrument whose notes struck a chord deep inside Maura. But to attempt to describe it seemed to lessen the experience and Maura began to simply allow the music to flow through her emotions, and wrap itself around her to ultimately seep into her soul. Never before had she heard such music, and somehow she realized that, quite possibly, never again would she be affected in this way.

One foot in front of the other, Maura made her way toward the music. Whether it was friend or foe she went to in the darkness had no bearing on her movements. She knew only that she must find the creator.

The music had grown quite loud now and Maura knew she was close. She felt no fear, no apprehension of what she might find. She knew in her heart that whatever it was, whoever it was, they would not harm her. Finally, she felt another presence, and knew that it was time to speak.

She began hesitantly.

"I don't know who you are, but I must know your name and how you come to make your music."

There was silence for a time, but when the answer came it was uttered in a decidedly male voice, one she was familiar with.

"You know me."

Maura, too, hesitated, then finally, said softly, "Your music speaks to me, Joseph," and the moment she said it, she felt that she had said too little.

"As I hoped that it would," he answered.

"Tell me, why are you out here?" Maura asked. She shivered and hugged herself.

"The music speaks to me also," Joseph explained. "And I feel in some ways, it speaks for me."

He raised, what at first appeared to be a long stick, but as Maura's eyes adjusted, she could see that Joseph placed one end to his lips and set his fingertips on several holes drilled along its length. The end of the instrument was shaped like the beak of a bird, with its mouth wide open. As Joseph's breath entered it, a sweet sound exited from the flute. It circled around them, and Maura stood, mesmerized.

When it ended, Joseph saw that Maura shivered.

"Come inside," he said huskily, inviting her to share the warmth of the colorful blanket he wore over his shoulders. Without hesitation, she complied and reveled in the weight of the blanket and the scent of the man who carried it and wrapped it around her.

"Do you know," he began, "that if a man and a woman stood together in my village, as we are doing now, everyone would consider them to be courting?"

"If I were a woman standing with a man like you in your village, I would be very proud to be courting you, Joseph." Maura said the words so quietly that he had to strain to hear. But as Maura laid her head on his chest and wrapped her arms about him, his cheek caressed the top of her head and she could feel him smile.

Time passed unnoticed and Maura did not know how long they stayed that way, as she listened to the rhythm of Joseph's heart. Reluctantly, she loosed her grip and turned, but Joseph pulled her back against his body, hugging her to him again. Maura lifted her eyes to the sparkling sky and broke the silence.

"You know, I saw thousands of electric lights at the Columbian Exposition in Chicago and I thought that was the most beautiful thing I'd ever seen. Until tonight."

Joseph lowered his head, listening quietly and taking in her scent. Soon, Maura began shivering again, only for a different reason. "Your flute music is not the only thing that speaks to me," she said, and Joseph pulled the blanket tighter around them both to block out the night.

"So."

Maura recognized James' voice behind her, as she washed out a shirt that would definitely need some mending before she returned it to its owner. She studied the frayed portions of the garment, making a concerted effort to ignore his presence in the vain hope that he would simply go away. After last night, she did not want him to spoil her happiness. She felt better today than she had for some time, but now James threatened her rediscovered confidence.

"I hear you have that Indian school teacher at your beck and call. Maura, Maura," he chastised. "Did you enjoy that group of redskins so much that you wanted another?"

"I will not let him goad me into speaking," Maura thought, rubbing at a stain for the third time, while biting the inside of her cheek to keep from retaliating.

James had not approached her since the confrontation inside the fort. Now he had found Maura at work at the laundry tubs and she was irritated by his visit more than afraid of what he would do.

"What could he possibly see in you? You are as big as a house, my dear, you and your little bastard Indian baby. Or do you know exactly who the father is? Oh, well. I think Walks Alone will live up to his name. He won't want you much longer. You cannot hide your shame, Maura. It precedes you everywhere you go."

There was a blessed silence for a time, and it took Maura a minute to realize that she had been holding her breath. Not hearing another sound, she turned slowly and saw that James had left. Apparently his plan now was to take one chip at a time from the wall she had built around herself. Maura exhaled and allowed her shoulders to slump. If she was to be truthful with herself, she felt as if James had just read her mind. He had asked her the very questions she hadn't wanted to ask herself.

What did Joseph want with her? She was nobody. He shouldn't waste his time on her. Her rational mind could form those sentences, but her heart felt something completely different. It had felt so wonderful last night, being held, feeling loved. There. She had said the word, if only to herself. Love. It had been so long since she had felt loved, protected, wanted. It was nice to pretend that it could go on.

She looked down at her burgeoning belly. Would Joseph remain after she bore someone else's child? A man that she wouldn't recognize if he spoke to her? The confidence she had felt just a short while ago was rapidly receding, as her thoughts centered on what her life would bring. The laundry lay in her hands, forgotten, as Maura watched a small log bob and twirl in the swirling water of the Missouri.

Suddenly, she felt someone behind her and his hands gripped her upper arms. "James," she groaned. "Please let me alone."

"What did he say to you?"

"Oh, Joseph," Maura's shoulders slumped in relief. "Well, it was nothing. He wasn't here long. But I'm glad it is you."

"He was here long enough. You should not have to endure his words. I must think of a way to stop him. His remarks cut you, so that I can almost see the wounds. I do not like it."

Joseph began to knead Maura's shoulders. Her eyes closed of their own volition and she sighed audibly.

"Let us forget him. Right now, you must slow down. You need to rest."

"I'm all right, Joseph, truly. You shouldn't worry about me. I'm stronger than you think."

"Then you must have the strength of ten men," Joseph grinned. "I already believe you to be the second strongest woman I know."

"Only the second-strongest?" she asked.

"Behind my grandmother. She is the wisest as well."

"I agree. I have never met anyone quite like her and I feel honored to be placed second to her."

"In all other ways, you do not place second." Joseph stopped his massage and held Maura's back close against him.

"So, I am third, or fourth?" She meant only to tease.

"You must know that is not true." He leaned in so closely that Maura could feel his breath against her ear.

"Joseph," she began, as she turned to face him. "I wanted to tell you how grateful I am for your support and for the time you have shared with me. I realize...."

"Grateful! Bah! Am I that stupid, that I believe there is affection where there is only gratitude?" He gripped her arms tighter and pulled her closer. "Are you satisfied with my 'support', or do you want more? I want more, Maura. I thought after last night, I believed we shared more than support and friendship. Am I wrong?"

"Oh, Joseph. Look at me! Really look at me."

"I would look at you every hour, every minute, every second of every day, for the rest of my life. Do you understand, Maura? Do you?"

"You don't know what you're saying." Her voice became louder and she enunciated each word. "I am carrying someone else's baby, and I don't even know the father. What does that make me?"

"A victim of someone's greed. And a mother-to-be."

Taking a deep breath, Joseph continued. "My people revere children. Each child is someone to treasure. It is an extension of one's self and of one's people. How do you feel about the child you carry within, Maura? You have never spoken of him."

"O'Brien! Ya got them clothes washed yet? Get busy and quit yer yakkin' with yer boyfriend. Daylight's a wastin'." Maura looked guiltily at the head laundress who stood nearby with hands on hips. "I'm sorry, Mrs. Armstrong. I'll get right at it."

"See that ya do!"

Maura turned back to the washtub and began to scrub again.

"Do not think that you do not have to answer me, Maura. I will be back." Joseph turned on his heel and walked determinedly back to the fort.

"I don't know which one is worse," Maura said aloud, "but their guilt is killing me."

Joseph stopped when he got to the fort gates, turned and looked back at Maura. He could see that she was bent over her tub, scrubbing an article of clothing. He felt in his heart that there was more going on than what she would say or show to him. He could not have prevented what happened to her that morning months ago, but it would always be a part of her. He did know, however, that he could help her heal, and he would do whatever was necessary to see that nothing, and no one, hurt her more.

Chapter Seventeen

"I've been thinking, Dr. Pierce...."

"Oh, for heaven's sake, call me Henry. 'Dr. Pierce' is a little too formal for me."

"All right, sir, I mean, Henry. Anyway, I was looking at the photographs again, and I believe there must be other clues in addition to them."

"What do you mean, Joseph?"

The two friends were sitting on opposite sides of the doctor's desk, working on solving the mystery of the attack on Maura.

"I've been trying to remember what was at the campsite." Taking a sheet of paper from his pocket and leaning over the desk, he showed the doctor what he'd done. "I've drawn what I recall seeing at the site, and I've started a list of things that I saw inside the wagon. But I there was something that I didn't see. Something large that had apparently been removed from it. There was a tarp inside, but it covered nothing. There had to have been something it was hiding. But what?"

"All you can do, my boy, is retrace your steps from the time you say you heard the shots. What did you see?"

Joseph considered the doctor's question. "I remember that once I got close, I saw the group of four or five, and they had a horse that appeared to be carrying something. But from a distance, I couldn't tell what it was. I went into the camp carefully, found the wagon driver, Shakley, and then Maura. I moved the tarp in the wagon and laid her on it to take her back to my village."

"Think about what was inside the wagon, Joseph. Can you remember?"

"The tarp, some wood, tools, flour, salt, hardtack..."

"Those were in there when you got there?" the doctor prodded.

"Yes."

"I heard a rumor at the time that a shipment of magazine rifles, which the army would start giving the men as standard issue, had been taken in the fray. Could those have fit inside the tarp you saw?"

"Definitely. If the guns were in the wagon, that would explain the attack. But how did they know the new rifles were in that particular wagon? Or was it just coincidence?"

"Joseph, I had another thought and it has nothing whatsoever to do with weapons. Even renegades have to eat. With all the foodstuffs you named in the wagon, wouldn't they have taken that as well? I may be shut up in this fort, but I've seen what goes on. The Indians are starving right and left, Joseph. Why would they leave the food? Wouldn't they at least take it for themselves, if not to pass it along to others?"

Joseph felt as if he had been slammed in the gut. "You're right. I wouldn't let my people take the food in the village because I was afraid we would be accused of the attack if the food were missing. Why didn't they take it?" he said, half to himself. "Unless...."

"Dr. Pierce! Dr. Pierce!" The shouts came from outside and something hit the door like a rock. Then it flew open and Andy Riegel, the young man Joseph had hired to carry the laundry for Maura, burst into the room.

"Dr. Pierce! Ya gotta come quick!"

"What is it, Andy?" the doctor asked as he rose from his chair and grabbed for his medical bag.

"It's Miss Maura. She's all doubled up and moanin'." Joseph didn't wait for any more explanations. He took off running, while the doctor followed as fast as he could. "Go on, Andy," he urged, planning to listen as he walked.

"I had to run an errand for Miz Armstrong and I told Miss Maura to wait for me if'n she got done afore I come back. But she went and tried to carry the basket herself and when I got there, the clothes was all over the ground and she was actin' like she was hurtin' somethin' powerful. So I came to git you straight away."

"Good job, Andy," said Dr. Pierce, patting the young man on the back as he came upon Maura, now lying on the ground with Joseph hovering over. "We'll take it from here."

"Maura." The doctor said the name calmly, hoping to convey that to his patient. He could see that she was holding her stomach and sweating profusely.

"She's in a lot of pain, Henry. What can we do?"

"Well, for one thing, we can't leave her lying out here in the dirt. Let's take her home."

"Right," Joseph agreed, inserting his hands in the tight space between Maura and the ground. He lifted her effortlessly and rose from his knees to his feet, heading for the fort.

"Joseph! I said, take her home!" the doctor shouted.

"I am. She will not lie on the ground to have this baby. I will take her to my quarters."

The doctor began running behind Joseph to try his best to catch his friend. "That's not a good idea, Joseph, and you know it. They'll never let you bring her in there. And even if you did get her to your door, they'd stop you and bring her back. They don't want her there. Please, Joseph! We can take care of her in her house."

"No."

A small voice interjected. "He's right, Joseph. Take me back."

"I will not. We are going inside now." And Joseph headed into the fort. He made it more than halfway to his door when the first command hit his ears.

"You there! You can't bring her in here. Get her out!"

Joseph ignored the speaker and continued, putting his hand on his doorknob.

"Walks Alone! That woman cannot go into your quarters. That's an order!" Col. Coffey commanded.

"Take her to my office, Joseph. She can have the baby there," Dr. Pierce suggested. But the compromise did not sit well with Joseph and he continued into his room.

Placing Maura carefully on the bed, he went to the water bucket, and then brought the ladle to her lips. "Drink," he ordered, and she took the ladle in her shaking hands and swallowed as much as she could. Then he found a clean shirt, ripped it in half, and dipped it in the cool water. He placed the cloth over her forehead. "Try to rest, Maura."

Joseph walked over to where the doctor stood, half in and half out of the room. "Are you coming in?" Joseph asked. "What is it? Do you need something from your office?"

The doctor's face was white and Joseph feared that following him so quickly had strained the physician's own health. "Henry? Are you all right?"

"What? Oh, yes, yes, I'm fine."

"You don't look so good, Henry. Maybe you'd better sit down."

"Right, that would be an excellent idea, my boy. Excellent."

Joseph studied the doctor, then retrieved the ladle from the bucket and passed it to the older man, who drank thirstily.

At that moment, several men burst into the room, and behind them followed Capt. James Cole.

"Ready to whelp, are you, Maura?" The captain waved his hand at the others with him, silently ordering their departure. The men looked at one another, then left.

"Really, Walks Alone, what do you think you're doing, bringing her in here?" Cole looked at Maura with distaste. "She can't stay, you know. It isn't right to subject the other ladies to this. I'm sure none of them have even seen a whore, let alone listened to one moan. I'm sure Maura has had plenty of practice in that, and while the men may enjoy it, I doubt the ladies would approve. Now get her out of here."

"Now see here, sir," Dr. Pierce interrupted. "I'll not listen to this."

"Oh, you'll listen, doctor, or your days here will be numbered as well. Coffey has been too lenient with you, and when he's gone, you may be assured that you will be reassigned elsewhere. But perhaps you enjoy treating whores. Some physicians do. There are so many lovely diseases to experiment with. And speaking of Maura, do take her away, back to her whorehouse. That was good enough for my mother and it will be more than sufficient for her."

"She stays."

Cole looked at Joseph, as if he hadn't heard right.

"Are you disobeying me?" Cole asked.

"I am under no obligation to obey you," Joseph pointed out. "While I admit that I am here under your good graces, I am not your subordinate. I am an entity unto myself while you, sir, are an officer of the United States Army who invited this woman to come here, then abandoned her after she was brutally attacked and almost murdered, all the while under the supposedly safe umbrella of that same U.S. Army, I might add. Now she is about to have a child and I believe she has already suffered enough through this ordeal without having to endure the further indignity of lying on a pallet on the dirt in order to give birth. She stays."

Joseph turned his back on the captain and began speaking to Maura in a low voice as he sat on the edge of the bed beside her.

"Walks Alone." The call was met by silence.

"Walks Alone!" said louder this time.

"Yes."

"If I hear one peep from these quarters while she is here, I will hold you responsible and whatever happens will be on your head, do you understand?"

"Yes."

Joseph had never turned to face the captain, whose boots now made thunderous echoes in the room as he stormed outside.

"I am afraid, Joseph," Maura said.

"There is nothing to be afraid of, Maura. Henry is here, and..."

"I'm not afraid of having the baby, I'm afraid of James...of what he will do. Especially, what he will do to you. He does not take orders. He gives them and expects to be obeyed. Please do not take him lightly," she pleaded.

"This is not for you to worry about right now," Joseph countered. "Think about the child you are to have, not the child who leaves the room when he doesn't get his way. Now," he continued, "are you comfortable? Do you need anything? Is there anything I can get you?"

"Joseph, we have a long way to go before this baby gets here and I'd rather that you didn't hover over me the entire time. I'm fine."

"Henry, what do you need, then? Henry? Henry?" Joseph looked around the room and found that his friend was still sitting in a nearby chair, staring at Maura and sweating profusely.

"Henry, don't tell me you're afraid of the good captain as well. I don't..."

At that point, Joseph was interrupted by a groan and the doctor leaned forward with eyes wide, motioning the younger man to move closer to him.

"Henry, what's the matter?"

"I'm afraid."

"Afraid? Of Cole? Of losing your job? Henry, you must know that he can't do a thing to you. You'll be fine."

"No, no, my boy. That's not it. I'm afraid..." Henry hesitated, and then whispered, "of the baby."

"The baby? Is there something wrong that you haven't told me about? Henry, whatever it is, I need to know now."

The physician leaned even closer and said in an even smaller voice, "I've never delivered a baby before," and with that, he collapsed back in the chair.

Joseph's eyes grew large and he straightened. "Come outside."

"I can't my boy, I'm weak as a kitten."

"Come outside," Joseph said forcefully. "Now!"

The doctor rose slowly and headed for the door, as Joseph assured Maura they would be right back.

When the door closed behind Joseph on the other side, he grabbed the doctor's upper arm and steered him to his office. As soon as they were completely alone, Joseph questioned, "What did you mean when you said you've never delivered a baby? There are children here at the fort, surely you helped with them? My God, Henry, you've been here, how many years?"

"I feel I must let you in on a little secret, Joseph. Perhaps I should have told someone before, but you know how it is. One little lie leads to another and pretty soon you're in so deep, your next stop is China."

"Henry, get to the point."

"Well, you see," the doctor's voice cracked a bit and after clearing his throat, he nervously went on. "I'm not really a doctor."

"What?" Joseph shook his head in an attempt to clear whatever it was blocking his hearing. "Say that again, Henry."

"Well, I am, but I'm not."

"What the hell does that mean?"

"Please be calm while I tell you this. It's difficult enough without you shouting at me."

"I'm sorry, Henry, but you must realize that this is not the most opportune moment for you to reveal this."

"I know, I know, but I kept thinking I'd have plenty of time to find someone to come and help when it was Maura's time. How did I know she'd go into labor early?"

"Well, if you were a real doctor, you'd have known that was a possibility," Joseph said evenly. "But of course, if you were a real doctor, you wouldn't need anyone to help, because you'd know exactly what to do yourself!"

"You really must calm down, Joseph. Someone's going to hear and you're just upsetting yourself."

"You're right, you're right. Please, continue."

"Well, to begin with, I was a druggist, with a comfortable business in Chicago. I was doing all right for myself...I had my own home, two servants, nice clothes, the works. Then came the great fire and my shop was totally wiped off the face of the city. I had been having a bit of wanderlust anyway, so I thought, 'why not?' and sold my home and most of my belongings. I packed up what was left, along with some tricks of my trade, and took off for the west.

"I had passed through Pierre and stopped here to seek protection for the night when I heard that the colonel was having, what seemed to be, chest pains. I ordered the young sergeant to lead me to him and I took one look, went to my wagon, mixed up my special concoction – bicarbonate of soda and water, administered it to him and within the hour his symptoms were gone. He'd just had indigestion, you see, but I was hailed as a miracle worker, and since the fort doctor had gone to Colorado Springs six months earlier and never returned, Coffey asked if I'd like to stay and sign on as the company physician. What would you have done? I said, 'yes', and I've been here ever since. That was nigh on 10 years ago. All along, I planned to tell someone, but since the Indian problem, sorry, my boy, was pretty much over, there was never any serious injuries beyond a broken arm or a severe cut. And I could pretty much treat illnesses with my medications and consults with my trusty manuals.

"As for delivering the other children, I was never required to do so. I was out of the fort when young Jimmy Thompson was born, and the other two ladies who have been with child did not want a gentleman attending the birth, so several mothers experienced in these matters helped out, and luckily, nothing went wrong.

"I've done quite well for myself, really, under the circumstances."

"I'm very happy for you, Henry. But now, you see, you've hit a brick wall, as it were and we must decide how to peel you off of it because those 'experienced mothers' are not going to help Maura. It's just us, so get whatever you think you'll need and pull yourself together because we have to get back to our mother-to-be. This baby is coming, Henry, like it or not!"

The closest thing the fort had to a doctor began to search his quarters for anything that resembled something necessary for childbirth. When he was done, the two men left the office and headed back to Joseph's quarters.

When they got there, Maura was on her feet, pacing the small room. "There you are," she said. "I thought you two had left me here to have this baby by myself. Well, don't think I couldn't do it. I don't need either one of you. Especially you, Mr. Walks Alone. You just keep on walking right back out of here, because Dr. Pierce is the only one I need right now. You don't have any business being...uh, oh. Here comes another one!" And with that, her right hand flew to support her abdomen while she bent forward to cope with the contraction that gripped her.

Henry looked at Joseph, his eyes rolled back in his head and he pitched forward into a heap on the floor.

"Guess that leaves me," said Joseph, mostly to himself, as he picked up the items Henry had taken to the floor with him and then placed them on a table.

"Maura, don't you think you'd better lie down now?"

"No, I don't. What's the matter with Henry?"

"I was quite young when my cousins were born, but I recall that my aunts didn't lie down in childbirth. I wonder, though, if you might not be more comfortable in bed," Joseph offered, in a temporarily successful attempt to evade her question.

"No, I would not be more comfortable. Besides, when I was young, I helped my mother several times when she mid-wifed for some women in our building. She always made them walk around for as long as they could before they had the baby. She said she learned that from her mother and it was best for the woman and the baby. So don't be trying to tell me what to do Mr. Know-It-All Walks Alone. You're a man, anyway. Leave me alone."

"No matter what you say, I will not leave you alone, Maura. I promise you that I will never leave you alone again."

Maura grew very quiet, and even though Joseph could tell that another contraction had moved in, she continued to stare at him, searching his face with her eyes. Finally, when the contraction had passed, she exhaled and spoke.

"Don't be promising me something you can't keep, Joseph. I have the memory of an elephant, don't you know, and I'll remember everything you say today. My mind isn't clouded by what's going on. Besides, I've been alone for most of my life now. That's just the way it is and I have a feeling that that's just the way it's going to continue to be. But I thank you for saying it anyway."

Two steps separated the pair, but Joseph knew there was an even greater chasm between them. While they had grown much closer over the past weeks, Maura's lack of trust bothered him. He knew that it was a defense mechanism on her part – everyone she had ever counted on, had been taken away in her life – her parents, William Shakley, and even to a certain degree, James Cole. She had a right to feel the way she did, but it didn't make life any easier for Joseph. He had to find a way to break through, but this probably wasn't the time.

"I hope you do remember what I said, Maura. I hope you remember it every day of your life and that you remind me every day of mine. Then your constant nagging will ensure that I keep my word. I wouldn't want to hear about it if I failed."

"I have a feeling you've not met failure many times in your life, Joseph," Maura said.

Joseph fingered the bone choker he wore constantly around his neck. "I've met it more often than I'd like to remember," he answered. "Too many times."

Maura watched the man across from her and felt that while he sat physically in the room with her, mentally he was very far away. She wanted to ask him about his thoughts, but another contraction hit her and her mind was occupied elsewhere.

It was at this point that Henry began to drag himself from his unconscious state. Rolling to a sitting position on the floor, he looked dazedly around him until his eyes fell on Maura. "Oh, no. It's coming, it's coming, and there's not a damned thing I can do. Oh, no. Oh, no," he groaned, plopping his head into the palms of his hands.

"What is the matter with him?" Maura asked, as Joseph moved over toward the older man.

"I'll explain later. I just don't think he's feeling very well right now, are you Henry?"

"I'll never feel well again. Never again."

Trying to get the man to snap out of his depression, Joseph began organizing the items the two had brought back from Henry's office, as Maura walked around the room. "Henry, come and tell me how you want these things arranged," Joseph called.

"It's no use, son. I wouldn't know what to do with those things any more than I'd know what to do with a plow. I'm useless. Just throw me out on the heap with the rest of the garbage."

"What is he babbling about?" Maura wondered. "Henry, what is wrong with you?"

"What's wrong? What's wrong? I'll tell you what's wrong."

"Henry!" Joseph tried to stop him.

"What's wrong is I know absolutely nothing about women having babies. There. I said it. Now she knows. Woe is me!"

Maura looked at Henry, then looked at Joseph.

"Sit down, Maura," Joseph ordered. "We have something to tell you."

Maura slowly sank into a straight-back chair nearby.

"Go on, then, tell her, Henry."

"No."

"Henry, you've already let the cat out of the bag."

Henry wrinkled his nose, as if he smelt something bad. "It's true, I don't know anything about babies. I don't know how to hold them, I don't know how to feed them and I especially don't know how to deliver them, because I've never delivered one in my life." Turning to Joseph, he gave the man a defiant look and snapped, "Are you happy now?

"Tell her why, Henry."

"Do I have to?"

"You might as well."

106

Henry looked Maura right in the eye and blurted, "I'm not a doctor."

"I know," she stated simply.

The jaws of both men dropped simultaneously. "You know?" they shouted together.

"I've known for quite some time," she said.

"How? Why? What gave me away? Does anyone else know?"

"Henry, I don't know about anyone else. I've never discussed it with anyone. I knew right after I first met you."

"I don't recall. What did I do? What did I say? How could you tell?"

"Oh, it wasn't what you did, so much as what you didn't do. You know little Johnny Riegel, Andy's brother? Remember when he fell and broke his wrist and the bone was sticking through his skin?"

Henry broke out into a sweat again. "Oh, yes, how could I forget? That was the most disgusting thing I'd ever seen. But, go on."

"Just a second," and Maura placed both hands at the base of her mother load, feeling the intensity of the contractions from the outside. Once it passed, she went on.

"Well, the minute you looked at Johnny's arm you went white as the snow in winter, kind of like you are now. Your eyes watered and your hand went to your mouth. I thought you were going to vomit right there and then. But you excused yourself, saying you needed some other supplies, ran back to your office and it was a good 10 minutes before you returned. Poor little Johnny's mother was just about beside herself by that time. She figured you weren't coming back."

"So that told you I wasn't a doctor?"

"Well, it was a good suspicion. By the time doctors have reached your age, sorry Henry, they've usually seen everything there is to see and then some. But that wasn't the only thing."

"I'm afraid to ask," Joseph said grudgingly.

"It was when Henry brought out some laudanum, for Johnny's pain, we thought. But after he dosed it out, Henry took it instead! Then of course, I think he realized what he had done and immediately gave some to the boy. I volunteered to help with the injury since I had watched my mother set my brother's arm after he had broken it falling out of a tree. I sewed up what was needed and that job done, Johnny was taken care of, and off to bed he went. I helped Henry back to his office where he laid his head on top of his desk and started to snore."

"I guess that's why I don't recall much about it," Henry admitted. "But why didn't you ever say anything?"

"Why should I? You're the kindest, most gentle man I've ever met and you sincerely care about people. That's enough to get them through just about anything."

Henry grabbed Maura's hand and kissed it.

"Now," Maura stated. "Although I myself have limited knowledge of doctoring and babies, I do know that when your water breaks as mine did just now, it shouldn't be long before the baby comes. And if you don't mind, I believe I feel like lying down now."

Both men leaped into action and almost dragged Maura over to the bed in their haste to help.

Unfortunately, Maura's prediction of a speedy labor did not hold true. Hours later, as she let the constant pain of her succession of contractors take control, Joseph said to Henry, "I'm worried. It seems to me that something must be wrong. I wonder if I should offer to pay one of the ladies to come and help us. Maybe Mrs. Armstrong would come."

"Well, that's a thought, Joseph. We're obviously not equipped with the knowledge to help her and she's wearing herself out trying to do this on her own. I'll go down to the laundry and ask Mrs. Armstrong for help."

Joseph sat on the edge of the bed next to Maura and, taking a cool wet cloth, wiped the sweat from her brow. The woman smiled weakly and squeezed his hand. "Joseph, I don't think I'm doing this right. Shouldn't the baby have been here by now?"

"I don't know, sweet one. I've heard that it takes longer for some women than others. Perhaps you are just one of those. You may have to fight hard for this child. Would you do that, Maura?"

"Yes," she said quietly, but firmly. "I know I have not talked about it but I want this child, very badly. Its conception was not my choice but its life is. We will stay together, and we will have a home filled with as much love as I can give it. There is just one thing that I regret, however," and saying that, she paused so long that Joseph felt it necessary to ask, "And what is that, Maura?"

"This might sound silly, but I really, really wish... I wish that this was your child, Joseph. That it was our child together. I want you to know, in case something should happen to me, that I have a great deal of love in my heart. Not only for this child, but for you as well. If you don't feel the same, it's all right, really it is. I'll always remember what you've done for me, the way you've cared for me. No one has cared, really cared, for so long." At that point, Maura's eyes rolled back and she collapsed and at the same time, the child slid silently from her body.

Henry burst into the room then, with Mrs. Armstrong in tow. "We're here!" he announced.

"It doesn't matter," Joseph said, tears flowing unchecked. "It's too late."

Chapter Eighteen

"You gave me quite a scare, son, telling me that. Why, I thought Maura here was a goner, and that baby of hers, too. But just look at the two of them! They're the most beautiful people I've ever seen."

"I agree," Joseph said, catching Maura's attention, as she held her new son. "The mother, especially, is very beautiful."

The statement caused the woman in the bed to turn a dark shade of pink and created a shy smile to replace the one that had already existed since she awakened to find her new son clean, and waiting to be fed. Mrs. Armstrong had long since left the room after taking care of the baby and changing the bedding. Now the trio sat and stared at the patch of red hair that topped off the pale skin of the child.

Joseph motioned Henry aside, to pose some questions that were perplexing him. "How can this be, Henry? There is no obvious evidence of native blood in this child. Is that possible? Or do we have yet another mystery on our hands?"

"You well know that I'm no expert, Joseph, however, I believe a possibility always exists for anything. Strange things can happen, you know. But have you considered that the white man in the photograph Maura took could have been the father? That's always a possibility as well."

"Yes, I had thought of that, but one of the first things she said to me after she was attacked was that 'he' looked just like me. So I believe that the man had to have had darker skin, darker hair. I'll ask her about it again, but not right now. She needs to rest, and there's something I need to do."

Maura's eyes were closed, as Joseph gently lifted the baby from her arms. "Let her sleep," he instructed the older man. "We'll be back soon."

Wrapping the child tighter inside the blanket, Joseph opened the door and stepped out into the warm night. He walked directly to the fort entrance and acknowledged the guard on patrol, as he passed through. He didn't notice the bright red glow from a cigar being held by a figure standing quietly nearby with second person, watching from the darkness.

"Where do you suppose he's going with that brat?" one asked, to which the other drawled, "To the river to drown it, I hope."

Joseph stood in the moonlight, holding the child tightly to his chest. "I am the only father you will know, my son. So it is my duty to present you to the four directions." After explaining his intentions to the blue-eyed boy, Joseph presented the new creation to the west, the north, the east, and the south and then to the heavens and the earth. The man then held the boy for quite some time, heartbeat to heartbeat, giving him his first lesson in listening to one's own heart.

"Yes."

"No."

"Maura, you will stay here."

"No, Joseph, I will go home."

"You are home. You will stay with me."

"I can't. We can't. This will be difficult enough, without trying to live under the constant stares and whispers of everyone here in the fort, especially James. I really don't think I could live like that. I want to take my son home. At least there, no one will bother us."

"I will not allow Cole to bother you. I am through with his manipulations, and his threats. I will see that he stays away from you."

"Joseph, I just don't feel comfortable here. I'm sorry. Night has fallen and I'm leaving tonight. If you want, you may help me carry my things and walk me to my door."

"You are not rested enough."

"I'm fine and Mrs. Armstrong said she would help me. She really has been very good to me. Besides, I'll have Andy to help me, too, and he can come and get you, if I need you."

"If. When. If you will not stay here, then I will go there with you."

"Joseph...."

"I mean it. There is no reason that I cannot. Once the Army is gone, we can move back."

"But it will be just as bad if you did that," Maura contested. "People will talk about an unmarried woman with a child, living with a man. They make no bones about how they feel already. For the past six months I have suffered malicious whispers from busybodies, who wouldn't know truth from idle gossip if it bit them in the bustle. I don't want my son to hear of these things."

"He will not hear of that."

"Joseph, I will not stay."

"He will not hear because when there is something you can do to solve a problem, then you must do it."

"What do you mean, Joseph?"

"I mean, I must go to Pierre within the next few weeks and I am hoping that you will go with me."

"Go to Pierre? You think I should move to Pierre to get away from the talk? I really don't know if that would help the problem. It would just be different people saying the same things. Word travels quickly."

"No, no, Maura. I do not want you to move there. I want you to go with me to find a minister and be married. I know it will not stop the talk. But it may help to stop your heartache."

Maura looked at Joseph, as if he had grown three heads. Her reaction did not stop his thoughts, however, and he continued, speaking quickly. "If you have a problem marrying a native when you are of white blood, please know that I would never force you into this, Maura. I would still be here to help you, in whatever manner you would allow. I know that a marriage between people of different blood is always fodder for gossip and our life would not be easy, but at least you would be a married woman and you would legally be under my protection. And with your permission," here he hesitated, swallowed slowly and breathed deeply. "With your permission, I wish also to find a judge and give my name to your child. I wish him to know me as his father. Even though we are not of the same blood, we have something in common, he and I."

"What is that, Joseph?" Maura's question emerged from between her lips more as a light breeze through a field of flowers than a sentence spoken.

Joseph moved in so close that Maura almost felt the need to take a step backward, but she didn't. He lifted his shaking hand, and as lightly and gently as he could, caressed the left side of her cheek, saying, "His mother is very special to us both."

Maura's face grew a lovely shade of pink and her eyes glowed, as they locked tightly with Joseph's. In the uncounted minutes they stood that way, her mind told her that a marriage of convenience such as this would, indeed, solve her problem, but she was convinced it was not love on Joseph's part. On the other hand, she had quit her job and traveled almost 1000 miles, fully prepared to marry a man she hadn't seen in years. Although she had known Joseph only a short time, she did feel a connection between them that could only grow with time. Perhaps, this could be the family she had been praying for. She had enough love inside her that she would make it work, for all three of them.

Before she could say a word, Joseph put his index finger to her lips and said, "Don't say anything right now. This would be a big step for both of us and I want to be assured that you were not rushed into making a decision.

"I will do as you ask and let you go to your home on your own but only for a short while. I am hoping that you will eventually allow me to join you there as your husband, or that you will change your mind and stay with me here. But if you choose otherwise, I will be near, no matter what you might say. I care about you, Maura. I do not want you to be alone, ever.

Joseph picked up the few things that Maura had needed after the baby was born and held out his arms to take her son into them. With an action that spoke more clearly than words, Maura did not hesitate in placing her son in Joseph's care. She placed her hand at his back and patted it gently.

"For a man with a name such as yours, you certainly have a little parade traveling with you right now!" she noted, smiling shyly.

"I would lead this parade forever, and hope that it would grow along the way," Joseph said, walking toward the door.

Maura opened it and allowed the two most important men in her life to exit ahead of her. She was nervous about seeing James on her way out but the three made it to the fort entrance and on to her tiny home, without mishap.

Opening her own door, Maura stepped through first, immediately noting the light that created a soft glow in the one-room shack. She could not say anything, however, as a rather large lump blocked her throat.

In addition to the lamp, someone had brought in a real bed frame, several quilts, and a cradle for baby Ryan, and on the small table, a vase filled with fresh wildflowers of every color.

She turned to shoot a questioning look at Joseph.

"I knew you would tell me 'no' when I asked you to stay, so I came here ahead of time and made a few changes to keep you and Ryan comfortable. I did not want you to sleep on the floor anymore and I know that my son would need a place to rest his head, as much as he sleeps."

"'Thank you' does not seem enough in exchange for all of this," Maura said, sweeping her hand across the quilts. Noting something else, she began to feel the stinging of tears in her eyes, as she brought her hand to a pile of books lying on the new nightstand by her bed. She lifted the top volume, and flipping through the pages, found it to be a copy of George Catlin's *Life Among the Indians*.

Joseph stepped over to the cradle and laid the infant inside, then carefully covered him with a quilt, which turned out to be a smaller version of the one on Maura's bed. After making sure the boy was comfortable, he turned to the baby's mother, and, placing one hand on her shoulder, took the book with his other.

"Henry told me that you were a teacher in Ohio, is that right, Maura?"

She nodded, almost imperceptibly.

"This book was with some others I have carried with me and I thought that if, as I hope, you stay in South Dakota, being the woman that you are, you will want to know more about its people – all of its people – my people. This man lived among the people of the Plains and can tell you more than I could. I can relate some things to you, but I have been away a very long time. Sometimes, I am unsure of my own ways.

"By the way, Henry has also made a suggestion, one that relates to all of this, but with all I have given you to think about, I believe I will save that for another time. You have much to think about already, and you will consider all I have said, will you not, Maura?"

"I will," she said, sitting slowly on the bed. "I promise."

"I will be waiting as patiently as I can for your answer."

"And so you left her there, alone?"

"Henry, what else could I do? One cannot bend a woman like Maura to do one's will. She must make her own decisions to feel comfortable. She has much distrust inside of her, not only because of recent events, but also because of what has transpired throughout her life. In order to build a life of trust, she must be the one in control, not me."

"Where did you get such wisdom in such a short lifetime, Joseph? You are far ahead of your time."

"I am not so much ahead of my time, as I am fighting not to be a prisoner of it. I am also fighting as best I can, to have the life I want. I want Maura and her son in my life. He will be my son. That is what Maura wished for, as she lay in labor. I was not sure at the time that it was not just the pain talking, but I have convinced myself that in her heart she truly feels a bond with me. I hope I am right in believing that."

Henry looked at the younger man, the one who had come to feel like a son to him, and said, "Joseph, my son, you know how I feel about Maura. I want you to know that there is no one else on this planet that I would trust her care with more than you. I can see your heart in your eyes, and I know that you love her, but you have not told her that yet, have you?"

"I have not used that word, no."

"You must do that, Joseph. The feelings are there, and women have a genuine need to hear those words out loud. Believe me, I know what I am talking about."

Henry did not speak for a few moments, instead, seemed to concentrate on the contents of one of the bottles on his desk. Joseph knew that the older man was struggling with something and it needed to play out on its own. Finally, Henry took a deep breath and blew the air from his lungs forcefully through his lips.

"I was engaged to be married, once, did I ever tell you that?"

Joseph's raised eyebrows gave Henry the answer.

"It was back in Chicago. I had my own home, my own business. I probably seemed like a good catch, but I never paid much attention."

A smile played on his lips and Henry's eyes grew bright. "Her name was Emiline. She wasn't the most beautiful woman I had ever seen, but she had...something. She literally ran into my shop one day. It had been drizzling and all of a sudden, a downpour emerged and pushed everyone out of the streets and into the shops. By accident, she had chosen mine. There were several others inside, some were even customers, but I didn't notice them. The light shone from her eyes, as if she had actually enjoyed the rain."

Here Henry stopped and seemed to gather his thoughts. "Her first words to me were, 'Don't you just love a good storm?' and from that moment, I was smitten. Most of the ladies I had known avoided storms, well, rain of any kind, as if it were acid. Not Emiline. She loved it! I helped the customers that had come in as fast as I could, praying the rain would continue to keep her there.

"I was 41 years old at the time, but I felt like 17. When the rain stopped, I walked her out to the sidewalk and wished her well. She began to walk away, then turned abruptly and said, 'Mr. Pierce, I will sound very forward, but please forgive me. May I come back to see you again, even when it's not raining?'" Henry's smile was so big while he relived that long-ago day that Joseph reeled from the force of the other man's emotion.

"Needless to say, she came back the next day, and then the next, and finally she began to meet me, as I closed my shop. We began courting, I met her parents, and we planned a life. I thought things were wonderful. But she'd press me for the words of love, and being the man I was then, I just couldn't say them. My own upbringing had been cold; there were no words of comfort, let alone love, in my home. I didn't know they were important.

"It wasn't until much later, when I looked back on things, that I realized she had gradually become more and more distant, pulling away. Finally, one day, she met me at the door of my shop, and told me that, although she felt a great deal toward me, she had found someone else, someone who could give her what she wanted, someone who could say 'I love you', someone who could do what I could not.

"When my shop burned, it was just one more loss that I couldn't face. My home was empty. My life was empty. I didn't care; I didn't want to live there anymore. That's why I came west. That's why I am alone to this day. Grab life as it comes by and hang on for dear life, Joseph. It may not come again."

As Henry rose from his chair, it toppled backward onto the floor. It seemed he hadn't noticed, as he made no effort to pick it up. Instead, he headed out the door of his office and walked toward the river. As he disappeared, Joseph looked at the chair lying on its back rocking from side to side like a cradle. He said a prayer at that moment that the keeper of the heavens would help him do whatever he had to do, in order to get what he wanted.

The next evening, as Joseph rode toward the fort following an afternoon ride, he was surprised to see Maura standing directly in his path. He reined in his animal, which stopped just inches from Maura's right shoulder.

"Yes."

A very small smile crept to Joseph's lips and began to spread like lava flowing from a volcano. Leaning on his saddle horn, Joseph reached for Maura's hand and grasping it tightly in his said, "Do you know, Maura, that that is the first time you have said that word to me since we met?"

"Yes," she said again, smiling rather coquettishly, Joseph thought. And he liked it.

Chapter Nineteen

Three weeks later, the little trio rode confidently into Pierre. Joseph had insisted that they leave the area of the fort under cover of darkness, the same moon that had seen them move Maura and her son from his quarters and back to her tiny home.

He and Henry had discussed the situation and agreed that until they had learned more about the infant's father, it was best to keep the child under wraps, allowing all concerned to believe that the baby's skin and hair resembled that of Maura's attacker. The fact was, that as the days passed, with the exception of his sky blue eyes, he looked increasingly like his mother and there was nothing to lead the two investigators to a viable conclusion as to his father.

As they rode through the streets of the city, Joseph already looked forward to the day they would leave. He felt certain that by then they would do so, having won everything his heart desired.

At the same time, Maura, though a bit more apprehensive about the turn of events, tried to be happy. She had been serious, and in complete control of her senses, when she had expressed her emotions to Joseph during childbirth.

She loved the man who rode besides her, holding her sleeping child snuggly in the cradleboard he had fashioned in the way of his people. Joseph had told her that a cradleboard made by a woman of his village would have been beautifully beaded, but she thought the one he had made, though he considered it plain, held a beauty that could not be compared. After all, Joseph had made it especially for Ryan, and that meant everything to her.

Maura was content with the turn her life had recently taken. She sincerely doubted that Joseph felt the same toward her, though he tried to tell her so, but it didn't matter. The three of them would be a family. That's just the way it was going to be.

They were on their way to the Pierre Community Church, a structure newly built on the city's west side. Joseph recalled seeing it on his previous trip and had filed its location in the back of his mind. Today, Joseph helped Maura off her horse and led the group to the door. They found it locked and were a bit disappointed, but Maura reasoned that the minister's house could not be far away, perhaps even next door, as many had been in her hometown.

A quick look down the street brought them to the first of their two choices – a plain clapboard house with a chicken running loose and a dog tied to a tree in the front yard. A knock at the door brought a dirt-smudged face pressing its runny nose against the new glass pane.

"Pa! Pa! There's an Injun at the door!" they heard from inside, and Maura looked nervously at Joseph. He winked at her and squeezed her hand.

Finally, the door was opened by a tall, stocky man wearing a stark white collar that contrasted dramatically with his black suit.

"Yes?" he asked, giving both Maura and Joseph a long, hard look, which ultimately settled on the blanket-covered infant carried protectively in Maura's arms. He looked back to Joseph, then seemed to choose Maura as the individual he wished to speak with.

"Ma'am? Is this man bothering you? Do you need my intervention?"

Flabbergasted, Maura said, "No, sir, he and I came together. We are searching for the clergyman of the church next door. We wish to be married."

"Married?"

The man only seems to speak in questions, Joseph thought, before speaking up in his own behalf.

"Yes, sir. Miss O'Brien and I wish to be married as soon as possible and we were hoping, no praying, sir, that you would help us."

"Praying? To who, Injun? Some animal? Some star in the sky?"

"Here we go again," Joseph thought, but kept his temper.

"We wish to be married right away. Can you help us?"

"Well, by the looks of it, I'd say you waited a mite too long to look for me."

Eyeing Joseph while he spoke, the minister turned to Maura. "Did this man take advantage of you, miss? I must say you are right in forcing him to atone for his sins. He is responsible, though being an Indian and all, he probably was a hard one to convince. They don't seem to feel responsible for too much. Of course, you must go before the Lord and confess your own sins, because if there's one thing I know, it's that it takes two, even though it's usually not the woman's idea. Now you two have a baby to think about giving a name to, and that's something you should have thought about sooner, might I say."

Maura didn't think her jaw could have dropped any further without hitting the ground. Taking a sidelong look at the man next to her, she expected to see that Joseph was about to lose his cool demeanor. Instead, she saw that he was smiling, and although the expression was rather unexpected, she waited to hear what he had to say. It didn't take long.

"I can see that you only have our child's welfare in mind, sir," Joseph began. "But speaking for myself at the moment, I'd like to tell you what my priority is."

"What's that?"

"To get my son and my wife-to-be as far away from you as possible. I can't fathom..."

"Father? I heard voices raised. Who is it? Oh!"

The question had come from a younger man who pushed his way past the older one, still blocking the doorway.

"I'm sorry, can I help you?"

"Who are you?" Joseph asked.

"I'm Reverend Thompson." When no reply came from the visitors, the younger man added, "I'm the minister at the church here," pointing next door. "And you are?"

Maura and Joseph traded looks, before Joseph finally found his voice. "I thought he was."

Following the direction of the native's index finger, Reverend Thompson realized what had happened and, addressing the older man, asked him to wait inside. "It's all right, Father. I'll take care of this."

"Get them out of here before your daughter wakes up and gets a look at him," he said, inclining his head toward Joseph.

"Don't worry, don't worry, I'll take care of it. You just go in and make sure she's still in her room."

"You let them know they're on the road to damnation!"

Waiting for the departure of the other man, the younger one hesitated, then turned to the couple waiting at the door, and offered his observation. "I'm not really aware of what actually transpired between you, but I have the feeling that an apology is in order."

"That isn't necessary," Joseph said, "because we're going to start over. My name is Joseph Walks Alone and this is Maura O'Brien and her son..." He looked at Maura intently, then changed his description, "I mean, our son, Ryan." Maura smiled and watched the minister for his reaction.

"Miss O'Brien and I wish to be married, and we were hoping that you would help us. We'd like the ceremony to take place as soon as possible and I'm hoping your response is a bit more positive than the other...gentleman's."

Rev. Thompson stepped outside and pulled the door to the house completely shut. "Will you all walk with me to the church?" he asked.

The group made its way toward the clapboard building. Reverend Thompson slid his hand into his right pocket and pulled out several keys strung together with a piece of cord. He chose a large skeleton key and inserted it into the church door. A loud click and the door swung inside where an odor of newly cut pine assailed their senses.

"Please, sit down," Rev. Thompson said, directing Maura to the rough bench at the front of the sanctuary. Joseph leaned behind her, lifting the corner of the baby's blanket so that he could see whether the infant had awakened during the initial confrontation. He had not, so Joseph replaced the covering, straightened, and placed his hands on Maura's shoulders.

"I wanted to get away from the house," the clergyman began. "My father-in-law is not a bad man, but I regret that his beliefs in any way led you to consider leaving. I will be happy to help you, but let me explain his reaction first."

"There's really no need, Reverend," Maura assured him.

"I hope that you both can find it in your hearts to forgive Louis, my father-in-law. You see, he was probably taken aback by the sight of you at the door. I don't mean to be personal, Mr. Walks Alone, but my wife, Louis' daughter, was killed in an Indian attack, on our wagon train on the way out here, several years ago.

"Oh my," Maura said quietly.

"My son and daughter, both of whom were quite young, witnessed the death of their mother. My daughter has never really been the same since that time and as you can imagine, it has cast a shadow over our family."

"I'm sorry for your loss, Reverend," Joseph said. "Both Maura and I have lost people who were important to our lives and we can empathize with your pain. I regret if my hasty reaction to your father-in-law in any way added to your family's distress. But I want you to understand how important it is to me, to both of us, to have this marriage and be together, now that we have found one another."

Maura's right hand reached backward to cover Joseph's right, which still rested on her shoulder. Together, they looked to the minister for his reply.

"I don't think it would be in anyone's best interest to block your marriage. I can see you are sincere and that what is between you is real. I would be happy to officiate, but I believe you might want to freshen up before you exchange your vows, wouldn't you?"

Exhaling audibly, then turning to smile at Joseph, Maura answered the minister by nodding her head. At that moment, the baby in her arms began to make his feelings known as well.

"I really don't feel that I can take you into my home, with my family there and all," the minister began, apologetically, "but I think our neighbor, Mrs. Williams, might have a room or two available in her boardinghouse. She's a member of this church and a very good and kind-hearted woman and I'm sure she'd love the baby. I'll walk over with you and make the introductions."

"Thank you Reverend. You've been very kind," Maura said, turning in the direction he had shown her.

It didn't take long for Maura and Joseph to find that Loretta Williams was a take-charge woman, whose bubbly personality seemed incongruous to her almost six-foot, bony frame.

"Now, you just make yourself at home and take care of that demanding young man of yours," she told Maura as she led her into a bedroom. "I have this adjoining room available as well, and I'll just let the three of you make use of it for a while too, seein' as how I don't have too many boarders right now. Of course, after you're married, you and the mister will be sharing a room, but newlyweds need to get away from the young'uns once in a while, if'n you know what I mean, dear."

Maura blushed at that statement and Joseph sent her a reassuring smile.

"Now, you need anything, you call out to Loretta, you hear? I'll take care of it if I can."

"Thank you, ma'am," Maura said, making her way to an oak rocking chair sitting on a braided rug in the corner of the room. The rocker, decorated with a pillow that fit just right into the hollow of her back, was just what the doctor ordered to allow mother and child to settle in.

Joseph placed Maura's bag inside the door of her room and watched her remove her child from the cradleboard, smooth his small brow and begin to softly sing, keeping time with the rhythm of the rocker. Finally, realizing he was staring, and although Maura had not noticed, he almost felt as if he were intruding on the intimate scene between mother and child.

Turning, he closed the door to the hall, moved across the room and opened the door that led into the adjoining room. The decor was sparse but neat and clean, and in looking at it, Joseph knew that Mrs. Williams took great pride in her ability to run her boardinghouse as she would run her own home.

Placing his case on the bed, Joseph took out a crisp, white shirt and another pair of pants and hung them in a nearby wardrobe. Shrugging out of his black calf-length duster, he reached into the inside left pocket before placing it on a hook in the wardrobe.

Bringing out Mr. Shakley's photograph of Maura that the woman in the next room still knew nothing about, Joseph felt the need to continue staring at her. "I don't know how I have come to this, but I thank God that she has agreed to allow me into her life, to make a family. I only hope that she will come to trust in me and believe that I wish to stay with her until the end of time." He placed the photograph on the bedside table, and then searched the bag for his string tie. Finding it, he laid it in readiness for the marriage ceremony.

As he sat on the edge of the bed, Joseph suddenly felt lonely and decided to seek out Mrs. Williams in the kitchen downstairs.

The woman's back was toward him, but Joseph could see that she was busily mixing something in a bowl. He brought a gold watch from the waist pocket of his vest and checked the time, noting that only several hours remained until he and Maura would be married in the dusk service. Mrs. Williams undoubtedly spent much time creating the meals that made her boarders happy and well fed, but Joseph hoped she would not mind if he joined her.

"You want to sit in here with me?" Mrs. Williams could not have looked more surprised at Joseph's inquiry. "Well, I'll warn you, if you do, I'll have to put you to work. That's just the way it is around here. And another thing, you've got to call me Loretta."

Joseph smiled, grabbed a small knife from beside the sink and pointed to a pile of potatoes on the table. "How about I tackle the spuds? I've always had a certain appeal for them," he stated in a serious manner, but when Mrs. Williams turned around and raised an eyebrow, they both ended in peels of laughter.

"You remind me of my John," she told Joseph, shaking her head. "Actually, he was always the better cook, though I'd have to die before I'd tell him that." Raising her head and looking out the window she added quietly, "Unfortunately, he died first and I never did get to tell him that. Wish I woulda'. He was a good man. Never met another quite like him."

"I am honored that you compare me to him, then," Joseph said. "I hope talking about him doesn't pain you overmuch," he said, setting a bowl on the table and taking the potatoes one by one to the knife. As she shook her head, he added, "When did he die?"

"Oh, my. It's been nigh onto 12 years now that I've been on my own. And I've not liked it one bit," she admitted. "If you don't mind, I guess your wedding plans are putting me in a remembering mood and I just feel like remembering out loud."

"I don't mind at all," Joseph told her.

Loretta began pouring the mixture from her bowl into three shallow pans as she spoke.

"He was probably the most obnoxious man I'd ever had the misfortune to have to listen to when we first hooked up," she began, and Joseph's eyes widened at the remark. "Oh, he was always pushing me to leave my friends and family and marry him. Why he took such a fierce liking to me, I didn't know at the time, but it just grated on me like fingernails on a schoolhouse chalkboard."

"There must have been some kind of attraction for you, wasn't there? You married him after all," Joseph noted.

"Oh, I was attracted all right, but admitting it was another story. He was so different, so...well...dangerous, I guess would be the word."

"I really can't see myself as dangerous," Joseph reflected. "Why did you say that I remind you of him?"

"Didn't I tell you? My John was part Indian. That's why it took me so long to warm up to him. I was playing with fire, as far as my family was concerned. And they wouldn't have anything to do with me after we set up housekeeping. But my John, he was the sun rising in the sky and the moon glowing at night. I never regretted letting him talk me into marrying him. He treated me with respect, asked my opinions, and loved me until I couldn't take it anymore. Then he went and died on me, and ever since then I see him in the sunrise, and watching over me all day, but even though I talk to him, I can't touch him, I can't be with him. It tears my guts out."

Joseph looked at Loretta Williams with a new understanding.

"I know what you speak of," he said. "If Maura were not in my life, it would be empty. Though we are to be married, she does not believe in me yet. Her level of trust is not what it should be for a husband and wife, but in time, I hope she will come to see that I will be with her as long as I live and should I leave her on Earth, my spirit will be with her wherever she goes. We are one, she and I, but she does not realize that to the fullest extent."

"I take it that there is much more to her story than meets the eye," Loretta reasoned. "That child is not yours, is it?"

"That child is mine, and will always be mine," Joseph answered vehemently. "It may have come from another's seed, but it is Maura's also, and because of that fact, as Maura will be my wife, that child will be my son. Its father was a coward, who would only give pain to a woman. My son will never know him and I will teach him to respect his mother and any other woman he comes into contact with. This I will do."

Loretta looked at the pile of potato peelings lying all over the table and pointed them out to Joseph. "I believe that you feel strongly about this, Joseph, but I think you should take it easy on my potatoes or I'll be having hash browns for supper instead of mashed."

Joseph looked down at the stub of a potato he held in his left hand. He had peeled away more than the skin, leaving barely enough meat for a child's portion.

Laughter filled the room and smiles greeted Maura, as she entered. "Well, you two are surely havin' a high old time here," she said, taking in the scene. "I just put Ryan down for a nap and thought I'd see where you were," she told Joseph. "I don't believe you missed me at all."

The laughter faded and Joseph stared intently into Maura's eyes. "Oh, I missed you. I will always miss you when we are separated, whether we are miles apart or in different rooms of the same house."

He turned to look at Loretta but the older woman had begun violently kneading some bread dough and she pretended she did not hear.

Chapter Twenty

"I now pronounce you, man and wife. What God has brought together, let no man put asunder."

The final words of the ceremony resonated from Reverend Thompson's lips as the newlyweds shared a shy kiss in the glow of the evening and the groom grabbed their son from his mother's arms to enfold him into their joy.

"Thank you," Joseph said to Maura.

"For what?" she wondered aloud.

"For marrying me. For allowing me to be a part of your life," Joseph answered.

Tears welled in Maura's eyes, as she looked into Joseph's and saw the truth reflected there.

"You have allowed me and my son into your life," she said, "We should be the ones thanking you for making us a family. That is something I have not had for many years and until recently, lost all hope to have again," she added. "I want us to be a real family, to have a home of our own. That means everything to me."

"You will always have a place to call home wherever I am," Joseph said, squeezing both Maura and the baby, as the new family officially celebrated its love.

The minister announced that, while she had been unable to attend the wedding, Loretta Williams now wanted a small celebration back at the boardinghouse. Gathering their things, the participants moved out of the church and into the back door of Loretta's home where they were greeted by a three-layer wedding cake decorated with frothy white frosting, and just-picked blue tinted cornflowers.

"I'm sorry I didn't have time to make a fancier spread," Loretta said, "But I figured this would do, with you two so much in love and all, I thought the cake and the celebration were secondary."

Both Maura and Joseph reached for Loretta and took her into their arms for a hug.

The small group, which ultimately included Loretta's other boarders as well, toasted the couple and enjoyed the confection while Ryan yawned sleepily in Joseph's arm.

One by one the party broke up and finally, all that were left were Loretta and the happy family.

"Well, Mrs. Walks Alone, I guess we should probably retire."

"You're probably right," Maura agreed rather hesitantly, but she allowed Joseph to walk her to her second floor room after giving Loretta a hug and thanking her for all she had done for them.

Still carrying the baby, Joseph switched the small body onto his left arm and used his right hand to turn the knob on the room adjoining Maura's. He walked in, and using only the light from the lamp in the hall, made a nest in the center of the bed and laid the child within it. Joseph gave Ryan a light kiss on the forehead, and then rejoined Maura in the hall.

Taking her by the arm, he led her toward her door.

"Joseph," she began, "I should have spoken to you before, but I..."

"I know, Maura. Believe me, I know what you want to tell me. I knew when I asked you to marry me that you were not ready for all aspects of a relationship, but I wanted you with me, and I believe that one day, you will trust me enough that we will be one in all ways."

"Joseph, I don't want you to grow tired waiting. I don't know when I will feel right about...everything."

"I will wait forever, Maura. But in the meantime, please allow me to offer my love by simply holding you. That will be enough."

"It won't always be enough, and that is what I'm afraid of right now," Maura admitted.

"When your fear is gone, I will still be with you. I promise you that."

Maura opened the door and led Joseph into the dark room.

Breakfast at Loretta's was a belly-busting affair.

"Have another flapjack, Joseph. You could use a little meat on your bones."

"Loretta, if I'm lucky, I won't explode from downing the two stacks of flapjacks, the bacon, the eggs and the milk, not to mention the pot of coffee, and Maura will just have to roll me out of here today. My poor horse will probably never be the same."

Giggles came from Maura, who was sitting on the opposite side of the table. Loretta held the baby while Maura ate her breakfast.

"Now you young folks need more to keep you going. You've got a busy day ahead of you and you'll need every morsel you can get. Why, Joseph, you've already been out and about today, doing who knows what and you being a man and all, you need more."

Loretta hurried to clean up the last of the dishes, as she planned to watch Ryan for a few hours while Joseph and Maura went further into town to find the judge that Reverend Thompson had suggested to discuss Joseph's adoption of the child.

After feeding him and changing his diaper one final time, Maura hesitantly handed Ryan over to Loretta.

"This is the first time I've ever left him," she worried aloud. "What if he gets hungry? What if he can't go to sleep without me? What if..."

"What if we just head on out the door?" Joseph said, turning Maura toward the door and pushing her into the morning sunshine. "He'll be fine, Maura. Let's go."

"I may not have had one of my own, girlie, but I've taken care of my share of young'uns. Don't you give us a worry now. We'll be just fine, him and me. We're going to take a walk out in the garden, pick some apples..."

"If you're going to take him outside, he'll need an extra blanket. I'll go get it," Maura said, doing an about-face and starting back into the house and toward the stairs.

"Whoa!"

The command caused Maura to stop in her tracks.

"Maura, if Ryan needs a blanket, I'm sure Loretta can find it. Let's let her take care of things."

"But..."

"But nothing. I'm not one to give orders, but I'll start now if I have to, Mrs. Walks Alone."

Looking first at Loretta, then at Joseph, Maura blew a kiss to Ryan, and then swept past her new husband and out the door.

"Well, come on! We've got things to do!" she called, as she left Joseph in the dust. The native looked at Loretta, shrugged his shoulders, and smiled. "Life will never be dull," he noted.

Judge Peter Brock lived on a quiet street, nestled in a cozy neighborhood of picket-fenced yards and freshly whitewashed houses located about seven blocks away from his office. He walked to work every day, enjoying the solitary activity and using the time to get his day in order in his mind.

His mind now wandered back to his breakfast this morning. Blackened toast, scorched eggs, inedible planks of bacon. "She tried," he said to himself, but noted the growling in his stomach. He'd have to stop by the hotel and have a real breakfast before he went to his office this morning.

The judge's wife, Sarah, had died almost three years ago. "Now there was a woman who knew the way to a man's stomach." He remembered the table groaning under the weight of the beef roasts, fried potatoes, vegetables of the day and, of course, dessert. No one in the territories could hold a candle to her pies.

"Melody, on the other hand, bakes pies that taste like candles," he thought, and suddenly burst into laughter, while crossing the street. Several passersby looked sidelong at the judge, and he knew they were wondering what had possessed him, but, dammit, well, it was true. "My daughter will have to catch a man with her beauty. She'll certainly never attract him with her cooking...or her intellect," he admitted to himself.

Unfortunately, all Melody had inherited from her beloved mother was her luxurious blonde hair, which covered a cavern that only echoed the trivialities that occupied her social schedule, he thought. This was illustrated by her choice of beaus these days – her favorite being an army officer from a nearby fort. The judge only hoped the man's company would move on before the pair got too serious...if they already hadn't. He wasn't prepared or willing to take his wife's place and ask for any intimate details of the time they spent together...time he could not order her to stop. He feared doing so would only ignite her stubborn streak and force her to move faster toward something he did not even want to think about.

"Oh, Sarah, I wish you were here," he said, staring into the bright sunlight overhead. He found himself talking to her quite a bit these days, but nothing ever came of it. "I really should stop," he thought, but he knew he wouldn't. He had spent 33 years talking to her; it was too late to stop now.

As he took a seat in the hotel restaurant and waited for his food to arrive, he remembered how thrilled they'd been when Melody had come into their lives late in life. Even though they were older, and had long since stopped expecting to ever have a child, they welcomed the small bundle and spoiled her incessantly. "Perhaps we went a tad overboard," he told Sarah silently. "But how could we not?" Melody was a bit wild, but it wasn't so bad that she could not turn things around, he hoped.

Maybe not too late for that, but it was too late for many other things – for Sarah, for their life together, for going back. "What will be, will be," he said aloud, and dug into a huge hunk of ham.

"He's not here? Well, when do you expect him?" Joseph stood in the lobby of Judge Brock's offices, speaking to his clerk, a small-framed man sporting a large mustache and a very pinched appearance.

"The judge is always a very punctual man. I'm sure something very important has delayed him and he will be arriving any moment now. Please take a seat...over there," the man said, pointing a bony index finger toward several chairs on the opposite side of the room.

Joseph looked at Maura, and shaking his head, led her over to the seats.

"I don't know what's wrong with me. I'm very nervous, Joseph," Maura said, whispering behind her hand.

Her husband reached over and took the hand in his and began to run his fingertips over the palm. The action unnerved Maura even more, but she did not pull away.

"Perhaps it's just because you're a new mother, newly married, who is sitting beside a handsome man who loves you very much and who would at this very moment like to..."

"Joseph!" Maura whispered loudly. "We are not sitting under a tree out on the prairie! Married or not, please try to control your tongue."

A slow smile formed on Joseph's face, as he looked into Maura's eyes. "I wish we were under a tree out on the prairie," he said. "Unfortunately, prairies don't have too many trees, but if they did, boy, I'd be right there with you..."

"Oh...you!"

At that moment, the door burst open to admit the form of the judge who went directly past the clerk's desk on his way to his office.

"Sorry I'm late, what's on the schedule today, Warren? I'm ready to get going." Taking off his heavy overcoat, Judge Brock threw it on a nearby chair then eased his weight into a large, red leather wingback behind an ornate mahogany desk.

Warren had skittered into the room in the judge's shadow and stood to one side, whispering. "Sir, there is an Indian and a woman, they're together, sitting out there. They've been waiting for you for some time but they don't have an appointment. I wanted to tell them to leave but I was...well, to be truthful, sir...I was a bit afraid."

"Afraid, Warren? Afraid of what, might I ask?"

Warren's face registered his shock at the judge's question. "Of what, sir? Why, of the Indian. He's all dressed up and all, but my God, sir, you know how they are. You just can't be sure what they're going to do. I was afraid that I would make him angry and...well, that he would hurt me."

"Hurt you? With what?" The judge leaned to the right and looked out into the lobby. "From what I can see, I can detect no weapon on his person."

Warren eyed the judge sadly. "Oh, my. Well I'm sure he has something hidden somewhere. You know how they are."

"No, Warren, I don't know. How are 'they'?"

"Frankly sir, being in the position you're in I'm sure you realize yourself..."

"Warren, just answer my question."

"Yes, sir. Well, they're sneaky, don't you know. They lie, they cheat and they'd sooner steal you blind than look at you. I've been keeping my eye on that one while he's been in here. I didn't see him take anything, but if you bring him in here, I'll take a look around and if I see that something's missing, I let you know."

"You do that, Warren. Say, by the way, what about the woman?"

"What about her, sir?"

"Did you keep your eye on her, too?"

"Well, no, sir."

"Why not?"

"Didn't see any reason to do so, sir. From what I can see, the only problem with her is that she came in with him."

"I see. So was it because she's a woman, or because she's white, that you didn't feel the need to keep your eye on her?"

"Well, both reasons sir. She seems nice enough."

"Warren, have you been paying attention to some of the cases that have come before me lately? I've had some white women in my court that were pretty sly thieves and even one that murdered her employer."

"Yes, but forgive me for saying this so indiscreetly Judge, but, those women were butt ugly. This one's not the prettiest, but she doesn't look like any of the criminal types you've seen lately."

"I think I'm beginning to understand your logic, Warren, and I believe it's something we're going to have to discuss further, but right now I think these people have waited long enough and if I were them, my patience would be wearing a bit thin while I witnessed this little whispering session, which I have no doubt they have already figured out was about them. Now get out there, Warren and send them both in."

"Yes, sir."

The little man scurried back to the outer office and put his desk between himself and Joseph before he told the waiting couple that the judge would see them now.

Maura glanced nervously in Joseph's direction as she rose from her seat. She felt the comforting warmth of his hand at her back, as he walked just behind her into the room.

"Judge Peter Brock."

"Joseph Walks Alone, and this is my wife, Maura."

"Glad to meet you folks. Please have a seat."

"Thank you, sir," Maura said, as Joseph led her to one of two empty chairs facing the judge.

"Now, Warren tells me that you two have been waiting for some time and I'd like to take this opportunity to apologize for my tardiness this morning," Judge Brock offered. "Please, tell me what I can do for you today."

Maura put her soft, white hand in Joseph's larger, darker one and held on tight, as his eyes locked with hers.

"Well, sir," Joseph said. "We're here to start our family" and he began to relate their story from the beginning.

Chapter Twenty-one

"And so you see, we both want this very much and I want to be able to know that Maura and our son will be taken care of, should anything ever happen to me," Joseph said in conclusion.

"Very good, Mr. Walks Alone, very sound reasoning. I can't blame you for worrying and I understand your wish to be together. Before my dear wife passed on, we were never far away from each other. I will consider your request Mr. and Mrs. Walks Alone, but I hope you can be patient for a little while longer, as it will take several days to work out the particulars. Rest assured that I will do everything I can to assist you. Now, just go out into the other office and Warren will give you an appointment for later this week."

An audible exhalation of breath came from both Joseph and Maura as the judge spoke.

Rising from their seats in one fluid motion, the man and wife each shook Brock's hand and exited the room. Once outside, Joseph took Maura in his arms and gave her a big hug. "We're on our way, Maura. Soon, we'll officially be a family."

Tears of joy glistened in Maura's eyes and threatened to flow down her cheeks. She blinked them away and smiled, as Joseph went toward Warren's desk.

"That's far enough," the little man warned with hand upraised. "I can talk to you from there." Leafing through the large appointment book on his desk, the clerk continued to eye Joseph warily and nearly jumped from his skin, as the Indian reached down and picked up a pen lying on the desk.

Breaking into a smile, Joseph held up the writing instrument and waved it in Warren's direction. "This is a greater weapon than any knife or gun I could carry. Remember that."

Warren's left eyebrow shot upward in confusion, then his face turned pink as he realized that the Indian had heard what he'd said to the judge.

"You just can't be too careful," he said in his own defense.

"Yes, you never know what kind of people you're dealing with," Joseph said pointedly.

At that moment, the outside door burst open and a ruffled, blonde figure ran through the outer room and into the judge's office, almost knocking Maura to the ground. Joseph grabbed his wife's arm and looked after the rushing blur.

"Melody, dear, you almost sent one of my visitors into the wall! Apologize, now!"

"Oh, sorry," she said dismissingly, not bothering to even turn in Maura's direction. She did, however, reveal her face as she rounded the desk to hug the judge from behind.

"Daddy, you'll never guess! James is in town and he wants to take me to lunch. I know I promised to go out with you but, well, I really want to go with him, Daddy. Say I can. But you know, even if you don't, I'll go anyway. I just don't get to see him as much as I'd like."

"You see him too much for my liking," her father countered, rising halfway and looking out his office door. "Are you all right, Mrs. Walks Alone? Please excuse my daughter's behavior. She's a bit impulsive."

"I'm quite fine, Judge Brock. Don't give it another thought," Maura assured him. It was Joseph she was worried about. His expression had changed drastically, as he looked on the scene in the adjoining room. "What is it, Joseph? What's wrong? If you're upset about what happened, I'm fine. Let's just go," and she tugged on his arm.

But Joseph stood stock-still and continued to look at the woman identified as the judge's daughter. He realized he knew her better as the mystery woman who had been in Captain James Cole's company in the hotel restaurant a while back.

"I'll be damned," he said aloud to himself, and the expletive caused Warren to raise his head.

"That's the only thing I'd agree with you about," the clerk noted before returning his attention to a folder of papers on his desk.

"What was that all about, Joseph?" Maura asked as the pair returned to their horses.

"It was nothing. I just thought I recognized her from somewhere, but it must have been some other obnoxious woman I was thinking of."

Maura giggled and swung her leg over her animal's back as Joseph did the same.

"I can't wait to get back to see Ryan," Maura said and Joseph smiled as well. He was surprised she hadn't said that long before now.

"You're going to have to wait a bit longer, my dear," he noted, turning his horse in the opposite direction to Loretta's.

"What do you mean? I thought we were through here."

"We have several more items of business to take care of before we see our son again."

"And those are..."

"The first is a surprise, the second is lunch," Joseph said. "I'm starving."

"How can you be starving after the way you shoveled the food in at breakfast this morning?" Maura asked in wonder. "I've never in my life seen anyone eat as much as you."

"If you knew what a joy it is to eat without worrying about someone taking it away, you might understand. Many years ago, I learned to eat as much as I could in as little time as I could and I am hard-pressed to do otherwise even now, although I do enjoy a leisurely meal when I can."

Maura looked thoughtfully at Joseph, then turned her gaze in the direction ahead. "I think there is much I don't know about you yet, Mr. Walks Alone."

"And I about you," Joseph admitted, adding, "but I plan on spending all the time that I can learning as much about you as possible."

"We have a lifetime," Maura noted.

"A lifetime."

Joseph pulled his horse along the street and swung down to tie the lead around the hitching rail. He walked to Maura's horse and raised his arms to help her down, then led his wife up the street.

"Where are we going?" she asked, suspiciously. "I have the feeling that you have something up your sleeve, sir."

"You might be right, Mrs. Walks Alone. You know me much better than you think."

She was truly shocked, however, when he led her inside Grant's Jewelry Emporium. The name implied a generous establishment, but the interior was dark and cramped. A clerk appeared from nowhere and stood before Joseph and Maura with arms crossed.

"Can I help you?"

"Yes, you can tell me what we're doing in here, because frankly, I'm a little confused," Maura stated.

"This is a surprise for my wife," Joseph explained. "I believe you have some things held back for me...my name is Walks Alone."

"Oh, yes! Mr. Walks Alone! Mr. Grant left strict instructions to take very good care of you. Right this way, sir," and the clerk showed the couple to a small room, which was not immediately evident from the front portion of the shop. "Please, have a seat while I get your things," and with that, the clerk hurriedly left the room.

While Joseph settled himself in one of the plush velvet-covered chairs, Maura walked around the room. Her fingers glided over the cold surface of the ornate marble-topped table in the center. A fainting couch graced one wall and moving closer, she felt the decadent, flocked wallpaper and began to examine a collection of oil paintings. Upon closer inspection, she noted that the first painting that caught her eye, as well as a group surrounding it, had been created by Claude Monet. She had seen another of his works at the Columbian Exposition.

"Joseph, this is beautiful. Where did you find this place? And by the way, you still haven't answered me, why are we here? How does that man know who you are? I don't like surprises that leave me as the only one in the dark."

"The light will come on in a moment, Maura. Just be patient and forgive me for this. It's a selfish move, but one that I hope you will like."

The clerk returned to the room carrying a tray covered with a silk cloth. He carefully placed it on the table and motioned to Maura to sit close by.

Lifting the corner of the cloth, the clerk silently slid the fabric away.

Joseph had been right, Maura decided, the light had come on - the glittering, shining lights of diamonds, rubies and sapphires.

"What is this?" Her softly spoken question was not really directed to either gentleman, just spoken in reaction to the array of gold and jewels set out before her.

Joseph leaned forward in his chair and, choosing a large, square-cut emerald ring, brought the jewel close to her head. "I thought this would complement your hair."

Maura could do nothing but stare, first at the brightly colored stone, then into Joseph's eyes. She was utterly speechless. Mistaking it for a dislike for the ring, Joseph placed it carefully on the velvet and picked up an opal. "Perhaps this would be more to your liking...or any of these really. It's for you to choose."

"Choose? Me? Why? Joseph, I just don't understand. What is this? How did that man know who you were?

"Whoa, whoa, whoa! I can only answer so many questions at a time. Let me see if I can remember them. First, choose? Yes, I brought you here to choose a wedding ring."

"Joseph, that's not necessary. We both know we're married. It's not important to me that others can see a wedding band."

"I knew that you would say that. Yes, I agree that it is not a necessary item for others to see. But it is important to me that both you and I wear a reminder of what we have promised each other, not only during the ceremony last night, but at other times as well."

While Maura considered his words, Joseph continued answering her questions. "Now, I believe that took care of the first four questions. We still have one remaining. Mr. Nelson – the clerk – knew who I was because I came here this morning before breakfast to ask the owner of this establishment to get some things ready for you to look at. I knew if I just brought you in you would turn around and refuse to look. I thought if I had something ready, it would be better, but if you don't see anything here you like..."

"Don't see anything I like? Are you crazy? I like it all, but Joseph, I don't see anything that looks like me. I'm plain, Joseph, if you haven't noticed. I'm not all shiny and sparkling and fancy like these jewels. I'd be afraid to wear anything here."

"I disagree that you're plain, that you are not shiny or sparkling," Joseph told Maura. "But since you're so vehement about it, maybe there is one ring on this tray that would be more to your liking" and with that, his right index finger pointed toward the far side of the tray. Maura's eyes followed and saw a gold band featuring a *claddaugh*, a symbol of love. Picking up the band, she looked closely and smiled at her husband. "That's more like it," she said. "I'd be proud to wear that."

Joseph's face broke into a smile to rival the brilliance of the gems on the tray. "I was hoping you'd say that. Look on the inside."

Maura's gaze questioned Joseph's statement, and then moved to the underside of the ring where she saw inscribed "*Wacinyan*".

Attempting to say the word on her own, Joseph closed his hand over hers and softly said it to her.

"I don't know what it means," she told him.

"You do not know now, but you will. When the time comes, I will tell you."

Taking the ring from her right hand, Joseph placed it on the third finger of her left and folded his fingers through hers. The shop clerk, who had been waiting patiently in the shadows of the small room, came forward. "Did you find something to your liking, Mrs. Walks Alone?"

"Yes, I believe I did. I do believe I did."

From his jacket pocket, Joseph brought out a larger version of the ring that Maura now wore and he showed it to her. Inside his was inscribed, "*Wicala*".

"Yours is different," Maura noted.

"No, for us it is the same," Joseph stated, and slipped it over his knuckle.

The couple made their way from the store and as Joseph opened the door, Maura gasped and turned. "Joseph, we didn't pay the man for the rings!"

"He has his money. I paid for both rings this morning."

"How could you know that I wouldn't choose one of the other rings instead?"

"We have not known each other long in the whole scheme of things, Maura, but I know enough of you that I knew which ring would appeal to you. Besides, if you didn't choose it, I would have bought another anyway. But I would have made you take that one as well."

Smiling to himself, Joseph wrapped Maura's arm around his and headed her past the horses and down the street.

"This day has been so full of unexpected joys and I am afraid to ask you where we are going now. But I'm thinking we really ought to get back to Loretta's and take care of Ryan."

"We have time to have lunch first. We will be there for Ryan his entire life. One more hour will not hurt" and Joseph led his wife into the Pierre Hotel where still another surprise awaited them both.

Chapter Twenty-two

"James, I just don't understand why I can't come to the fort and be with you. I'm almost 18 years old now. You don't want to be marrying an old cow now, do you? That's what I'll be if you keep me waiting. You wouldn't do that to me, now, would you sugar?"

James Cole had never wanted to pay much attention to the young blonde across from him at the table. It was her large breasts and her daddy's money and prestige, not necessarily in that order, that had attracted him to her in the first place. It certainly hadn't been her conversational skills. In fact, he was sure at this moment, that she had no skills at all, although, he thought, he hadn't tried every venue. She might prove to be quite skillful in some very important areas if she had the right teacher. And he was quite certain he was up to the task.

Unfortunately, the little bitch hadn't so much as offered. Oh, she'd hinted enough, but he wasn't stupid. He knew the moment he broke through her barriers he'd have to marry her and he wasn't interested in her in that way, in the least. Her daddy on the other hand, could prove to be quite useful. The problem was, the old man was smart. He'd have to tread carefully to get what he wanted. The girl, on the other hand, well, a body would need a stick of dynamite to get her attention away from herself, and James just wasn't interested enough to work that hard.

Right now, though, his own attention was centered on a couple that had just entered the dining area of the hotel.

Maura O'Brien's hair was hard to miss anywhere, but the soft lights of the room created highlights in the red waves that were doubly difficult to ignore. And she was with that redskin devil, Walks Alone. There was something about him that James absolutely abhorred. It wasn't just the fact that he was an Indian. It was something more.

"James? James? Are you listening to anything that I'm saying?"

"Why yes, darling. How could you think that I wouldn't hang on your every word? I just recognized some people who walked into the dining room, that's all, and they momentarily took my attention away. It won't happen again, I assure you."

"Oh. You mean the Indian and that slut woman with him? They were in Daddy's office earlier today. I didn't pay too much attention but I did hear Daddy say something to Warren about their little boy. I just don't understand why that could be so important it could take your attention away from me. I haven't seen you for so long."

His luncheon companion's comments finally drew James away from the scene before him.

"In your Daddy's office about their little boy, you say. Well, well, well. That's mighty interesting."

"Oh, well, if you're truly interested in them, James, I can ask Daddy more about it, but really, I don't know why you'd want to waste your time on them."

"How right you are my dear. Why waste my time on them when I have a much more interesting conquest before me."

The comment drew a giggle and a knowing look from the opposite side of the table and James was barely able to keep back a snort. "If she only knew," he thought. The girl was actually becoming somewhat of an albatross around his neck with her constant hints of marriage; something James had no intention of carrying through. He was more interested in her 'Daddy' and the power he wielded through his judgeship. "The potential is limitless," he thought, as he considered the ways he could garner that power and use it to his advantage.

"But all in good time," he said aloud, without really realizing that he had done so. "All in good time."

"What was that, James?" his companion asked.

"Oh, never mind, my dear, never mind. Now, where were we?"

Joseph had spotted the pair as soon as they had entered the dining room, and he persuaded the hostess to seat Maura and himself elsewhere in the room. They could never be far enough away, he thought, not wishing to spoil the day for either Maura or himself.

He had been right in the judge's office when he had thought he had recognized the girl as being the one he had observed with James Cole on that earlier visit to Pierre. And when he had heard her refer to "James" as she spoke with her father in his office, he had been convinced. He had no immediate concern for the judge's daughter, but right now, he really did not want Cole's presence to ruin Maura's joyful mood.

Unfortunately, Maura's attention was soon drawn to the area where James was seated when a waitress inadvertently splashed a drop of tea on the skirt of the captain's dining partner.

"You bumbling idiot!" came the shriek from the blonde. "Look what you've done to my dress! I'll have your job for this! Where's the manager?"

"Oh, please, miss. I've got babies at home to feed. It was an accident, it was. If you'll just hold still, I can dab it with a wet cloth and you'll never know..."

"I'll know, all right. I've a memory a mile long and I'll remember you. You'll pay for this. Manager! Where's that manager?"

"Joseph what can we do? That poor girl didn't mean a thing and it was just a drop of tea," Maura observed. "I can't believe that woman is going on like that. I'm going over there. This is ridiculous."

It was all Joseph could do to catch up with Maura, as she rounded the tables in her path.

"Excuse me," Maura began. "I really couldn't help overhearing and though I know this is none of my business..."

"You're right," the blonde said. "It is none of your business. Now get out of my way" and rising from the table she looked at Cole and started in on him. "James, aren't you going to say anything? What kind of gentleman are you to not come to my aid?"

"I hadn't realized you required help in making a scene, my dear. It seemed to me that you were taking care of that all by yourself. But, might I point out, you've completely ignored someone who will make this a bit more interesting. Maura, how nice to see you! I see you've come to join the fray, but I'm afraid from my dear companion's perspective you are on the wrong side...once again, I might add. I see you've brought along your Indian...friend. But where's your son, my dear? I am quite interested in seeing just who he looks like."

His statement hit its target with full force and Maura felt as if the wind had been knocked out of her.

"How did you know that I had a son?" she asked quietly.

"Oh, my! Was it a secret, my dear? I'm so sorry, but if you didn't know, the woman wronged by the waitress is Judge Brock's daughter, Melody. We've been seeing quite a bit of each other, and, the funny thing is, she just told me moments ago that you and Walks Alone had been in her father's office earlier today to discuss your son. And now here you are before me. You have a habit of showing up when I least expect it, Maura."

Joseph placed his hand on Maura's shoulder and turned her to look into his eyes. "It doesn't matter. Don't let him bother you."

As if awaking from a dream, Maura shook herself and recalled why she had made the trip across the room in the first place. By now, the dining room manager had indeed made an appearance and was attempting to soothe the disquieted patron.

"Now miss, the hotel will take care of everything. We do apologize for the inconvenience...."

"Inconvenience? Inconvenience? This... this dolt, ruins one of my best dresses with her clumsiness and you call that an inconvenience? I want her fired, do you hear me? Do you hear me?

"Yes, miss. It will be taken care of, I assure you. Now, if you would just sit down, we'll remove her from the room and you can continue your meal if you so wish. We'll supply a bottle of our best champagne, on the house of course. And we'll give you a voucher for a new dress at the shop of your choice."

Melody smiled slyly to herself, as she returned to her seat. As if she could not see the waitress' tears or hear her cries of innocence, the girl appeared to act as though the incident hadn't taken place. Reaching into her handbag, she brought out a silver compact and checked her appearance in its mirror. As she did so, Maura watched in fascination.

Joseph finally pulled her back toward their table and moved her chair out to allow her to sit down. After pushing it back into place, he returned to his own seat and noticed that Maura had a questioning look on her face.

"What is it, Maura? You're not letting them bother you, are you?"

"No, it's not that. It's silly, really."

"With a look like that on your face, it can't be silly," Joseph observed.

Maura sat very still for several moments and Joseph said nothing, allowing her to collect her thoughts.

"She had a silver compact."

"Yes, I saw it. Many women have silver compacts."

"I know, and that's why I think this is probably silly, but, hers looked familiar."

"Familiar? How so? What made hers different from any others?"

"I don't know. I didn't even see it up close. It just brought back memories, that's all. Let's just forget it and finish our meal. I'm ready to get back to our son, how about you?"

Joseph smiled in answer and speared a slice of meat with his fork, bringing the food to his lips. He thought the taste of the food couldn't please him half as much as Maura's automatic use of the word "our".

The happy pair returned to Loretta's, putting the scene at the restaurant behind them. Though they had only been gone a few hours, to Maura it felt like days since she'd seen the baby. Walking three to four steps ahead of Joseph, even though she continued to hold his hand, Maura hurried into Loretta's warm kitchen.

Expecting to find the older woman there starting some tasty morsel to treat boarders at supper, Maura was thrown when she saw no sign of Loretta or Ryan, no boarder filtering through, nor any odors of baking bread or cakes, though several pans were askew on the stove. Her hand hit the swinging door on the opposite side of the kitchen that led them into the dining room and on to the parlor. The sight that greeted them there robbed the breath from them both.

The two forms they sought lay sprawled in a rocking chair in the corner of the room. Though her eyes were closed and her face somewhat contorted, Loretta's arm still held the small body protectively on her lap. Down the front of her dress, from chest to where it disappeared under Ryan's body, was a large, dark red stain.

Maura could not speak, as she inched forward in the silence of the room. Her hand seemed to reach out of its own accord, shaking slightly, fingers softly extended in a motion seeking answers to questions unasked.

Just as the tips were about to touch the baby's skin, an ungodly sound rivaling the cries of lost souls in the depths of hell echoed throughout the room and caused a reflex movement in Maura that backed her away from the baby and into her husband's arms. The same hand that had just seconds ago reached for her son now covered her mouth to slam the door on a scream that was inching its way up the back of her throat and threatening to spill into the room.

Both Maura and Joseph held each other as if their lives depended on the tightness of their grip.

"What the hell is going on here?" Joseph yelled.

"Saint's preserve us!" yelled Loretta. Her sudden move, as she bolted from the rocker, forced the chair to tilt onto Maura's toe, eliciting a scream that awakened the child from his sound sleep and caused him to wail like a banshee.

As the noise began to fade and Maura stopped hopping on one foot, some semblance of order was restored. Joseph pulled Ryan from Loretta's arms and the older woman began to focus her eyes on the small group standing before her.

"What's the problem with you two?" she questioned rather loudly. "The young one and I were just taking a wee nap and you come in yellin' like an angry mob."

Maura tried to put her fears into words. "Loretta, we didn't know what was going on. There was no one about when we came in and with you and Ryan lying so still in the chair, it looked, well, it looked like...oh, I can't even say it!"

"It shoulda looked like we were taking a nap, that's what. And what's wrong with that? We had a busy morning and we sat down for just a moment before you two came bustin' in. Why'd ya have to yell like that anyway? Can't a body have a little quiet time?"

"Quiet time? Quiet time?" Joseph's voice escalated, as the phrase was repeated and continued loudly as he explained, "While we wondered whether you were dead or alive, we found out quick enough when you let out a snore a trumpeting elephant would envy! My God, Loretta, it scared us half to death!"

Loretta's face turned red and she stammered in her own defense, "Well I don't know what elephant would be tootin' around these parts, but I do know that you're exaggeratin' more than a little, Joseph Walks Alone, because ladies do not snore. Now you apologize to me at once!"

"Didn't your husband ever tell you that you snored, Loretta?"

"He mighta mentioned it a time or two but he always said it was like music to his ears."

"He must have loved you a great deal, Loretta," Joseph quipped, which resulted in an elbow to his ribs from Maura. "Another thing which may have contributed to our concern, was your dress."

"My dress? Now what I wear ain't good enough? Why, I'll...."

"Loretta, calm down and look down."

Loretta glanced at the front of her dress, and then took another look. "Oh, my! I forgot about that."

"What is that stuff, Loretta? We thought you were hurt, or killed," Maura said shyly.

"Don't you worry none honey. Old Loretta was cookin' up some beets and when the baby started a fusin' up a storm, I mighta spilled some beet juice."

"You mighta?" Joseph repeated, looking at the cook for some clarification.

"All right, I did. Land sakes, you'd think it was against the law."

"Well, anyway, we're just very happy that everything's fine and all is right with the world."

"You're certainly in a good mood now, Joseph. You two must have had good news from the judge."

"That we did, Loretta. In just a few days, our little family will be official and we can go back to the fort and begin our lives together."

"I can't wait," Maura said, taking young Ryan from her husband's arms and heading toward her second floor sanctuary to spend some mother-son time.

"I can't either," Joseph said quietly, as he watched them leave the room.

Chapter Twenty-three

Joseph, Maura and Ryan had plenty of quality time together over the next several days. The little family took long walks, rocked in Loretta's porch swing and watched the sun melt into glorious evening pinks, purples and gold.

During the baby's naptimes, Joseph and Maura left him under Loretta's watchful eye while they sorted through some of the school supplies still stored in a city warehouse. He also asked for her input as he made a list of other necessary items for not only the classrooms, but for the living areas as well. Many of the students would be staying at the school during the various sessions and Joseph wanted them to be comfortable in their new, strange surroundings.

Maura was proud that Joseph asked for her opinions and seriously considered what she had to say. But in the back of her mind, she wondered why this school held such importance to the man who had so recently begun to stake a claim to her heart. Even now, as she lay in her bed, she knew he was downstairs at the kitchen table, a single lamp illuminating the papers he worked almost feverishly to fill with his thoughts, as if, should he not write them down quickly enough, they would disappear between conception and script.

Without consulting a timepiece, Maura knew it was quite late and since they were scheduled to meet with Judge Brock the next morning, she wanted Joseph to get some rest, so that he would be ready. She had a feeling that this would be a day they would all remember.

Sliding her feet into new slippers her husband had purchased for her,

Maura donned her cotton robe and headed for the stairs. The soft glow of lamplight guided her way through the house until she came to the kitchen doorway. Quietly, she leaned against the doorjamb, folded her arms and lay her head against the cool wood. With eyes closed, her lashes intertwining, Maura stood and listened to the sound of Joseph's pen traveling across the writing paper.

Opening her eyes, Maura was surprised to see that Joseph's eyes were turned in her direction, though his pen never stopped.

"I didn't think you were aware that I was here," she said simply.

A crooked smile formed on Joseph's face, first in amusement, seconds later conveying affection.

He placed his pen on the table, and then surrounded it with an arm on either side of his paper. Looking intently at his hands palm side down on the furniture, then shifting his gaze toward the woman in front of him, Joseph spoke softly.

"There are few things of which I am unaware. I am aware of the cadence of your footsteps as you move across the floor. I am aware of the scent of lavender when you come into the room. And I am aware that the lamplight softens your features and curves to the point that I must physically attach myself to this table so that I do not frighten you with the intensity of my longing."

The native's soliloquy stopped, but the words lingered in the air like the rumblings of thunder after a storm has subsided.

A long silence followed, but finally Maura noted, "I only came down here to ask you to get some rest. Perhaps I'd better go back upstairs."

"No," Joseph ordered lovingly. "Stay."

And the two words, though delivered seconds apart, were melted together by the heat in the room.

Placing his foot on the seat of the chair opposite his, Joseph pushed gently in silent invitation, as well as an act of reassurance that she would be close, but far enough away at the same time.

She took her time, because everything within her screamed for her to run the other way. But something held her feet to their spot, and then moved them into the room and toward the chair. She sat as if ready to leap away at a second's notice, but several deep breaths helped calm her.

Joseph's hands now turned palms upward in a beseeching movement, which pleaded for her to place hers on top. She did, and they sat together thus for quite some time, listening to the thunder of their respective heartbeats and reveling in the warmth of their hands covering each other like down filled comforters.

The moment was broken when thunder from outside the house replaced that of the inside, causing Maura to jump several inches in the air, to land with a thump. The pair looked at each other and began to laugh, finally clearing the air and allowing them to enjoy each other's company.

"I feel like a cup of tea," Maura said, rising and making her way toward the stove.

"I think you do too," Joseph said, "All warm, silky and scented." Maura stuck her tongue out, turned and began to heat the water. "I'll make a cup for you as well, on the condition that we change the subject."

"I was rather enjoying myself, but if you have something else you'd rather discuss..."

"I do. I came down here to ask you when you were coming to bed."

"I thought you said you wanted to change the subject."

"Oh, you! You know what I mean. You've been working far too long. We've a meeting with Judge Brock in the morning, in case you've forgotten, a meeting to make us a family. I don't want you falling asleep and missing out on everything."

"I appreciate your concern, my dear, but let me assure you, I have every intention of remaining awake and lucid for our meeting. I wouldn't miss it for the world."

Maura poured the now boiling water into a china pot containing tea leaves and let the mixture steep. Removing two cups from the cupboard, she placed one in front of Joseph and the other in front of her seat. She placed the pot of liquid on a cloth in front of her and sat down.

"You're being much too quiet, Maura. What's really on your mind?"

"I've been thinking about how passionate you are about your school, and how much work is involved in starting something like that. As far as I can see, it will have no equal here or perhaps anywhere."

"What's your point, Maura?" Joseph asked, picking up the teapot and pouring for both of them.

"My point is...and if you don't wish to answer me, I'll try to understand, but I feel that I must know. Why is this school so important to you, Joseph? It seems as if it consumes you."

Silence was the initial answer, as Joseph stared into Maura's eyes.

Just at the moment she thought he would bolt from the room, he breathed deeply and began.

"When I was 16 years old, my family's way of life, as they had known it, was already gone. I would never be the warrior my father, grandfather and uncles had been. We were told to be farmers." Joseph almost spat the word as he said it once, and then repeated, "Farmers! Of what? Grass? Raising prairie dogs instead of hunting buffalo?

"The Indian agent did not care that our children were sick from eating the government's tainted meat or that our old ones were dying from the cold. Their job was to assimilate us into the white world. To get rid of the 'Indian' in us, and to replace it with white ways.

"To this end, they came with great wagons and stole our young people from the villages, taking them away from everyone and everything they had ever known. Our families could only watch. While I would have been considered a man in our world, the white man deemed me still a child and still able to have the Indian taken out of me easily. I did not want to go. I fought them as though my life depended upon it, and in a way it did." Joseph gathered his thoughts, and then went on. "I was not strong enough though. They beat me and I was rendered unconscious. I did not see the tears of my mother or hear the angry words of my father. And I would never again. I never saw my parents alive again outside of my dreams."

Joseph hesitated for several seconds, looking out the window and Maura did not know if she feared more that Joseph would stop or that he would go on. She listened as he continued.

"They took us to the Indian Agency where they stripped us of our clothing and moccasins and gave the boys the white man's pants, shirts and shoes and the girls dresses, undergarments and boots. They forced us to wear them even though the shoes cut into our feet so badly that we bled and the clothes were so uncomfortable we could not breathe. They cut our hair.

"Then they loaded us into railroad cars like cattle and took us a thousand miles from our home, away from our families, so that we would not be tempted by the old way of life.

"We were enrolled in an Indian school, but the last thing they would have done is teach us about Indians. There were many nations there from the Plains as well as those from further southwest. We were thrown together in one big pot and mixed and chopped and boiled until we did not know what or who we were anymore."

Joseph had raised his arms onto their elbows. He sat and stared at his hands, turning them this way, then that, as if he had not seen them before. Then the hands went to his face and touch either side. His eyes broke away and looked at Maura again and he seemed to return to the kitchen for a moment before his memories again took over.

"With all the other children there, did you have no friends, Joseph?" Maura prodded.

"Friends? Yes, I had some friends, most of whom acquiesced and after an initial period of fighting back, they began to speak the white man's tongue fulltime, enjoyed dressing in the new clothing and forgot where they came from."

"Maybe it was easier for them to do that, Joseph," Maura noted quietly.

"I'm sure it was."

"But you did not take the easy route, did you?"

"No. My way was not easy."

"Were you alone in that?"

"For a while, no."

"Tell me, Joseph."

Several bolts of lightning shocked the sky before the man at the table rose, walked to the window and spoke again.

"The weather tonight reminds me of him," Joseph remembering, chuckling just a bit. "He was a storm of much intensity." Walking behind Maura's chair, he placed his hands on the back of it and leaned forward, then changed their position, putting them on her shoulders and massaging the tired muscles.

"What was his name?"

"The white school gave him the name Benjamin – after Benjamin Franklin - which they added to a portion of his Arapaho name, Long Rider. He hated his white name, of course. I considered him to be my brother, as Benjamin in the Bible is Joseph's younger brother. We were like brothers." Joseph hesitated; then said more forcefully, "We were brothers. We fought, we played, we laughed, and in the darkness of our room at night we secretly longed for the old life – he with his Arapaho and I with the Sicangu – and we made plans to return home to our brothers and sisters."

Joseph smiled as he recalled, "He never called me 'Joseph', even when whites were around, he used my real name and told me that we must leave this place and never come back." The smile suddenly disappeared.

Maura waited quietly for several minutes, then reached behind her and took Joseph's hand in hers.

"What happened?"

"We had tried on several occasions to run away and make our way back home. We knew it would not be easy, but we could not stay. Our punishment, after being hunted down by dogs, was, to say the least, severe. But we kept trying anyway.

"The last time, it had snowed for several days and showed no sign of stopping. We thought that all the snow would make it more difficult for the dogs to track our scent, so we dressed warmly and carried several blankets in packs we had fashioned from our bed sheets. We knew they would not stay dry, but they would be easier to carry.

"We got away after the final bed check. The moon was just a sliver – only enough light for us to make out any trees before we ran into them. Unfortunately, it was not enough to help me see a small ravine. I fell, breaking my left leg. I knew I could not continue, but I pleaded with Long Rider to go on, to leave and never come back. And that is exactly what he did."

"He left you?"

"I crawled back toward a farmhouse, and the next morning, the farmer found me as he was going out to feed his livestock. I was half frozen and so weak I could not raise my head, but he got his rifle and kept it trained on my head while his son rode to the school to turn me in. It wouldn't have been hard for anyone to realize where I had come from."

"What happened to you when you got back?"

"They beat me with a switch, then set my leg. I would not scream. I would not give them the satisfaction. I believe they were disappointed."

"What about your friend?"

"It was several days later when they came to me. I had not told them that we had gone off together, but they knew. We were inseparable. They knew. They took great pleasure in telling me that they had found him, still alive but in a bad way, in the woods about 15 miles away. They took their rifle butts and slammed him repeatedly about the head and body, then tied his wrists together and pulled him through the snow back to the school. He was dead before they got there. They used him as an example for anyone else who tried to get away and each time I looked out my window I saw his grave."

"Oh, Joseph, I don't know what to say."

"I was happy."

"What?" Maura asked, incredulously.

"I was happy for him. He did what he wanted to do. He left, and because he died before they got him back to the school, he never came back. He was, and still is, enjoying the old life on the other side of the mountain. I hope to see him again when it is time for me to cross over."

Joseph ran his fingers through the length of his black hair.

"I did not try to leave the school again. The fight was taken out of me. I was a coward, compared to him."

Joseph fingered the bone and bead choker he always wore, and the action, which Maura had seen before, finally struck a chord with her.

"That was his, wasn't it?"

"Yes. His aunts had made it for him and he smuggled it with him by hiding it in his pants. Nobody, not even a male white, wanted to touch an Indian's privates. He had left it behind, hidden in his mattress, because he was so sure he would be going home. I took it and have worn it ever since, so that I will never forget."

"And so you wanted to start this school close to your students' homes so that what happened to you would not happen to them?"

"Yes. I have long dreamed of a school that will allow the children to talk about their families, their way of life. They would be able to visit their homes, keep things that are important to them. We would not try to beat their 'Indian' ways out of them, but teach them to embrace them alongside the teachings of the whites. Their world is changing very quickly. They need to have the white man's education to compete in his world, but they need to remember their heritage as well, and I will assist them in trying to straddle the two," Joseph vowed, then added, "And I would very much like you to help me in this."

Maura turned and, placing her hands on either side of Joseph's face, used her thumbs to wipe the tears that had for so long been streaming unchecked from his eyes. The same thumbs wiped her own tears and mixed them together.

"Was that the idea of Henry's that you wanted to tell me about?" she asked.

"Yes. He must receive the credit. He told me that you had been a teacher in Ohio and had come here believing you would be a teacher again. He suggested that I ask you to work at the school." Quietly, he added, "He told me you loved the children back home very much. I hope you will love these children as much. You know, Henry has much confidence in you...and I do as well. You have been given a gift, Maura. Please work with me and use it again."

"I will."

And the two people stood holding each other, as the bright yellow sun began to rise amongst the scattering gray clouds in the eastern sky.

In a room not far away, a tall figure leaned across a massive desk, looking his adversary in the eyes.

"You understand what I want you to do, then?"

"Yes, I understand, and you must know that it goes against every principle that I have held dear in the 40 years I have held this office, but you have given me little choice."

"I don't give a damn about your principles, and if you really did, you wouldn't even consider what I've asked. But you're going to do it, aren't you? I'll send everything you hold dear to hell if you don't. Believe me.

"Then send me, too. It'll be all I deserve after this."

"It would be my pleasure."

"I only hope you join me there. The devil enjoys a good fight."

The wide grin was impossible to miss, even in the darkened room.

"I am the devil, sir."

Chapter Twenty-four

"Maura! Joseph! I have a message for you!" Loretta yelled up the back staircase. She knew that at least one of the two was up, as she had heard the baby caterwauling not long before.

The sound of heavy footsteps caught her ears and she turned to check on the cornbread in the oven. Breakfast was just around the corner and most of her boarders were already seated and waiting.

Joseph appeared in the doorway and Loretta pointed to the piece of paper lying on his plate at the table. Joseph picked it up, smiled and headed back the way he had come.

"That boy, he's got somethin' up his sleeve, I can just tell," she said, shaking her head and taking a large knife and slicing the still hot bread she had just removed from the big old cook stove.

Taking the steps two at a time, Joseph reached the top with little effort and proceeded to quietly open the bedroom door. The sight that met his eyes never failed to knock him backward a bit. Mother and child together in the rocker, the sound of soft crooning echoing off the walls.

Maura tore her eyes from her son and glued them to her husband instead.

"What was it, Joseph?" she asked.

"It's a message from Judge Brock. He wants us to bring Ryan with us to the appointment today."

Two strides took him to his wife's side where he knelt on the rag rug covering the hardwood floor.

"I don't know if you realize what this means to me," he said, unable to hide his absolute joy.

Maura reached out with a free hand and cupped the side of her husband's face.

"I know. Oh, how I know. For having lived a thousand miles apart, we have much in common, you and I. We both want this little family very much."

She sat back and closed her eyes. "Ever since my parents died, all I have wanted was a place to call home again." She reopened them and sat forward in the rocker before continuing. "You are providing that for me, Joseph. My heart is so full, I don't know how I will ever let more in."

"Your heart will stretch, Maura, I have no doubt. Now, are you two ready to go? It's almost time for us to officially become the Walks Alone Family!"

An hour later, the three made their way to the judge's office. Maura carried Ryan and Joseph stepped up to the door first, swinging it open to allow entry for his wife. Following her in, he waited a moment for his eyes to adjust to the darkened interior after leaving the bright sunlight. Just six hours ago, as the rain came down in sheets and lightning filled the sky, Joseph would not have expected the sun to be out in such radiance this morning. He felt it could only be a sign of the day's events.

Maura was already speaking to Warren as Joseph joined her. The clerk was normally squirrelly in Joseph's presence, but he seemed even more agitated today, as he informed the pair that the judge was indeed in, but was in conference with several other people at the moment. He hinted that they could leave and come back, but Joseph planted himself in one of the curve-back chairs directly opposite Warren's desk and settled in.

Maura gave Joseph a look of warning to which he replied, "You're no fun."

The steady tick, tick, tick of the grandfather clock in the corner was the only sound in the room until a rather large belch reverberated, having originated from the smallest person in attendance. Maura and Joseph stared at the baby, then looked at each other and began to laugh.

It was at that precise moment that the door to the judge's office opened and the weary face of Judge Brock appeared. The gentleman stepped into the doorway and beckoned them to enter. Warren began to say something to the judge but the elder man waved him off.

"Please sit, Maura, Joseph. I see you got my message and brought the boy."

The office door closed behind them and the faintest click of the lock that followed was masked as Joseph replied, "Yes. We are very happy we can be together on this occasion," and Maura nodded her head in agreement.

Judge Brock's chair creaked loudly as he sat down heavily behind his desk and took an audible, deep breath. "There is something that I must tell you and I won't beat around the bush. I'm afraid that things will not work out quite the way I had hoped when last we met."

While the judge hesitated, Joseph interjected, "Sir, if it's more time you need, that's fine. We still have many things to do while we're in the city, we can wait, as long as it won't be too long. We're rather excited."

Maura held the baby closer, a shiver beginning on her spine and traveling its length. "Something's wrong, isn't it?" To her the judge's face looked more like a shriveled apple than a robust man. She definitely did not share Joseph's optimism.

Both parents were caught off guard when two figures emerged from the darkened corners of the room on either side of them. One, a woman, dressed in a dark skirt, short dark jacket and crisp white blouse. An equally dark hat was pinned tightly to her head.

On the woman's left was a gentleman whose stature was easily a third higher than hers. The regulation army jacket he wore was obviously made for a man much smaller than his six and a half-foot frame, with the sleeves taut and bulging from what could only be explained as large muscles constricted inside a too narrow fabric tube. His tight blue wool pant legs as well offered testimony to his strength and both Maura and Joseph were speechless as they stared in disbelief. The man's small blue cap bore the army insignia but barely covered the top of his head.

Joseph soon recovered his wits but since Maura's lack of speech was due more to fear than simply surprise, she was slower to recover.

"What's going on? Who are these people? Why are they here?" Joseph demanded rising onto his feet.

The giant moved a step closer but the judge raised his hand. "Mr. Walks Alone is entitled to an explanation."

"You're damned right I'm entitled. Neither of us suspected that there would be anyone else here and since this...this...Goliath is looking at me like he hasn't eaten for three days, I'd like to know what's going on. Is my family in jeopardy?"

"No one is going to be hurt, Joseph," Judge Brock assured him, adding under his breath, "at least I pray not, if you cooperate."

"Cooperate!" Joseph's shout was a 180-degree turn from the judge's tone. "Tell me what is going on or we will leave!"

"No, no, son. Sit down. Let us speak as rational people."

"You'll excuse me if I'm not feeling very rational right now, Judge. But I will sit down. Just promise me that nothing will happen to my family."

The silence in the room grew to such proportions that the tick, tick, tick of the grandfather clock in the outer room broke through the walls to fill Joseph's ears and served to build the level of Maura's growing hysteria. She was still incapable of speech, but her eyes spoke volumes, as they bore first into the judge, and then sought out Joseph's face as a sanctuary against whatever foe awaited them.

"You can't make that promise, can you?"

The question was posed as if Joseph were asking the judge about the weather.

"No."

Never in her life had Maura imagined that one word so softly spoken could carry such weight. She felt as if she were Atlas, as she looked down at her sleeping babe and prayed she could keep the weight of the world on her own shoulders.

"What is happening, Joseph? What are they going to do?"

"I don't know, but I'm sure the judge will be telling us, won't you, sir?"

"We did some checking after you two left the other day, and it was brought to my attention that since your wife is legally a ward of an officer in the U.S. Army, that this matter falls under his jurisdiction, not mine."

The statement was enough to arouse Maura from her stupor. "A ward of an officer? In the U.S. Army, you say? Where did you get such an idea? I'm of age! I can do what I please. They have no say over me!"

"I'm afraid they, or rather, he, does, my dear."

"Don't you 'my dear' me, sir. Somethin's amiss here and we're gettin' it straightened out now, once and for all. You'll be tellin' me where this nonsense is comin' from and who this officer is or I'll be knowin' the reason why." Maura's brogue was becoming more and more pronounced, as she became increasingly upset.

Judge Brock began sifting through a short pile of papers in front of him and finally found the one he was looking for.

Tilting his head back to get a better view of the sheet through his small spectacles, the judge asked, "Maura, is your maiden name, O'Brien?"

"Yes, I've made no secret of it."

"Then you might remember this," and he began to read from the parchment. "I do hearby certify that on the third day of October, in the year of our Lord, one thousand, eight hundred and ninety-three, the following two people were united in marriage by proxy in my presence – Capt. James Theodore Cole of Fort Sully, South Dakota, and Miss Maura Cieran O'Brien of Lima, Ohio in the United States of America. What God has joined together, let no man put asunder." The judge stopped, adjusted his spectacles, then continued, "And it's signed by what appears to be 'Rev. W.T....'"

"Hanrahan. Rev. W.T. Hanrahan," Maura offered softly. "Where did you get that?" She then spoke louder as if awakening from a sound sleep, "It means nothin'! James made me sign papers after I got to the fort. They were to make sure the proxy marriage was put aside, he said. I trusted him!" She looked at Joseph who just sat, staring. He turned and slumped in his chair.

"Don't ya see? It was James. Did he not give ya those papers? I know he has 'em. He said he'd be needin' 'em when he found himself a proper wife." She stopped, and then added, "a pure wife."

No one spoke for what seemed like an hour, and then the judge addressed the crying woman still tightly holding her baby. "Maura, you can't be married to two men at one time. That's against the law. Your marriage to Captain Cole stands as is, I'm afraid, until I receive evidence to the contrary, and your marriage to Joseph is null and void."

"No. He can't do this."

"It's the law, Maura. And there's another thing. The baby...he belongs to Cole. Since you were married before the baby was born, Cole is considered to be the child's father until he denies him under the law, and to my knowledge, he has not done that."

"He never wanted him! He wants nothin' to do with him!"

"I'm afraid there's more. Captain Cole has ordered your immediate return to the fort, Maura, whether you want to do or not." Maura sat reeling from the judge's words.

"You must understand, under the law, I must follow his wishes, no matter my own opinion, and Mrs. Welstead," the judge pointed at the dark lady from the corner, "is here to take the baby to a foster home while all this is sorted out. Now..."

"No! You can't do that! You cannot take my baby! He needs me! Joseph! What can we do? You know I'm telling the truth! Joseph? Joseph?"

In Joseph's eyes, the walls around him were crumbling. He knew the woman next to him was telling the truth, as she knew it. She was incapable of a lie of this magnitude. She could have never let their lives bond as they had she known. He was not bothered by the fact that she had never mentioned the marriage by proxy. If she thought it was done, then it was done, or should have been. He knew who the culprit was.

"Cole. Where is he?" was all Joseph could get out.

"He couldn't be here. He has sent Corporal Thorpe in his stead. The corporal is to escort Mrs. Walstead to the baby's new home. He will then take Maura back to the fort to her husband. Capt. Cole trusts you will cause them no trouble."

"Let them take our child and my wife with no trouble. Oh, absolutely. Of course there will be no trouble because this will not happen," Joseph stated emphatically. "You will not take them."

"I will, Joseph. She is not your wife. She has never legally been your wife and that is not your child." The judge spoke as if to a toddler.

The woman identified as Mrs. Walstead stepped forward and reached to remove Ryan from Maura's arms.

"You're not takin' my baby," Maura said, and got up to take flight. Joseph rose in slow motion. Watching Maura and the baby out of the corner of his eye, he thought first to strangle the judge, but in the blink of an eye realized that the man was just trying to do his job. Instead, he turned and flew at the giant beside him who had worked his way toward the desk. With a right to the left eye, Joseph began his assault on the one man, in the absence of Cole, he could turn his aggression toward.

Unfortunately, though Joseph was an experienced fighter, it had been a while since he had been involved in hand to hand fisticuffs and even his well-honed skills proved to be too little to handle the giant before him.

The difficulty was compounded by Maura's pleadings, which were falling on deaf ears. Then the cries of his mother awoke the infant who took one look at the stranger holding him and loosed a wail that should have been heard from blocks away. All this proved a distraction for the Indian and while he was able to land a few good hits, one backhanded blow from the corporal felled the man fighting just to be a husband and father.

Joseph flew backward, his head striking the corner of the judge's desk and the world closed in until there was nothing but blessed silence.

Maura took one look at Joseph, then another at Ryan and could not decide whom to attempt to aid first. She knew she could take the woman, although doing so with the baby in the woman's arms would be the challenge.

In the seconds that followed, Maura determined that the woman wasn't heading anywhere anytime soon, so with a cry from her Irish warrior ancestors, Maura leaped onto the back of the giant and began pummeling him about the head and neck.

"Oh good Lord," the judge said, as he held his head between his hands and shook it back and forth. He had convinced himself in the wee hours of the morning that the couple would be complacent; that they would see that he was only doing his job. He would have helped them fight this tragedy he had been forced to act out. But the final scene was nothing like what he had envisioned and was, in fact, getting worse by the moment.

Maura began twisting the corporal's ears, as he circled the room, attempting to shake her off, and his cries were music to her ears. They were short lived, however, as Warren unlocked the door and struck Maura on the head with one of the judge's law books. She dropped to the floor like a sack of cornmeal.

The people in the room who remained conscious looked at one another before moving into action. Mrs. Welstead quickly stepped over the bodies and left the building with the baby. It occurred to the judge that he didn't even know where the woman was taking the child, but he was sure he would be using every trick in the book to find out.

The corporal bent down and gently picked up Maura, then threw her over his shoulder without a second thought. He headed out the door and deposited her in the back of his wagon, heading back to the fort.

Warren, who was panting a bit from the effort he had put forth in wielding the book, observed, "I never thought she would have caused such a fracas."

"I told you to keep your eye on her, didn't I?" the judge asked, recalling the couple's previous visit.

"That you did, sir, that you did. Now, what are we going to do with him?"

Judge Brock looked down at Joseph and grabbed his coat from the nearby rack. "Help me get him up, Warren. We'll put him in my buggy and take him back to his boardinghouse. That's the least I can do."

The judge knew he was in no shape to be attempting to lift a young man, but he bent to try and waited for Warren to pitch in. Receiving no such aid, Judge Brock lifted his head and looked at his clerk. "Are you going to just stand there, Warren, or are you going to help me? And just so you know, your answer had better be the latter."

"Yes, sir."

The clerk reluctantly placed his hands under Joseph's shoulders and began to lift. "Are you sure he's unconscious sir? You know how these people are. He could be trying to trick us and the minute our hands are full, he'll open his eyes and pull out a knife and slit both our throats, not to mention taking our scalps."

The judge dropped Joseph's booted feet with a reverberating thud. "Yes, Warren, you're right, that's exactly what he's going to do with his head busted open and blood pouring out. And I'm sure he kept his knife well hidden while all the time he only used his fists on the poor corporal. I'm glad you have that end of him because he'll probably turn around any second now and kill you first."

The clerk turned white, and then pink as the judge ordered his employee to move out the door with Joseph in tow.

"I was just trying to make an observation," Warren said defensively. "If you're not careful in this town, you could wake up dead."

"After what I've done, I think I'd be better off dead, Warren, because when he wakes up, I'm the first person he's going to want to see and it isn't going to be pretty."

Chapter Twenty-five

Loretta handed the two-inch steak to Joseph and he held the cool meat over the throbbing, swollen mass he used to use as an eye prior to the fight.

The two were in the kitchen, Joseph sitting in a chair at the table, Loretta carefully examining the gaping wound on the back of his head caused by the contact with the judge's desk.

"Head wounds always make ya bleed like a stuck pig," Loretta noted as she pulled at the edges of the cut, then tried to staunch the flow of blood. "I think this one's gonna have to be sewed."

"My head already feels like a sledgehammer's pounding in it, quit messing with it!"

"I reckon it looks like a sledgehammer's already pounded ON it, Joseph. How big did you say that man was?"

"Whatever you have to do, do it quick. I have to go, Loretta," he said, removing the steak from his eye and attempting to rise.

"You'll do no such thing. Sit!" and she pushed his body back to the chair and forcibly bent his head forward. "You can't help Maura or the baby in this condition and I can't see a thing while you're squirmin' around. Now do as I say."

Joseph could only groan as he thoughts swirled back to the events of the morning. He had finally regained consciousness on Loretta's fainting couch in the parlor several hours after the judge and Warren had deposited him in her care. Apparently, Judge Brock had told the boarding house owner much of what had transpired and she was able to piece together the entire story, adding what bits of information Joseph could remember.

"Time is of the essence, here, Loretta. The baby was taken away, and Maura could be hurt, perhaps facing that rattlesnake that planned this whole thing. I've got to help them. Maura would never forgive me if I lost Ryan, but even if I find him, I don't know if I can take him."

Loretta reached for the needle and thread while she listened. Closing her left eye tight, she steadied her hands and aimed for the eye of the needle.

"What am I going to do, Loretta? Who do I look for first? And if...when I find them, what can I do? I trusted Judge Brock! I trusted him!" Joseph shouted, pounding the table with his free hand. Loretta could not see his face, but could hear the quiver in his voice as he vented his grief. "And because of that, in the judge's words, 'under the eyes of the law' Maura belongs to another, and Ryan will never be my son. I will trust no man again."

"Joseph Walks Alone!" Loretta began. "Don't you go saying such things! Why I remember just not too long ago, you and me were in this kitchen and you were tellin' me that even after all Maura had been through, you thought she oughta trust in you. Now here you are saying trust ain't something that's ever gonna be in your vocabulary again. Well, let me tell you somethin' boy. I can't make you trust anybody but I can tell you from experience, you have to trust your heart. If your heart tells you that Maura is your wife and Ryan is your son, then by God, you'd better believe it. As soon as you're feelin' better, you hightail it to the fort and get your wife back, then you can fight together to get your son back. That's what it's gonna take and if I know you, you are the person to do it. That's my opinion, that's my advice and that's it."

"Are you done?"

"I just told ya I was. Now hold still," and Joseph remained stoic as Loretta poked the needle though his skin and rejoined the tissues.

When she had snipped the thread and was returning her needle to her darning box, Joseph turned in his seat, took her hand and asked, "What would I do without you, Loretta?"

"I don't know, boy. I just don't know. And that's why," she grabbed her hat which was hanging on a hook just inside the back door, and plopped it on her head, tying a tight little bow under her chin, "I'm goin' with ya."

"Oh, no. This is my fight, Loretta."

"Oh, yes. You're in no shape to be headin' out anywheres in your condition and I figure you'll be needin' a driver in case you pass out agin. We'll tie your horses onto the back of my wagon, load up your stuff and take it on to the fort."

"Loretta, could we just leave the things here for a while? I don't know..."

"Well, I know, Joseph. That wife of yours will be wantin' her clothes and that baby will be needin' all kinds of things once you two get him home. Now I'll go up and fetch 'em while you get the wagon ready."

"Yes, ma'am," and though Joseph's head was pounding louder than a hammer on a railroad spike, he started to do her bidding, but stopped.

"What about the boardinghouse? You can't just up and leave your tenants, can you?"

"Oh, hell. They know how to cook and make their beds. They're all paid up to the end of the month, then if I'm not back and they wanna leave, let 'em. We've got business to attend to. Besides, knowin' those men and how they've fallen for Maura and the baby, I'd not be surprised if they insisted I go anyway, and if we waited around ta ask 'em, they'd just wanna come too. That's extra baggage we don't need. I'll leave 'em a note and we'll be off."

What seemed like too many hours later as they neared the fort, Joseph pulled on the reins he had taken away from Loretta and stopped the horses. Placing his elbows on his knees he looked toward the horizon, the outline of the fort just beginning to appear.

"You know, Loretta, I hope I haven't made a mistake letting you come along. I just don't know what we'll be facing when we get there, and if the situation gets as ugly as I fear, I'd feel badly if you were caught in the middle on my account."

"Land sakes, boy, you're a worrisome creature. You remember that word we were discussin' earlier - trust? You just gotta trust Loretta. I'll take care of things and I'll take care of myself. I've been doin' it now longer than I'd like so believe me, I know what I'm gettin' into."

Joseph reached over and gave the woman the biggest hug he could, given the circumstances. "I'm going to give you a better one when this is all over," he told her.

"I reckon you'll owe me quite a few hugs by then. I'll be keepin' a record, so you don't get away cheap."

"I'll be ready, Loretta." Joseph took a deep breath, and as he did, Loretta whistled through her teeth, taking him by surprise and he watched as she grabbed the reins again and gave them a sound crack, sending the wagon and its occupants lurching toward their destiny.

Totally unaware that Joseph was on his way to the fort, Maura sat cross-legged on the straw-covered floor of the solitary confinement cell in the fort stockade. No one had come in or spoken to her since the big ox that had brought her here had shaken her awake in the back of the Army wagon, picked her up, threw her over his shoulder and dumped her in the cell, closing the door and locking it.

No one had answered her calls for help and as far as Maura knew, there was no one in the building. She was able to hear quite a bit of commotion going on outside and wondered what was happening. She reasoned that whatever it was must be much more important than her "crime" against James or even he would be in here now, making her life a living hell.

Just the thought of the man made Maura fume. She could not fathom why he felt the need to do this to her. What joy could he possibly get out of such cruelty? Hadn't he done enough over the past several months, and hadn't she been through enough without having the most precious thing in her life taken away?

"Where has he taken my son?" she wondered aloud and began to pray that wherever he was, Ryan was alive and being well cared for. "We'll find you, honey. Don't you worry! Mommy and Daddy will come for you."

That thought led to Joseph, and Maura recalled that the last time she had seen him he was lying in a pool of blood on the floor of the judge's office, unconscious. She said another prayer for her husband, and then really began to consider her predicament.

"I'm alone," she thought to herself, "and Joseph promised me he would never leave me alone again. What will I do? I have no idea what I'm going to be facing here or if I'll ever see Joseph or Ryan again."

Tears began for the first time, as Maura allowed self pity to envelop her. She began pounding on the floor with both fists until finally, the self-pity turned to rage – against James, and against what was happening to her and to her family.

"Maura Cieran, would you listen to yourself?" she shouted out loud. "Get off your back porch and make something happen. You know that Joseph wouldn't have left you alone if it were physically possible. He will be here. Do not let James do this. He wants you to fall apart. Well, that will be the day, I say.

"I signed those papers, he knows it and he will let the judge know. Somehow I will make him. He has to give this up. I will not allow my family to be torn apart," and rising swiftly to her feet, Maura proceeded to beat the living daylights out of her wooden cell door. Screaming anything she could think of, to get someone's attention, she continued her onslaught until she heard the outside door open and click shut.

"Who's there?" she questioned. "Let me out of here. I've done nothing wrong. I demand to see the colonel. I've got a few things to say to him, starting with why I'm being treated this way."

The sound of someone rifling through the desk on the opposite side of the door was the only answering noise. Finally a drawer slammed shut, keys jingled and shuffling footsteps stopped just outside the cell door.

Maura stepped back to allow entry to the person outside, even though it may be a foe. "It's somebody at least," she said under her breath, and she would try to get him to take her to the fort commander.

The lock clicked open and the door moved toward her. Then a pair of glasses nesting in a mass of unkempt hair appeared before her.

"Henry!" she cried, and hugged the older man until he called for her to stop.

"You're going to squeeze the life out of me, my dear. Now, let's get you out of here. I don't quite know how, but we're going to manage, by golly! We've just got to think. I was going to start without you but I figured that two heads were better than one."

"Oh, Henry, I'm so glad it's you. Why is it you, by the way? What's going on out there that everyone else has ignored me but you?"

"The whole fort's in a tizzy, Maura. My goodness, you don't know! Coffey received a telegram ordering the immediate abandonment of the fort. The troops are needed further to the west, so they're moving out -

lock, stock and barrel. Only a small contingency will be left behind for a month or so, to make sure everything's taken care of."

Maura's eyes grew wider and wider with each bit of information she heard. "Are you leaving with them, Henry?" she inquired, hoping for a negative answer but expecting the opposite.

She got what she wanted. "No, I've already handed Coffey my resignation. I've decided to stay on here and if Joseph would let me, I want to volunteer my limited services to his cause at the school. I think I could at least help minor aches and pains if nothing else."

"Henry, you underestimate your worth. Of course Joseph will want you to stay on. He'll be delighted and so will I...well, we will be, after we get through the trouble we're in right now. Oh, Henry, did anyone tell you? James had the baby away from me and...James! Is he leaving, too? Do you know if someone brought the baby here?"

"Maura calm down. I've heard bits and pieces of what happened, and I can't believe that even Cole would do this to you. I apologize that I didn't get to you sooner, but up until about 15 minutes ago they've been watching the stockade door like a hawk. I don't know if they're expecting Joseph to arrive soon or if they expected me to attempt to come to your aid. I can think of no other reason because as you well know my dear, there is no one else within this facility who would try to help you."

Maura nodded sadly.

"However, I have not seen the baby." The statement brought a whimper to Maura's lips, but Henry continued. "But, Cole is not leaving yet so there is still hope that they could bring him here. Cole, my dear, will be left in charge of the soldiers that will remain. On one hand that is good, on the other, I'm afraid that puts you right under his thumb. We've got to do something soon, because there will be no Colonel Coffey to keep a tight rein on him. We could be in for some trouble."

Maura's heart sank as she listened to her friend.

"Dear, you must tell me every detail of what has occurred so that we can best make a plan to fight this thing." Maura complied and when she was finished, Henry asked, "Do you know what happened to Joseph? Do you believe we can expect him to come back here?"

"I pray he will come if he is able, Henry, but I don't know. I have doubts about his feelings toward me after what the judge told him." Henry began to protest but Maura waved her hand. "You didn't see his face, Henry. I did. He probably believes that I purposely lied to him so that my child would have a name." Maura looked intently at Henry and studied every line in the man's face and searched his eyes for the answer to her next question. "You believe me don't you, Henry? You know I could never do such a thing. I would have been perfectly happy on my own, with my son. We would have made it work, but...."

"But, you fell in love, didn't you?"

"How did you know? I haven't even told Joseph. He doesn't know, and that's why I believe he may think ill of me."

"Nonsense," Henry snorted. "He knows and he feels the same. He thinks you don't trust him, so he was waiting to tell you, to build a relationship you could count on. You two really must think that the rest of us aren't quite all there," he said, tapping the side of his head and accidentally knocking his glasses down crookedly on his nose. He adjusted them as if nothing had happened and continued.

"Why, it's as plain as the nose on my face how you two feel about each other, so why can't either one of you see that? You've been so busy dancing around the issue that you're missing the tune. Wake up and enjoy what life is trying to hand you Maura, and fight for it with every breath in your body. I assure you, you'll regret it if you don't."

Maura stared at Henry, and then threw herself into his arms. "You are the dearest, most wonderful man on the face of this Earth, Henry Pierce. What would I do without you?"

"I'm sure you'd get along fine, my dear. I don't know what your husband would think of what you've said, but I thank you. Now, if we're quite through, I believe we have some work to do, Mrs. Walks Alone."

"I believe you're right, Dr. Pierce," she answered, placing an emphasis on the title preceding his name. Henry smiled, grabbed her hand, squeezed it, looked out the door and said, "Come on!" While the fort was otherwise occupied, Maura was unceremoniously dragged from the stockade, down a wooden sidewalk to Henry's office.

"By all the Saints you're fast for an older gentleman!" she exclaimed, after the door banged shut behind them.

"I'll take that as a compliment."

Loretta halted the horses not far from the fort, watching, as row after row of soldiers and wagons filed from the gates and headed westward.

Loretta was confused and after checking Joseph's reaction, she asked, "I thought it was just me, but you look a little peeked yourself. What the Sam Hill's going on? It looks like mass desertion!"

"I'm not sure what it is. The fort is scheduled for abandonment, but it couldn't be this soon. I heard nothing about it before we left. They wouldn't just up and leave like this, would they?"

"You know these fellers better'n me, Joseph. I haven't been in these parts for years and to tell you the truth, I don't have much use for the army. My John never had a good word to say about it and I guess that kinda rubbed off on me. If they're leavin' I say good riddance. Leaves more room for us. I just hope Maura's still here."

"Me too," Joseph said quietly, taking the reins and letting the horses guide themselves through an opening in the formation.

Capt. James Cole was standing in the doorway of the commander's office, watching the line of soldiers move out. A broad grin threatened to ruin the tight-lipped visage he had plastered on his face. He could have laughed out loud when Coffey had received the telegram. "He is so gullible, and such a half wit. If he had given any thought to it at all, he would have realized that something wasn't right, but I knew I could count on him to follow any order given, like the sheep he is."

Cole had arranged for the telegram from Pierre before he had left the city. The telegraph operator had looked at Cole sidelong as he listened to his request, but a few shiny gold pieces accidentally dropped on the counter seemed to assuage the man's conscience.

The telegrapher didn't know how close he had come to meeting his maker that day, as Cole had mulled over the ease at which he could have done away with him, if he had given him any trouble. But in the end the captain had admired the operator's greed and had convinced himself that he really wasn't worried that authorities might be told of what he'd done because anyone who cared would be long gone by the time word had spread.

Meanwhile, Cole was left in charge of the fort with a small company of men, most of them loyal to his cause and would question nothing.

"I had to get them out of here now," he said aloud. "It's not as if they wouldn't have left eventually anyway. I'm in the right on this, they'll see. When everything goes according to my plan, they'll understand."

Quick movements drew his attention away from the column of soldiers and equipment and to a pair running silently down the planks, which served as walkways to keep too much mud from being dragged into the offices.

"Well, well, well. It seems as if the good doctor has helped my little bird escape a bit sooner than I thought he might. But that's quite all right, they're not going anywhere, that's for certain. They can sweat just as easily in the doctor's quarters, as in the stockade."

This time, an outright laugh escaped Cole's lips. "I can't wait until Walks Alone gets here, which I figure shouldn't be too long now. Then this is going to turn into quite an interesting confrontation. They'll regret trying to make me look the fool," and he smiled to himself, reached inside his uniform jacket and brought out a cigar. He ran the length underneath his nose, then popped an end into his mouth, struck a match against the wall and lit the other side, inhaling deeply.

Seeing Joseph's wagon pass through the fort entrance, Cole slowly blew out rings of smoke then said simply, "Let the games begin."

Chapter Twenty-six

Maura saw Joseph and Loretta at the same moment and her first instinct was to run out the door. "No," Henry ordered, grabbing her arm. "Let me go. I'll bring them in here."

The native had stopped the team just outside the entrance to his quarters. Searching the grounds for something that would tell him what was happening, his eyes met Cole's, as the captain lounged in the doorway of the commanding officer's quarters and for the first time in years, Joseph's blood ran cold.

"This is not good, Loretta," he said, jumping down from the wagon and reaching up to help the woman from the conveyance. Joseph knew that the abandonment had indeed begun and that Cole would be left to oversee the facility's final days. He had believed this would be a time of hope, as his dreams for the school began to reach fulfillment, but with the events of the past day, Joseph was certain things were not going to come as easily as he had thought.

"Is that, him?" Loretta asked, glancing at Cole from the corner of her eye.

"You have always been a perceptive woman, Loretta, and this is no exception. Yes, that is Captain James Cole and right now we are going to ignore the hell out of him. We've got to find Maura first and the place to start is with..."

"Joseph! Over here, son!" It was Henry, running towards them as fast as he could, finally coming to a stop in front of Joseph.

"Oh, my boy, I'm so glad to see you." The older man turned so that his back faced the captain and he added in a lower tone, "We're being watched, son. Maura's safe in my office, waiting. Let's go there and we can make our plans. Cole's not going to do anything, anyway, until he's sure the troops are gone."

The trio crossed the grounds together and entered the darkened doctor's office where Joseph was hit full force with arms wrapping around his neck. The scent of lavender pervaded his nostrils, giving him a hint of who the assailant might be.

"Oh, Joseph! I knew you would come. Well, at first I wasn't sure, but then I thought about you and about us and I just knew you would come."

"That sounds suspiciously like trust to me," Loretta whispered from behind the couple.

Joseph squeezed Maura until she thought she might burst, but she didn't complain, just held on tight to her man.

Finally, Joseph broke free and took Maura's face between his hands.

"I promised you that I would never leave you alone, and I will always keep my promises if I can. Together we will fight this. We will find our son and bring him home and be the family that we both want to be. This I also promise."

"I believe you."

The three words were spoken softly but hit Joseph's ears with the force of an explosion.

The tender moment was interrupted, however, as Henry tapped the native on the shoulder. "I hate to break you two up, but the last wagon just left the fort and Cole's men are gathering. I think we might be in for some trouble."

"I agree, Henry, but I believe the only way to combat this is to face it head-on. I'm going out there."

"Not by yourself. I'm going with you."

"Maura, no."

"Yes."

"Now she starts saying yes," Joseph said to himself, as he opened the door and walked out with his wife.

"Where is he?"

"Whoever are you referring to, my dear?"

"You know perfectly well to whom I am referring, James. Where's my son?"

Joseph and Maura had found Cole standing near the flagpole where his men had gathered to hear their instructions for the remainder of the day. The fort was a mess as those who had departed had simply thrown aside the items that couldn't fit into their wagons and those soldiers left behind were to put the area back in order.

"Tell me!" she demanded, at the top of her lungs.

James' eyes narrowed and his face contorted in a smirk as he began to speak.

"Even though your friends have helped you out of the stockade, you are still a prisoner here, Maura. My prisoner now, as it turns out, and I do not allow prisoners to speak to me in that manner. If you are as intelligent as I know you to be, then you must follow the rules, Maura, and the first rule is to keep your mouth shut. If – and I do emphasize that word, if – you ever see your son again, it will be because you've been a good girl and you've done exactly what I've told you to do."

"I am not your prisoner, Cole. Feel free to give me the information that my wife asked for."

James didn't bother to face Joseph as he answered.

"Your wife? She is no more your wife than I am. You two may have been playing house but I have a piece of paper that says she is married to me. You are no one, Walks Alone, and as for the boy, you have no right to know anything about him."

"I am his father."

"Are you, really? I find that highly unlikely and since his mother will remain legally tied to me, unless I decide otherwise, he will never, ever be your child. So you see, Walks Alone, your name is quite appropriate, don't you think? Maura will never be your wife and," here James searched for a name and finally looked to Maura, a wry smile on his face. "Why, you know, my dear, I don't even know the boy's name. Isn't that funny? Perhaps you ought to tell me what it is."

"No."

"Oh, well. It's not really necessary, anyway. Perhaps a new name would be good for him and it would be amusing as well. His own mother wouldn't know what to call him. Yes, I'll have to think about that."

"Why are you doing this, James? What have I done to you to deserve this? And Joseph? Why are you punishing him? He has done nothing to you but you are destroying us, destroying our family. You weren't interested in me or my son before, why are you now?"

"As for him," and Cole waved in Joseph's direction. " He's made me look the fool one time too many."

"It wasn't difficult," Joseph commented dryly.

"You see! There he goes again! There is no way that he could get away with such insolence as he's shown me were he in the Army. I deserve respect," he shouted, clenching his teeth and poking himself in the chest with his index finger to emphasize the point.

"You deserve much more than that, and with my dying breath I will see that you get it," the native promised.

Ignoring Joseph, Cole moved closer to Maura. "As for your inquiry about my interest in your son, that's a good question, and one that I will answer. Your son, my dear, fascinates me because he makes the perfect pawn. Such a tiny, disgusting little thing, but he's proven very useful so far, and I believe he will become even handier in the days to come. Oh, yes," he stopped, grinned and continued, "there is another, far more interesting reason, but I'll save that for another time. Besides, we have several more guests arriving and when that happens, things should really heat up."

Maura's face crumpled and her shoulders slumped as she listened.

Ever so gently, Joseph took her hand in his and squeezed it.

Finally Maura was able to get out, "I don't understand you."

"My dear, you don't have to. Now, I'm growing terribly bored with the lot of you and I have quite a bit of work ahead of me, seeing as I'm in charge of this fort now, so you will excuse me." Cole turned and began to make his way toward the commanding officer's quarters when he stopped, turned and announced, "Oh, yes, Maura. I'll give you, say, until dusk this evening, to decide whether you will be staying in the stockade, or living with me in my quarters."

At Maura's answering gasp and protests from Henry and Joseph, Cole noted, "We are married, now, aren't we? I seem to have the papers to prove it. That's what you came here for after all – marriage, a family. I can give you all of that, and more, though it may not be quite what you had in mind."

"I'd sooner die in the stockade than live with you. That is my decision," she retorted.

Cole looked her up and down and finally pointed at a corporal standing nearby. "That can be arranged, Maura. You there, Dexter, isn't it? Take my wife back to the stockade. Lock her in and give the key to me. Such nasty accidents can happen when one escapes from jail, I've heard. I'd hate for any kind of tragedy to befall you."

The corporal grabbed Maura's arm and was hit full in the chin by a right cross from Joseph. The quiet grounds were then alive with the sound of guns being cocked and raised, all pointing at the Indian.

"Joseph, I'll be all right. Let them take me," she pleaded, pointing out, "I need you and I can't lose you now. Please be careful."

"I don't like this," Joseph said to his friend, as they watched the small procession to the stockade.

"She'll be safer in there than anywhere else, as long as we can keep an eye on him," Henry said, moving his head toward Cole, as the captain retreated into his new quarters. "Besides, we've got some work to do."

"Wait a minute. I've got one more thing to ask him," and Joseph took off running to catch up to the officer before he shut the door.

"I thought we were through, Walks Alone. I've told you, I've said all that I will say."

"There's another subject you're avoiding."

"I avoid nothing. What is it this time?"

"This fort is to be turned over to me. Colonel Coffey should have left the papers granting me the property after the Army leaves."

"Oh, yes," Cole said slowly, walking toward the large commander's desk. He skirted around it, and sat in the swivel chair just in front of a blazing fire.

"I do recall seeing such a paper, Walks Alone, but I'm afraid there was an accident," and he looked at Joseph sorrowfully, as he explained.

"You see, while the colonel was packing up, he asked for my help in sorting what papers should go with him, and which ones should be destroyed. In our haste, I believe that I took the paper, which looked amazingly like this one," and he picked up a sheet of white linen from the desk, "and I turned to warm my hands, like this," holding his fingers outstretched over the flames, "and then the paper just, well, went up in smoke, like this," he said, as he watched the flames lick the edges of the paper and move quickly to swallow the entire document.

"Don't you see? I'm so very sorry, but there's nothing I can do. Perhaps you can go back to Washington, and get another one. In the meantime, I'm afraid you can't have the fort. It's under my protection, and I will guard it with my life."

"Your life is not worth the ash in that fireplace," Joseph told him.

"Why, Walks Alone, if I didn't know you better, I'd say you had threatened me. But I know you for the lily-livered redskin that you are, and I'm sure I just misunderstood, didn't I, because if I thought you were serious, I'd have to kill you."

"The only thing you have misunderstood is me. For your sake, I hope you soon begin to understand all that I am, all that my family and this school means to me, or it is you who will die, though perhaps not by my hand. You are a man with many enemies and your time on this earth will end in the time it takes for a rattlesnake to strike. Know that my family will be returned to me and this fort will be turned over to me, on schedule."

"Yes, yes, I hear you, Walks Alone. Why you bother spouting all your drivel is beyond me. Now, it's time for you to go. I have more important matters to attend to," and Cole waved his hand, dismissing Joseph from the room.

As the Indian walked out the door, he encountered his friend who had been listening to every word.

"You're right, Henry. We've got work to do. Let's get to it," and the pair moved as one toward the doctor's office.

Chapter Twenty-seven

"When did Colonel Coffey get the abandonment order, Henry? We heard nothing about this before we left and it's been less than a week."

"A rider came through the gates yesterday like the devil himself was after him. After he saw the colonel, Coffey brought the troops together and made the announcement that they'd been ordered to leave within 24 hours, heading for Wyoming. Beyond that, no one confided one thing to me, especially after I handed Coffey my resignation and told him I wanted to stay here and help you out." Henry caught what he had just said and, turning just a touch pink, said, "I guess I should have said something to you first. I hope that's all right with you, Joseph. I thought you might need some help with the school children, seeing as how they can get sick and all. If there's anything more serious, I can ride into Pierre and bring a real doctor."

An uncomfortable silence filled the room, as Joseph stared at the man who had impersonated a physician for so long. Henry began to sweat and adjusted the worn collar of his shirt just a bit, as he cleared his throat. "I guess I could catch up with them, tell them I changed my mind. Or I could just mosey on up the road by myself, maybe make a fresh start somewhere else, if you don't need me," he added quietly.

"I'm sorry, Henry," Joseph began.

"That's all right, son, don't you worry none. I shouldn't have spoken so soon, not before I'd talked to you first, anyway. There's plenty of other things I can do, I just don't know what they'd be off the top of my head, but you can count on old Henry, he'll think of something. I've done it before and I can do it again. Never mind that I'm a lot older now and it gets harder and harder to start over..."

A smirk crossed Joseph's lips.

"That's right, you are old, Henry," he said, and the comment earned him a look that would melt nails.

"Don't get me wrong, I don't mean anything by it. You said it yourself."

"Uh huh," Henry said with a doubtful tone.

"I just mean, I think, and I believe Maura would agree with me, that you should probably stay here with us, so while you're busy looking after the children, we can look after you, too. We'd love it if you would stay. I'm just ashamed I didn't think to ask you sooner."

"Nothing to be ashamed of, my boy," Henry said, beaming from ear to ear. "We'll do each other a favor, then. I get a home and lots of people to share it with. I'll never be lonely again. A fellow couldn't ask for more."

"Well, he could, but it probably wouldn't do him any good," Joseph quipped.

"Right, well, I think before we get started figuring out what to do about Cole, you should really introduce me to this beautiful lady you brought with you, Joseph. Don't believe I've ever seen her before because I'm pretty sure if I had, I'd remember it."

"Oh, my! Sorry! In all the confusion, I completely forgot. Henry, this is Loretta Williams. She owns the boardinghouse in Pierre where we were staying before, well, before everything fell apart. She's been a great help to us and she volunteered to come to our rescue now as well. I don't know what we'd do without her. And Loretta, this is Henry Pierce, our..." Joseph hesitated, and then finished, "doctor."

"Pleased to meet you, ma'am. I'm just sorry you had to come under these circumstances."

"I wouldn't let the two of 'em deal with this on their own for nothin'," said Loretta. "Of course, I didn't know that a fine man like you was awaitin' here. But glad I came anyway."

"Well, now that we have the introductions wrapped up, Henry, we really have to figure out what's going on here. I believe there's more to this than meets the eye."

"I agree, Joseph. Perhaps we should start at the beginning."

"Sounds like work. So while you boys are doin' your figurin', I'm gonna head on over to the stockade and see what I can see. I'll keep Maura company, if they'll let me. I got a feelin' from the way the captain talked, they're gonna be keepin' more than just a watchful eye on her from here on out."

"Thank you, Loretta. You don't know what this means to me," Joseph told her.

"Oh, I'm thinkin' I've got an idea," she said meaningfully, turning the doorknob and stepping out into the sunshine.

Henry and Joseph sat quietly together, saying little about what had just happened. When the conversation did begin, it was Joseph who first rippled the still waters.

"I don't know that we can win against Cole, Henry."

"We have to try, son. You can't just sit back and let him take everything you've worked so hard for. You've got a lot at stake here. Think about that and just get mad, son. I know you're not usually an angry man, that you're not prone to violence, but you've got to do something bold. Sometimes using your brains just isn't enough. Sometimes you've got to fight fire with fire. That's the only thing a man like Cole is going to understand."

"I know you're right, Henry but the last time I fought for something, I lost someone, a dear friend. I don't know if I could live with myself if something happened to Maura or Ryan or to you or Loretta. The responsibility is not something that I take lightly. I know that I have a lot at stake – it's my family, for God's sake. It's the home that both Maura and I have wanted, the life we had thought was right at our fingertips. I just can't believe that my wife is sitting in a jail cell, my son is missing and I am sitting here like a lizard warming itself on a rock."

"I'm listening to what you're saying, but I think that were our roles switched, you would tell me that even a lizard on a rock can be a dangerous predator when his insect prey believes the lizard is only sunning himself. That's what you have to be – a predator – with you know who as the prey."

"Henry, just when I think that I'm ready to teach, I find I am the student again."

"My boy, though we haven't known each other long, I've learned a great deal from you. I'm just repeating it."

"Well, then, Henry, let us begin thinking like the lizard instead of the insect."

"I'm with you, son."

After reviewing what had happened in Pierre, Joseph told Henry, "Cole has obviously been planning this for some time, the question is, why would he keep Maura's proxy wedding certificate after he'd made her sign papers declaring it null and void? And where are those papers now? If they're here at the fort, we've got to find them and take them to the judge. I don't blame Judge Brock for any of this. What choice did he have, given the evidence Cole provided? Knowing his daughter's relationship with Cole, I have to believe Brock is just another of Cole's pawns in this underhand game of chess."

"I've heard nothing but honorable things about the judge ever since I came to this area," Henry agreed. "But even honorable men can trip. Let's not rule him out of this game right now. We'll put him toward the back of the wagon – still in sight if we need to haul him out."

"All right," and thinking a moment to himself, Joseph ran his hands through his dust-covered hair, then down his face. "I know this sounds ludicrous, but I suggest we begin where this whole story starts."

"In Pierre?"

"No, in Ohio."

"What?"

"You heard me, Henry. I'm considering what Cole has been like since the day I met him. He has a reason for everything he does. So we must start at the beginning, with his out-of-the-blue offer to marry Maura. She told me she hadn't seen or heard from him for years prior to his letter."

"You really believe this goes back that far? Are you out of your mind?"

"Perhaps, but his thoughts are as twisted as a spring whirlwind. A normal man does not think like he does. So we must perform mind contortions to match his own."

"This sounds like a lot of work," Henry said, "and a little scary too."

"I will not force you to help, Henry. You have aided Maura and me many times over the past months. You have done your duty. If you wish to mind your own business, now is the time."

"I don't have any business of my own to mind, son. I'd rather help mind yours, if you'll let me. 'One for all and all for one', you know. Think of us as two musketeers, you and I."

Joseph's shoulders visibly relaxed, as Henry cast in his lot with him.

"I'm very glad to hear that, Henry. I need you."

"Oh, I think I need you more, son."

An hour later, the two still hadn't come up with any hidden meaning to Cole's proposal to Maura. They were beginning to discuss her photographs at the scene of the attack when the office door opened and Loretta slid in, bearing a large wooden board on which were several plates and three cups of coffee.

"That smells wonderful, Loretta. Where did you get it?"

"Well, they wouldn't let me stay with Maura very long, so after I left the stockade I decided to find the kitchen. When I walked in, I found the young lad who had been left in charge and he was lookin' mighty sad. Seems he's never fixed a meal in his life and soldiers are expected their supper, so I sidled up to him and taught him a thing or two about cookin' for a bunch of people. Now we're just fast friends. Might come in handy, you never know," she winked, and looked for a place to set the makeshift tray. Finding no clear spot, she looked at Henry and said, "Land sakes, man, your place could use a woman's touch. Have you ever cleaned in here?"

"Well, I...."

"Never mind, I can see you haven't. Let me tell you that's gonna change while Loretta's here, believe you me. Now, clear a space so I can set this down or I'll take it back where it came from!"

Both men rushed to pick up books, move bottles of Henry's magic elixirs and brush the dust off the small table that at one time may have been used as a dining surface rather than a hodgepodge repository.

"I have to apologize. There wasn't much in the way of meat to work with. I don't know if the men that left took everything or if they didn't have it to begin with, but Private Montgomery and I made do with what we had. It ain't the fanciest dinner I ever made, but it'll fill up your hole."

Cornbread and beans filled the plates and were soon gone, as Joseph and Henry ate with gusto. They asked for second helpings, and then sank back in their chairs. As Henry looked around, then lifted his arm to wipe his mouth on his sleeve, Loretta's hand shot out and stopped it, and with the other she passed him a cloth to mop his lips.

The action triggered a thought in Joseph's mind and he suddenly rose from his seat. "Here I am eating my fill and Maura is sitting in the stockade. I don't know if she's even had anything to eat yet. I'm going to go see."

"She had a plateful, just like you, Joseph," Loretta assured him. "I made sure she got some, afore you or any of the other men in this place."

Joseph smiled sheepishly. "Thank you, Loretta. I can't believe I didn't think of it until now."

"That's only because you two were busy puttin' your heads together, tryin' to figure a way to get her out. She'd be the first one to forgive you."

"I hope so. Anyway, I'm going over to make sure."

As Joseph closed the door behind him, Loretta eyed Henry.

"Well old man, are you gonna help me with these dishes or are you gonna just sit here like a rock under my wagon wheel?"

"I shall be pleased to assist you, madam," Henry said, with a flourish of his hand and a nod of his head. Loretta flicked a napkin at him and laughed while Henry feigned being wounded by the assault. Finally, the two headed out the door with the dishes, talking and giggling like school children.

At the same time, another pair was sharing time in the stockade, unfortunately on opposite sides of the bars.

"I don't want you to be in here, but I'm not sure yet how to fight him. Cole is in control here, Maura. I could call in some help, but I'm afraid that by the time any arrived, neither of us would need them anymore."

Reaching through the bars, Maura took Joseph's hand in hers. "I know that you will do everything in your power to find the evidence that will get me out of here. In the meantime, I want you to know that I don't mind it in here, really. Of course, I'd rather be with you, but in some strange way I feel as if I have to be here to prove a point. James is in the wrong on this and he will have to realize that. He will pay for what he has done to me, to us, and to our family. I only pray that Ryan is safe and well cared for and that he can be back with us, very, very soon."

"I will join your prayer for our son. In addition, I will pray for his mother, so that she can draw upon the strength and faith that I know she already possesses, to get through this ordeal. I do not like being separated from you, because together we are as a rope – separate strands that, wound together, make the whole stronger."

"You will have to be strong for both of us, Joseph. I can do very little here, but you – you can move mountains. And I know you will."

Joseph bowed his head, saying a silent prayer for his family, then squeezed his wife's hand and said, "You place your trust in me, and as much as I have always wanted you to trust me, right now, I have many doubts as to whether I deserve it."

Maura began to protest, but Joseph continued. "I want you to know, however, that I will do whatever I can to make sure that you and Ryan are reunited. If, for some reason, I cannot be with you..."

"Joseph, no! Say that you won't do anything foolish. You won't face James yourself. With his control of the fort, he could do anything and get away with it."

"Maura, I want you to know that I have already made sure that you will be well taken care of, financially. Henry is holding my will..." Seeing that Maura was ready to protest, James placed a finger on her lips and began again. "Henry is holding my will, which leaves most of what I have to you. My wife will never have to worry about where her next meal comes from, or whether she will have to wash other people's clothing in river water to make ends meet. That I promise you."

"Joseph, that is one promise I can live without. I don't care about any of that. I would rather have you than your money," Maura said breathlessly. "I don't want you to even talk that way. We will be together," she enunciated her words forcefully.

Her husband smiled and leaned his head against the bars. Releasing Maura's hands and moving his arms through the bars, he hugged her to him best as he could.

"I cannot wait for the day that we do not have these iron bars between us and I can hold you as you should be held."

"I can't wait either, but..."

"That's enough. I'm kinda tired of listenin' to the two of ya yammerin' on and on. Cap'n Cole told me ta limit you two's visits anyway and I'm thinkin' this is long enough. Come back tomorra, when there's somebody else sittin' here to listen to ya."

"I'll be leaving in a moment, corporal. Just hang on to your long johns."

"Well, ya don't hafta get personable about it," the corporal replied, indignantly.

Joseph rolled his eyes and Maura giggled despite her circumstances.

"I'll be fine, Joseph. Don't worry about me. I'm not going anywhere."

"In knowing Cole, I would ask you that should he try to take you anywhere but here, you would make sure that I know about it."

"You will be the first to hear my screams and his cries for mercy. I won't go quietly."

"He underestimates us, Maura."

"Yes."

When Joseph returned to the doctor's quarters, he found Henry squinting into the eyepiece of the microscope as he peered at the photograph that Maura had taken just after the attack near the reservation. The older man was seemingly oblivious to Loretta who was puttering around the quarters, placing books on bookshelves and lining bottles on a large table. Periodically, she'd lift a cloth from across her shoulders and send up a cloud of dust from whatever surface she was currently attacking.

Henry looked up and motioned Joseph over to the desk. "I've been looking closer at the second photograph Maura took, and I think I've found something."

"What is it, Henry?"

"Well, you remember the first photograph, the one that revealed the blond holding the dark wig?"

"How could I forget? That image is seared into my brain."

"Well, I just thought that I'd take another look. I think we got waylaid after looking at the first one, what with Maura going into labor and all, and we never really got to the second photograph. Well, this is it and I think you ought to give it your full attention."

Joseph looked quizzically at Henry, but moved around the desk and as the older man gave up his chair for the younger, Joseph leaned over the eyepiece.

"A face that was blurred in the other photograph has come clear. Cole keeps accusing someone from the reservation in these attacks. I wonder if we could find someone who might be able to recognize this man. Do you think there's any chance?"

"Yes, there's a very good chance. I know him. It's Two Hawks."

As night closed in on the fort, Joseph and Henry stood outside the doctor's quarters. Henry had graciously given up his cot to Loretta and the men were planning on wrapping up in blankets on the floor. Both were tired, but sleep couldn't find either one and they had decided to move out on the walkway. Sitting on wooden chairs, they spoke to no one, their only company, the guards patrolling the periphery of the fort and the occasional fly that lingered past season.

The temperatures were turning cooler, as fall firmly grasped the region. It was reminiscent, Joseph realized, of his first meeting with Maura, almost one year before. So much had happened since then. The native shook his head.

"What is it, Joseph?"

"I was just thinking about how much could happen in a year. Last fall, after I had brought Maura to our camp, Two Hawks looked at her with such hatred, but never did I think he was capable of endangering his own people by attacking others. I'm not quite sure what to do.

"I could leave here, go to the reservation and confront him, but I am torn. I do not wish to be parted from Maura or you and Loretta, at this time of conflict. I'm thinking that Two Hawks can wait until Cole is dealt with."

"I think that's wise, Joseph. One thing at a time. Two Hawks will still be there when this is all done."

The two men remained silent again for some time, each buried in their own thoughts.

"I wonder who the other 'guests' are," Henry pondered.

"Guests? What guests?"

"Don't you remember? Cole said something to us about 'several other guests coming' and things should heat up then. I wonder who he was referring to."

"Well, for Maura's sake, I hope one of them is Ryan. I don't know what Cole did with him, but if he's planning on using him as a pawn as he said, he'll have to bring him here sooner or later."

"You're right about that, son. I just..."

Henry stopped speaking when a movement drew his attention to the stables. He hit Joseph on the leg and pointed in that direction. Both watched and counted as three, four, and then five men worked quietly, despite some obvious haste, to saddle and mount their horses. Riding single file toward the gate, the group was allowed exit by the guard on duty.

"What do you suppose they're up to?" Henry questioned.

"I don't know, but I'm surprised they didn't see us sitting here."

"We're in the shadows, and even though there's a full moon tonight, that may have played in our favor, I guess. Either that, or they just didn't care."

"Who were they? Did you see any faces, get any details?" Joseph asked.

"Only one."

"What was that?"

"I saw the embers from what I'm going to assume was a cigar."

"Cole."

"That'd be my guess."

Silence again permeated the air, and then Joseph said to Henry, "Are you thinking what I'm thinking?"

"Only if you're thinking to invade his office while he's gone and look for those papers."

"Great minds think alike, Henry."

"Yours and who else's?" the older man said, and he could see Joseph's smile despite the darkness of the night.

"Let's go."

"You check the desk, I'll look around the bookshelves."

"Right," Henry agreed, pulling open drawer after drawer in the large piece of furniture.

The two had moved quickly from their seats down the walkway to Cole's quarters. The door had been locked, but a few quick maneuvers with one of Loretta's hairpins had done the trick and gained them entry.

Henry had raised an eyebrow in the half-light to which Joseph shrugged and responded, "One of my teachers at the Indian school was a graduate of the local county lock-up."

"Don't you think Cole might believe his office to be too obvious a place to hide Maura's papers? After all, he knows we're here and that we might try something like this. He's not stupid."

"No, he's not. But he's not the sharpest pencil in the box, either. In trying to out-think us, he may just do the obvious. Even if this doesn't work, we had to try."

"You're right. We're lizards."

Joseph coughed and smiled in the moonlight that filled half the room, flipping through volumes on the shelves, then opening trunks and feeling under the bed.

"I don't know how I'll know if I have the right paper since I can't even see my own face in this mirror," Henry complained. The natural light did not permeate the darkened portion of the room where Henry searched.

Joseph moved closer and put his face toward the frame hanging on the wall behind the desk.

"Henry, you can't see your face because that's not a mirror."

"What the heck is it then? Oh, it must be a picture of some sort, it's got a wooden frame. Don't really see Cole as being an art lover, though."

"There has to be a match around this cigar smoker's desk, ah, here's one. Let's take a closer look," Joseph offered.

He struck the match along the wall and the flame sputtered and finally held. The two men stared at the oil painting. Joseph immediately recognized it as a copy of a work that he had seen on his European travels.

"I know this painting. It's called *The Marriage Contract*." Pointing to various parts on the canvas he noted, "See the couple seated to the left, and the group of men to the right discussing the document with the girl's father? I saw the original several years ago while visiting in England." Joseph blew out the match, but continued to stare through the darkness at the painting.

"What is something like this doing here, in a fort in South Dakota? And, by the way, what were you doing in England?" Henry asked in wonder.

"If I'm right, this painting is here because it has a very specific use. I can't picture Cole as someone who collects art for arts' sake. As to the other, I'll tell you about it another time."

Taking the painting in both hands, Joseph lifted it from the peg on the wall, baring the plain, whitewash beneath. Laying it on Cole's desk, Joseph decided to take a chance and light a nearby candle.

Having done so, he brought the light closer and began removing the small nails that held the wood back in place. Two sides were done when he carefully slid the back from the frame.

Several papers were revealed.

Both men were afraid to pick them up.

"We can't have been that lucky on our first try," Henry said. "It just doesn't happen."

"You look at them, Henry."

"No, I think you should."

"I can't."

"Well, one of us has to. We've been here for quite a while and we don't know when Cole will be back. I really think it should be you."

Joseph hesitated further, but reached out and picked them up. Turning them over, hand shaking, he began to look through them.

"These are the ones, Henry. I recognize this as the one Judge Brock was reading from in his office, but the other one I'm not sure of."

"Don't take time to read them now, Joseph. Put the painting back together and let's get out of here."

Joseph rolled the papers and pushed them into his shirt pocket. Replacing the wooden back was no trouble and he pushed the small nails back in their holes. While he did so, Henry tried to straighten everything they may have knocked askew.

While hanging the painting, Henry heard a noise and looked out the front window.

"Joseph, they're back! We've got to hurry!"

Joseph blew out the candle, took a last look around, and before heading out the door, stopped beside Cole's box of cigars. Lifting the lid, he was assailed by the aroma of the tobacco and he inhaled deeply.

"What are you doing? Come on!" Henry whispered loudly at the door and began waving his arms in frustration.

Joseph chose two cigars and added them to his pocket, replaced the lid, then followed Henry to the door. Taking out Loretta's hairpin, he reversed his action of the hour before and the two slipped through the shadows as the men unsaddled their horses in the dark stable.

"You gave me heart palpitations, boy! What were you doing?"

"Counting coup."

Chapter Twenty-eight

"Do you think he knows?"

"I believe he would have wasted no time confronting us if he realized that something was amiss in his quarters, and we would have been the first ones he suspected."

"Yes, I guess you're right, but my stomach's been twisting and turning all night. I think I've had about enough bicarbonate of soda in the past 12 hours to last me for the rest of my life. I'd like to stop worrying about it."

"Then do so," Joseph said. "He would have been here by now."

"Reminds me of *The Count of Monte Cristo*, when Edmond Dantes went behind his enemies' backs to get the goods on them. Too much excitement for an old man like me."

The two had made it back to the doctor's quarters without mishap and had watched from the window, as the men filed out of the stable and returned to their beds. Cole had been the last to leave and he had made a visual check of the grounds before closing his door behind him.

Henry and Joseph had put the papers in one of Henry's colored bottles and placed it on a shelf, preferring to wait for daylight before trying to read them. Then, they had bedded down on the floor, but neither had slept much.

Joseph prayed that what was on the other papers would benefit Maura's case. He hoped they were the documents she'd said she had signed after arriving back at the fort, making the proxy marriage null and void. He wanted to reread the Ohio document as well. There may be something useful on it.

In the morning, after Loretta had whipped up enough breakfast to feed what was left of the army, Joseph took a tray to the stockade.

The private on duty allowed him only 10 minutes, and while that wasn't enough, Joseph told himself that they had only to be patient and would have a lifetime.

Maura smiled as Joseph walked into the door.

"I was hoping you would come."

"I wanted to start the day with my wife. Did you sleep all right? Were you warm enough?"

A giggle met his ears. "Oh, Joseph, you worry too much. I'm fine." She looked over Joseph's shoulders and moved in closer. "I don't want to say this too loudly, but the private is a softy. He gave me two extra blankets from other cells, saying they weren't being used anyway and I might as well have them. They don't smell too good. If I could, I'd give 'em a good scrubbin', but they're certainly better than nothing."

"I'm glad. I'll take that into consideration later," Joseph promised.

Maura placed her hands on her hips and used to best Irish brogue to address her husband. "Now, Mr. Walks Alone, ya wouldn't be plannin' on doin' somethin' none too smart, are ya? You'd best be keepin' yourself safe for me."

Joseph smiled and reassured his wife. "Aye, that I'll do. I'll be keepin' meself safe, all right, and me wife as well."

"Now don't you go givin' me any of your blarney. You'll listen to what I'm sayin'."

"You know when you get upset, your accent becomes thicker and thicker? It's very appealing." Maura looked askance at her husband who continued, "I think Mrs. Walks Alone had better stop worrying. Everything will be all right."

"Are you sure, Joseph? Have you heard anything about our son? I can't stop thinkin' about him – where he is, who's takin' care of him. Will he remember me?"

"Remember you? How could he forget," Joseph reached through the bars and touched the side of Maura's face, "that beautiful vision that greets me at the start of the day, the sunlight that warms me and the moonlight that comforts me? You're a rare being, Maura, and don't you forget it. Your son will remember his mother. She's impossible to forget."

His thumb caught a tear that slid down Maura's cheek and he brought his arm back through and kissed the damp spot where it had been.

"The person who has to do the remembering is you," Joseph stated authoritatively. "You must remember that not only do I love you, but Ryan loves you, and even Loretta and Henry love you and we're already working hard to get this whole business straightened out. I can't tell you about it now," he said, moving his head in the direction of the guard who was making no bones about listening to their conversation, "but you will know soon enough. Just hang onto that."

"I will," Maura said quietly, grabbing for his hand.

"Time's up!"

Joseph looked at the guard and smiled.

"Just let me say goodbye."

"Only if you're quick about it."

"I will."

Turning back to Maura, Joseph squeezed her hand. "I have to go now, but I will be with you in here," he said, pointing to her heart.

"Always," Maura said.

Cole was out on the parade ground, putting his small group of men through drills when Joseph walked from the stockade back to the doctor's office.

The eyes of the two met and in that instant, made a silent promise.

"Well, what are they, Joseph?"

"The first one is definitely the document that Judge Brock was reading in his office. When or where Cole got it back, I don't know. The second is the paper that Maura had said she signed, making their proxy marriage null and void. But there's something very, very interesting that is not here."

"What's that? Don't tell me we have to go back!"

"I'm not sure yet. But what isn't here is Cole's written authorization of the proxy. In order to have a marriage, shouldn't both parties be involved?"

"Oh my God! You're right, Joseph. You don't suppose he kept that somewhere else?"

"He may have, but I don't understand why he would have. I should think that he would keep them together. This may make all the difference in the world. If he never authorized a proxy marriage, then this was never valid to begin with, and she and I are still man and wife."

"You've struck gold, man! All you have to do is present it to the judge."

"But why would Cole be so adamant about Maura going through this ceremony if he were not going to carry through on his end? What was he up to here?"

The sound of hooves and wagon wheels met their ears and once again, the investigators were interrupted in their ponderings.

Peering out the window, Henry relayed, "There's a petite blonde getting out of a coach. And she's heading straight for Cole. Wait a minute! She's not alone. There's an older woman... she's carrying something...looks like...either a huge loaf of bread...or maybe a baby?"

"A baby!" Joseph leapt to his feet and dashed to the door. Throwing it open, he ran outside and stopped. The blonde was the judge's daughter and the older woman was a stranger to Joseph, but she carried a form wrapped in a blanket, which he wholeheartedly believed to be his son.

Close enough to hear the greetings between Cole and Melody Brock, Joseph heard the girl whine, "You went without me? How could you, James? You know how I enjoy it and I've always been a help to you, haven't I? Are you punishing me for something?"

"No, no, it just wouldn't have worked out this time, Melody. You had my son to care for, remember?"

"Ahh," and here Joseph thought she would spit, "your son. My surprise, you mean. Anyway, I can't believe you'd leave me with this...thing to take care of. All it does is mess itself and cry. Thank God this woman did everything. I can't even bring myself to look at it. I told her what to do, of course, and she did it, fed him and everything," here Joseph saw Melody scrunch up her nose. "I wouldn't have touched the smelly little bundle of joy for all the money in the world."

Melody smiled, hearing her own words, then corrected herself. "Well, maybe I'd touch him, but only for as long as it took to get the money."

Cole laughed uproariously, then settled sufficiently to say, "That's what I like about you my dear. Truthful to a fault, and greedy too! A girl after my own heart."

"I'm after more than your heart, James."

"I know, my dear, but beware of what you seek."

"Oh, James, I have missed you. It's been hell being cooped up with this, this baby, and that woman, yuck. I don't know how you talked Daddy into this, but this is one time that I wish he had won. I didn't like it at all." She sidled in closer, if that were possible and added, still loud enough for everyone to hear, "Now, were I to be cooped up with you, that would be another matter."

Joseph had had about enough. He was ready to spring into action, when he felt a hand on his arm.

"Easy, son. Slow and easy."

Joseph patted the older man's hand, and then moved forward.

"Cole!"

"Ah, Walks Alone. I knew you'd be just a moment away. Come to congratulate me on my son, have you?"

Bile rose in Joseph's throat as he thought of his son under the care of this girl and the thought crossed his mind that if he wasn't careful, Ryan could be spending his entire life with the man standing in front of him, and learning how to be just like him. The thought revolted him.

"If you were expecting me, then you know what I've come for."

"I suppose you're referring to little what's-his-name here. By the way, darling," Cole turned away from Joseph, addressing the judge's daughter, "Did you think of a new name for my son yet?"

"He's not your son," Joseph said, separating each word through clenched teeth. Then taking a deep breath, he visibly regained control.

"Are you sure about that, Walks Alone? Are you very sure?" Cole had turned his full attention back to the Indian. "Because, I happen to believe that he is – legally and in every other way. And so he shall stay with his father, that's me, whether you or my wife like it or not."

"Your make-believe family will not last, Cole," Joseph promised.

"Yes, well, I'm tired of listening to you again, Walks Alone. You really must try to curb your desire to tell me about every little thing. I really couldn't care less about your opinions, so do yourself a favor and desist. Besides, I must hurry. As soon as I get Miss Brock and my son settled, my men and I will be responding to the latest attack by members of your reservation."

Joseph raised an eyebrow and Cole continued, "I told Coffey this would happen when word got out about the fort abandonment, but would he listen? No. The army should never have planned this abandonment. We are still needed here and I'll prove it to them. There are still too many renegades out there attacking innocent settlers.

"Oh, I forgot, they're probably friends of yours," and here, Cole looked eye to eye with Joseph, "or even you could be involved, Walks Alone. Yes, why didn't I think of it before? I'll have to seriously look into that. In the meantime, don't go anywhere, or I just might find you meeting with your friends, and then the matter is in my hands and I will not be responsible for what happens in the line of duty.

"Come my dear," said Cole and led Melody Brock, the wet nurse and baby Ryan to their quarters adjacent to his.

Joseph remained where he stood for several minutes, and then walked back to where Henry stood just outside his office.

"I don't know why I bother," he said, sweeping past his friend.

"I do."

"As soon as he leaves, I'll bet good money that Miss Brock will want to get away from the baby. Then we'll make our move."

"What are we going to do?"

"We're going to return Ryan to his mother."

"Joseph, do you really think we can?"

"I know we can."

It wasn't very long before Cole led his band of men out the gates, leaving only a handful of soldiers to guard the fort. A short time later, Melody Brock came out of her quarters wearing a split skirt, blouse and coat ensemble, turned and screamed, "You keep this door locked, you hear me? Don't let anyone in but James, or me and for heaven's sake don't go taking one of your walks. I'll be back soon." Melody pivoted and sashayed to the stable, where she ordered a horse saddled, and then rode out toward the river.

"This is it, Henry. Let's go."

"I'm getting too old for this sort of intrigue," Henry said, but followed close behind his younger friend anyway. They made their way to the quarters they assumed the wet nurse still occupied and knocked on the door.

"Now what?" they heard faintly, coming from the opposite side and the portal suddenly pulled wide open to reveal the form of the nurse. She took one look at the two men, stepped back and motioned them forward.

Surprised, Joseph almost hesitated, but recovered and moved in quickly with Henry right behind.

"I'm rather surprised you let us in, Miss..."

"Buckley. Marjorie Buckley. And if you didn't come, I would have gone out lookin' for ya."

Joseph and Henry looked at each other, introduced themselves formally, and then turned their full attention to the nurse.

"I know who ya are all right. Miss High 'n Mighty pointed ya out to me and told me to stay far away from ya. I figure that's enough reason to join up with ya 'cause I'll tell you, if that woman doesn't stop orderin' me around I'm afraid of what I'll do. I know God put everbody on this Earth for some reason but I'll be damned if I can come up with a good reason for her to be breathin', other than to make everbody else's life hell so's heaven looks real good about now."

Joseph could barely contain a snort and Henry was smiling from ear to ear.

"Then you know what we want, and you'll help us?" the older man asked.

"One thing I know, that baby should be with his momma, and she should be with him. I'd help you for that reason alone, even if I didn't work for 'Miss Nose-in-the-Air Shrew.'"

Marjorie Buckley's voice got louder and louder as she spoke, finally ending in a shout. "Oh, sorry," she said, realizing how she sounded. "The baby's asleep and here I am screeching like a hooty owl."

Joseph walked over to the large basket in a corner that served as Ryan's bed. He bent at the knees, squatting, and leaned over the make-shift crib, taking one of the baby's hands in his.

"So I'm assuming you are not staying here willingly," Joseph stated, as he looked down at the boy. Returning his gaze to Marjorie, he questioned, "How did you get hooked up with these people anyway?"

"Well, I've known Miss Brock for years, unfortunately. I really didn't think she was such a bad 'un 'til I had to live with her. I came to know her because my brother, Warren, works for her father."

"You are Warren's sister? If you'll excuse me, you don't act a thing like he does."

"I know what you're talkin' about. He got kinda uppity after he started clerkin' for the judge, but he ain't no better'n anybody else, he just thinks he is. Anyway, he knew I needed the money, so he got me this job."

"Do you have children, Marjorie?"

"Yep, well, no. Me and my husband, we lost our baby just about a week or so afore Warren brought me in to take care of your boy."

"I'm so very sorry," Joseph said sincerely.

"Thanks, but that's the fourth baby I've lost. I guess I'm so used to it now, don't even expect to see 'em alive anymore. My momma had seven of us after we first come out here but Warren and me was the only ones what lived. Don't cotton much to doctors, nothin' personal ya understand," she said, addressing Henry, who nodded his head. "But me and my husband Horatio, we keep on a tryin'. He likes tryin', if you, ah, get my drift."

"Yes, well," and clearing his throat nervously, Joseph continued. "And what about Cole? Had you known him?"

"Him? No, I don't know much about him except for what she says," and switching to a high-pitched squeal, Marjorie did an admirable job imitating her supervisor. "James is sooo handsome, James is sooo important. James, James, James."

Then restoring her own voice and thoughts, Marjorie added, "James makes me wanna upchuck my supper on his shiny black boots. If ya ask me, this James is using her and she either can't see the buffalo for the chips or she's usin' him just as bad for her own purposes. From what I've seen, neither one of 'em does nothing that don't benefit 'em one way or another. If I had time to waste thinkin' on it, I'd try to figure 'em out, but I don't see the point, really."

"I see you are a great judge of character, Marjorie," Henry observed, adding, "I hate to be the one to break this up, but don't you think we'd better get out of here before Miss Brock returns?"

"Yes, you're right, Henry," Joseph agreed. "Marjorie, the plan is simple. We want to take you and the baby to Maura. She needs him very badly right now, and I can see that you understand that. The thing is, we have to wait for an opportune time when Miss Brock will be away longer and we can make sure we get you secured before she comes back."

"I overheard the two of 'em talkin' about goin' somewhere's tonight. Maybe that would be a good time."

"Tonight?" Joseph scrunched his eyebrows and looked at Marjorie. "Are you sure? He's already out with a group of soldiers. Is he planning on returning, then going out again? And where would they go?"

"That one's for you to answer, mister. Personally, I don't care, as long as she's gone, and I'll thank God for every minute I don't have to listen to her."

"Well, if she does leave, come to the doctor's office and get us. We'll take you and the baby to Maura in the stockade. If you don't mind, the plan is to find the key and lock you in together. If we take the key and find the skeleton, they won't be able to get you out." Joseph tried to reassure Marjorie that she'd be safe with them.

"Hell, this sounds as easy as takin' a nap. But, this Maura, she doesn't scream at ya or think she's better'n anybody, does she? I'd hate to trade one harpy for another one."

Henry laughed out loud. "I don't think you have to worry about a thing, Marjorie. Maura's probably one of the nicest people you'll ever meet, and very sincere. She loves her son and she'll love you because you've taken such good care of him. She's been very worried, and I know you've been the answer to her prayers."

"Well there musta been nothin' fancy to her prayers, then, if'n I'm the answer to 'em."

"Give yourself more credit, Marjorie. You've kept a precious baby boy well fed and safe. There's not much more anyone could ask of you."

"Well, Miss High 'n Mighty would think of somethin' else to ask of me but right now I'm thinkin' I'm not gonna give her the chance."

"Just be careful, Marjorie," Joseph warned. "Go along with her as usual, at least until she leaves tonight. We don't want Miss Brock or Cole to suspect that we're up to something."

"Right. I'll do whatever you say, Indian, 'cause I'm finally seein' light at the end of the tunnel."

"If you're lucky, you could be on your way home very soon."

"Yeah, but there is one thing wrong with that."

"What's that?" Joseph asked.

"I'll never get paid for doing this, even though it is the right thing to do."

"You're very mistaken, Marjorie. Because you're doing the right thing, your pay will come from me. You'll be generously compensated, I assure you."

"Well, I'll trust what you say is true. And now," Marjorie said, as she opened the door, "you two better skeedaddle on out of here before Her Highness gets back."

"Don't forget, come get us if she leaves tonight."

"Oh, I won't forget. This is gonna be the most important night of my life."

"I hope we can all say that," said Joseph, and pushed Henry ahead of him this time, preferring to follow his friend's lead.

"Don't worry, Indian," Marjorie called after them. "I'll take good care of your son."

"I trust you will do that, madam."

Chapter Twenty-nine

Loretta sat silently between Henry and Joseph, chewing her food and looking from one man to the other. Both were obviously lost in thought, and Loretta was eager to find out what consumed them. She wanted to be patient, wanted them to know that she wasn't just a busybody, but finally, the dam burst.

"All right. I've sat here all evening waitin' for one of you two to say somethin', but I'm tired and I'm cranky and I'm not gonna wait any longer. What is going on? You've both been quieter than a corpse in a room by himself."

Joseph smiled and looked at Henry.

"I suppose we had best let her in on things."

"I agree. I'm getting rather used to her delicious cooking and I have a feeling that would stop if we didn't," Henry said.

"Now you listen to me, old man. I wouldn't stop feedin' ya and you know it. Looks to me like nobody's fed ya proper in a long time, and I'm here to see that's taken care of. I think there's a lot of things around here that needs taken care of by a woman."

"I never noticed anything wrong with my quarters," Henry said exasperatedly. "I have everything just where I need it and don't you go touching my things and putting things out of place, just to please yourself. You don't live here, you know. You're my guest, and I can change that, too."

"Old man, you don't know what's good for ya. Why I oughta...."

"All right, all right, you two. I didn't know we were going to get into a

204

lover's spat when this conversation started."

"Lover's spat!" Loretta and Henry shouted the words simultaneously, and then Henry was the first to find his wits.

"Joseph, this woman drives me crazy. I don't know if I can take this much longer. She might have to go live in Maura's old house until all this is straightened out."

"Maura's old house? That sounds good to me, old man. Talk about crazy. All these bottles with who knows what in 'em and books with who knows what all over 'em and paraphernalia that ain't seen a dust rag since who knows when. You need me, old man."

"Quit callin' me 'old man'! I ain't old... Ah! Here I go talkin' like her now. I used perfect English before you came here slangin' and cuttin' off all your 'g's'."

"Why, I'll..."

"Excuse me!" Joseph interjected, trying to be heard above the din created by the verbal pugilists.

When they stopped, Joseph reported, "I'm going to visit Maura and stay out of your way. Try not to start breaking anything or throw any punches while I'm gone, will you?"

Loretta and Henry looked at one another, then innocently at Joseph. Shrugging, Henry continued eating, as though nothing had happened and Loretta violently speared a piece of beef with her fork, popped it into her mouth and grinned.

Joseph left the room and headed to the stockade to see his wife. There was very little activity within the fort since Cole and his group still had not returned from their investigation into the latest attack. The native couldn't help but wonder, though, where the captain planned to take Miss Brock that night after he got back. Perhaps it was just to be a lovers' tryst, he thought. But knowing Cole, and now after hearing more about the judge's daughter, he decided there had to be more to it.

As if thinking of the devil would make him appear, the sound of hooves materialized into Cole and his men, as they entered the fort.

Joseph walked purposefully toward the stockade, choosing to ignore the captain. He had no idea, but would not have been surprised, that Cole's face had melted into a mask of hatred as soon as he spied the Indian, but he made no attempt to follow him, as his blonde paramour immediately accosted the officer.

Maura looked up as Joseph opened the stockade door. Earlier, he had brought some books for her to read and she relished every page, thankful for the distraction that kept her from spending every waking moment thinking about her situation and the fact that her son was, for now at least, lost to her.

"Studying?" Joseph asked, noting that Maura was reading a math book in her unguarded cell.

"Yes. I thought I would use the time wisely and positively, by going over some of the texts you brought me. They aren't quite as interesting as the fiction, of course, but it's been a while since I've taught anyone and I don't want to let you down. It won't be long until the school gets started and I want to be ready."

Joseph exhaled heavily. With everything else that had occurred, he hadn't told Maura that Cole didn't plan on letting him have the fort, and until he could do something about that, he wasn't sure that the school would even be a reality. But, in the meantime, he wanted her to keep her positive attitude and hoped it would rub off on him. He had no plans to tell her otherwise.

Instead, he changed the subject.

"How did you like Loretta's beef pot roast this evening?" he asked, as he rifled through the nearby desk drawer and came up with a large set of keys. Walking toward the cell, he tried key after key until he finally found the one that unlocked his wife's door.

Not missing a beat, Maura rose and went into Joseph's arms. "It was quite good, as usual."

"I have to tell you, when I left Henry's quarters I had to order the two of them to be good. They were arguing like a couple that had been married for forty years."

"Wouldn't it be wonderful if the two of them could work something out? To be together, I mean. I think they'd make a cute couple."

"'Cute' is not the word for what I just left," Joseph recalled. "I wouldn't hold my breath on that one, Maura."

"Oh, well," she said, settling into a chair and patting another for Joseph. "So tell me something, anything. I'm starving for some kind of information.

Since the fort got word of the latest attack, I don't even have a guard to talk to anymore. Talk to me, Joseph."

"I'd like to do more than that but I'll hold off for now," he said, smiling wide.

Maura raised an eyebrow and Joseph continued.

"I do have something to tell you, but you have to put down your book, and you have to promise not to get too excited because I don't know for certain that this will work out as planned right now."

Maura slowly closed the volume she'd been studying and looked intently at her husband.

"Ryan is here."

"What!" By now she had jumped up and grabbed her husband's forearms.

"Why didn't you say something sooner? Is he all right? Who is he with? He's not with James, is he? When can I see him? Oh, Joseph, this is just wonderful news! I can't believe it! I've been making myself insane wonderin' about him - where he is, if he's all right – and now you tell me he's here! Oh, thank you, Lord. You really do make all things possible."

"I'm not quite sure which of your questions to answer first, but I'll just tell you what I know. First of all, he came to the fort with the judge's daughter."

"The judge's daughter! Is she helping us? What's happening? Explain it to me. I can't believe..."

Joseph held up a hand to stop her. "I think this will work better if you try to refrain from speaking until I am done."

Maura put both hands over her mouth and sat down, but looked at Joseph with more than a twinkle in her eyes.

"I can see that you are very excited, wife, so I will continue."

She nodded her head.

"No, Miss Brock is not on our side. She is here for Cole. As for Ryan, he has a wet nurse. Henry and I had the opportunity to visit with her at some length this afternoon when Miss Brock went for a ride. It seems the nurse is Warren's sister..."

At that statement, Maura's eyes rolled.

"I know, but she differs much from her brother. Anyway, she is not, to say the least, enamored of Miss Brock and wishes to help us."

Maura began hopping up and down on her seat.

"She told Henry and I that Miss Brock and Cole planned to go out of the fort tonight. I don't know if that will actually happen, but if it does, we will bring Mrs. Buckley and Ryan here.

"The fact that you have no guard is in our favor because we plan to lock them both in with you..."

Maura's eyebrows rose.

"We plan to lock them in with you and hide both the key to your cell and the skeleton key to all cells so that they can't get to Ryan or you. Both of you will be safer locked together until Henry and I can get this sorted out. It won't be long, I promise. We already have a clue that I hadn't expected, but I'll tell you more about that later."

"Can I talk now?"

"Yes."

"I love you."

A broad grin transformed Joseph's tired face.

"I love you, too, Mrs. Walks Alone."

"Am I still Mrs. Walks Alone?" Maura asked, suddenly looking very dejected.

"You are, as far as I am concerned. And, I forgot this bit of news; Henry and I infiltrated the devil's lair and discovered a few things. Today I sent Andy Riegel to Pierre to bring back the judge. I believe he needs to see something and I am unwilling either to leave or to let anything out of my hands."

"Joseph, is this what I have prayed for? Did you find the papers that I signed?"

"That, and something else has come to mind that I must ask the judge about. I wasn't thinking clearly in his office..."

"That knock on the head probably didn't help..."

"No, it didn't, but even before that, I was caught off guard. Now I have had some time to think and I believe I have caught your former fiancé in a bad move."

"Just be careful. I was excited at first, but now that I hear everything is so close at hand, I'm afraid, Joseph."

"You are a strong woman, Maura. Continue to be so, and we will have our family again, I promise you."

"If you promise, I know it will be so."

Joseph was silent for several minutes, and it caused Maura some concern. "Is there something else?"

Her husband took her left hand in his right and brushed his thumb back and forth over the wedding band she wore.

"Do you remember when we got our rings?"

"How could I forget? That day will live with me until the day I no longer breathe."

"You asked me, then, what the word meant that is engraved inside your ring. I told you I would tell you when the time came."

"Yes."

"The time is now." Joseph was very quiet as he chose his words. "The engraving inside your ring is the language of my grandfathers for "trust". There were many times that I felt you did not trust me, but I believed that in time, you would come to know that I spoke only the truth." Maura opened her mouth as if to protest, but shut it quickly when Joseph raised his hand.

"You know that I, too, have a word engraved inside my ring. It is my grandfathers' word for 'believe', because I wanted a reminder that if I believed, you would come to trust. I believe that our day has come, Maura. You do trust me, don't you?"

"Yes, yes, yes." Maura looked deeply into Joseph's eyes and hoped her words would sink in just as deep. "I trust you with all my being, Joseph Walks Alone. Please use the word of your grandfathers and trust what I say."

"It is so," he said quietly, and reached for his wife.

Several hours later, the occupants of the doctor's quarters were awakened by a faint knock on the door. Henry was the first up, as Joseph had slipped into the deepest rest he had had for several days and it took him several seconds to realize what was happening.

When the door was opened, the moonlight revealed the face of Marjorie Buckley and in her arms was Ryan.

"They just left," she whispered, entering the room.

"They left?" Joseph was incredulous. He could not believe he hadn't heard anything but Marjorie put his self doubts at rest.

"I wouldna heard 'em either if I wasn't so excited about 'em goin'. One more minute listenin' to her prattle and I was about to slit my own throat."

"I'm glad you didn't, Marjorie."

"Well, thanks. I like to think somebody'd miss me when I'm gone."

"How long ago did they leave?" Joseph inquired.

"Just about five minutes ago. I waited just a few to make certain they was really gone, then I picked up the baby and hauled us right on over here. I didn't see any of the soldiers on duty. I can only wonder what they're up to."

Joseph considered his next move only a moment before he began delegating tasks.

"Henry, I want you to take Marjorie and Ryan to the stockade and lock them in with Maura. Here's the cell key and the skeleton key. I found them both earlier this evening. They should be safe enough in there. Loretta, you go with them and keep an eye out for anyone heading toward the stockade. It's imperative that Marjorie and Ryan are locked up and the key is nowhere to be found when any soldiers come in."

Henry was curious. "What are you going to do?"

"I'm going to try and find Cole and his cohorts."

"In the dark? How can you?"

"I have to. I want to know what they're up to. I don't think this is a moonlight stroll. They're up to something or they wouldn't care how much noise they made as they left or who saw them go."

When no one moved, Joseph ordered, "Let's go!"

They opened the door slowly and Joseph looked out. Not seeing any sign of life, he motioned the others toward the stockade while he headed stealthily to the stable. Clicking his tongue against the roof of his mouth, Joseph watched his horse's ears shoot in the air and the animal used its teeth to loosen the rope securing it to the stall, and then walked over to its master.

"You have learned your lesson well," Joseph complimented the horse, as he rubbed his neck. "But now you must use another one. We must track the others and I will count on you heavily for your skills. Let's ride, old friend," and the native swung up onto the bare back of the horse and used his knees to guide the animal out of the stable, then away from the fort.

Once outside, Joseph stopped and lifted his face to the stars, feeling the sharp blast of an icy wind beginning.

"The sooner we get going, the sooner we will find them and be back in our warm beds," he teased and the two made their way through the darkness.

Near the river not far away, six figures grouped together to ward off the wind as they planned.

"I did not expect this so soon," one said. "We have only just completed one attack. I do not think this is a good idea."

"I don't really care what you think," another replied. "You will do as I say or you'll meet your maker. I have no use for sniveling children. Stay with me or die right now. What will it be?"

"I see you brought the woman again. I had hoped she would no longer ride with us."

"Why? Because she has more guts than you do? She has proven herself on other raids, you know that. Besides, she insisted on coming tonight, didn't you sweetheart?"

"I can't let you boys have all the fun. You left me out of the last one, so I deserve to be included this time."

"That you do, my dear. Now, I believe it's time to stop this gossiping and get on with what we came out here to do."

"What's our target tonight?"

"The fort."

Members of the raiding party straightened suddenly, as they sat on their horses. The first speaker protested vehemently.

"No. You are crazy. They will kill us before we have a chance to kill them."

"There is no 'they'. There are only a few men guarding the fort as we speak and most are loyal to me. If we kill a few guards, it doesn't matter. They are expendable. I want the army to see that the fort is still needed."

"Bah. I have no use for the fort or for the whites. The last thing I need is for those who have left to return. I joined you to have the chance to kill whites – any whites and if you continue with this plan, you may be next."

"Do you want me to shoot him?" the female asked.

"No, Melody. You've tasted blood before but it's prudent to be patient. Besides, it's more amusing to keep him alive. And I rather enjoy the fact that at any time, he could put a bullet in my back. It makes life rather exciting, wouldn't you agree? But even he should know that he's nothing without me."

Just feet away, Joseph knelt in the tall prairie grass. Though the vegetation was dry, he had managed to move through quietly so that he could hear the conversation. He wished he hadn't.

Moving slowly backward, he returned to his horse and headed back to the fort, having heard enough. He was not surprised by anything he had overheard. Suspicions had long been boiling in his head and the more he had denied it, the more he had come to accept them as fact. With Cole, Miss Brock and Two Hawks involved, many clouds were beginning to dissipate from the picture.

As Joseph made his way back to the fort, the scene continued to play out behind him. Cole grabbed Two Hawks' arm. "What's it going to be, my friend? I don't need you. We can do this by ourselves. It's just that I thought you'd jump at the chance since your old friend Walks Alone is at the fort."

"Joseph," Two Hawks spat out the name, then emphasized his disgust by spitting on the ground at Cole's feet.

"Joseph is a white also. He may look like his warrior grandfathers, but he has given up the old ways and taken on the ways of the whites. His blood is tainted and I would be happy to watch it sink into the dirt."

"Then you will help us?"

"Yes, I will come, but only for Joseph. He is mine."

"Then we have a deal."

"Maura, I'm going to lock you in," and Joseph did just that. Then, handing her the keys, he ordered, "Do not, under any circumstances, unless your life is in jeopardy, give those keys to anyone. Do you understand?"

"I'm not an idiot, Joseph. I heard you and I understand."

"Good. No matter what you hear going on outside, don't even stick as much as the tip of your nose out the door. Do you understand?"

"Joseph Walks Alone, I'm just about to hit you."

"All right, all right," he said, trying to calm her. "I just don't want anything to happen to you, that's all."

"I know you don't, Joseph. But I'm a big girl, and so is Marjorie and so is Loretta. You've given us guns and keys and we're perfectly capable of handlin' whatever comes our way."

"I hope so, because if I don't have to worry about you I can concentrate on other things."

"You mean James."

"Yes," he said slowly, "and the rest. We can't assume that the others are any less dangerous."

"Please be careful."

"I will. I want us to be together again. But that can only happen when Cole is no longer a threat, and this may be our only chance."

"I love you."

"And I, you," then softly caressing his son's head, Joseph headed out of the stockade, and did not look back.

"Henry! Did you find more weapons?"

"You bet I did, son. Looky here!"

Joseph's eyes were drawn to Henry's desk where rifles, shotguns and handguns had replaced Dumas and bottles of medicine.

"Loretta and I scoured the place and this is what we came up with. Would it do any good, do you think, to talk to the soldiers that are here and warn them at least?"

"I don't think so, Henry. If they're not in this with him, they'd never believe their commander was capable of such actions. We'll leave them to their fate and worry only about ours."

"I guess you're right. I'm having a little trouble believing myself. Why, if you're right, this has been going on for some time, maybe even since the attack on Maura's friends. Do you think he knew it was her in that group?"

"I can't stop to speculate now, Henry. Let's just hope that Andy can get back here quickly with the judge. If we're still alive when that happens, maybe we can convince him that something should be done about Cole. I don't know how he will react, though, if he does not realize the extent of his daughter's involvement in all of this. But if he doesn't help us, we may be doomed."

"Joseph?"

"Yes, Henry."

"I want to tell you something, just in case."

"You don't have to Henry."

"Yes, I do. I want to."

Joseph stood still and gave his friend his full attention.

"I know I haven't always been the best help to you, but I hope in some small way I have come to your aid."

"Henry..."

"Just a minute. In the past year, you have come to mean as much to me as Ryan means to you. If I had my life to do all over again, I would want a son like you. You, and Maura, have come to mean a great deal to me. I treasure our friendship, and whatever happens tonight, I don't mean to lose any of it. I will give my all for the family I feel we have become."

Joseph walked toward the older man and put one hand on Henry's shoulder and held out the other. Henry grabbed it, then pulled Joseph in for a hug. Then the two stepped back, each grabbing several weapons, and as Joseph yanked the leather thong out of his hair, setting it free, he followed Henry out the door.

Chapter Thirty

No soldier guarded the fort this night.

"Where do you suppose they are?"

"I would say they have decided that while the cat's away, the mice will play. But in this case, it may cost them their lives," Joseph noted.

He and Henry were watching the darkness beyond the gates for any signs of movement.

"When do you think they will be here?"

"Any time. They do not suspect that anyone knows what will happen, so they are probably in no hurry. They have all night. And under the cover of darkness none would realize who they were. Cole can get away with anything at this point."

"Except with us."

"Yes."

Six, dark-haired, buckskin-clad riders approached the fort with caution. Even though Cole had left trusted men on guard duty with instructions for them to distract the rest, he had learned long ago that anything could happen, and they must be wary.

He jumped down from his horse and walked up to the low wall. Slowly walking back and forth, he sought signs of movement, with only the moon and a few torches to illuminate the grounds. Seeing none, he motioned to the rest to follow.

As they began to cross the parade grounds, an unarmed soldier chose that unfortunate moment to exit the latrine. Melody Brock took aim and fired, the bullet hitting the man directly in the chest.

Cole turned and slapped her. "What the hell did you do that for? He was one of ours."

"So?" she questioned, smiling, as she wiped the blood from her mouth with the back of her hand.

The shot brought other men running from the barracks, some still pulling on pants or boots.

Someone yelled "Injuns!" and bullets began flying. Some of the soldiers were shot in the back by their own comrades who were in on Cole's escapades and loyal to him.

It didn't take long for the target group to be annihilated, and while some of his own men had been killed in the fray, Cole felt no remorse.

"They gave their lives so that this fort will go on. They knew what was at stake here."

Two Hawks began walking the grounds, rolling over bodies and searching for one face in particular. "I do not see Joseph. You told me he was here."

"I am here, Two Hawks."

Joseph stepped out of the shadows near the doctor's office. Henry followed close behind. Joseph had tried to keep the older man from coming with him, but his efforts proved fruitless.

"Hiding in the dark like a woman."

"Simply waiting until you finished killing your own. I see you have brought some friends."

Two Hawks shook his head. "I have no friends."

"What is it you want?"

"I came to see you dead." Two Hawks looked sideways at the group waiting to see what he would do. "They have other plans."

"I can't wait to find out what they are."

"You will not care what they are when you are no longer breathing. You have been like a stone in my moccasin for too long."

"Then I invite you to try to remove the stone, though I would point out, that sometimes what one has believed to be a stone turns out to be part of his own foot."

Joseph handed his rifle to Henry and stepped closer to Two Hawks who slipped a long, wicked looking blade from the beaded knife sheath tied at his waist.

"Do you use a knife to take a stone from your moccasin, Two Hawks?'

"No."

"Then put down your weapon."

Two Hawks replaced his knife in its sheath and stood opposite Joseph on the grounds.

Joseph stepped closer, holding his hands out at his sides. "Two Hawks, know this. I will willingly face death at your hands if you will answer my questions."

"I owe you nothing, but be quick."

"Why did you join these people? They are murderers of their own kind; their actions have only harmed our people."

"They want the same people dead that I do – especially you. I do not care what their purpose is. I know only that I can revenge what has been done to us by the whites."

"Revenge? How many whites have you killed? Five? Ten? At most a hundred? It will never be enough."

Joseph moved even closer, his eyes fusing with Two Hawks'. "Are you making them suffer a slow, agonizing death? Are you making them watch their children starve, or freeze to death? Are they forced to do as you say, dress as you say, eat what you give them? Are you taking their lands, raping their women, ripping their children from their homes and taking them so far away, they are the same as being dead?

"These are the punishments you would have to mete out in order to achieve 'revenge', Two Hawks. Can you tell me that is what you are doing? If you can, then kill me now."

Two Hawks stood rigid and watched the sky, as the morning sun began to reveal its first rays. It was some time until he spoke.

"It is true that I cannot rid our people of the whites. I have done what I could, but I have failed. I have heard what you said, and you speak the truth. If you die, He Who Walks Alone With Wild Horses, it will not be by my hand," and Two Hawks turned, walked back to his horse, mounted, then rode slowly toward the fort gates.

A shriek filled the air. "Are you just going to stand there, watching him go? Kill him or I will!"

"Melody, my dear, you are young. Some day, you will realize that some things are just not worth wasting your time doing."

But the judge's daughter hadn't learned that particular lesson yet.

Pulling a revolver out of its holster, she shot Two Hawks in the back. The Indian stopped his horse, looked back, and then slid in one fluid motion to the ground.

All eyes went to the woman.

"Melody, I will stop bringing you along on these forays if you insist on killing everyone in sight."

"James, I cannot believe that you would let him out of this fort. He knew too much."

"Who was he going to tell, Melody? Who would believe him?"

"I didn't think you cared whether he lived or died."

"I don't, but the point is, you cannot just shoot anything or anyone who moves just because you feel like it. It was endearing at first, but you'll soon be drawing too much attention."

"No one will miss him. And thanks to me, we can say that he was one of the ringleaders of the group, brought down by Captain James Cole. You'll get a promotion."

"I get my own promotions, thank you. In the meantime, put that gun away. That is an order."

"Yes, sir!" Melody struck a pose with her hand in a salute.

Cole grabbed her shirt and pulled her close enough that she could smell cigar tobacco on his breath. "Don't you ever, ever, mock the United States Army, do you hear me, Melody? You're beginning to irritate me and the more you do so, the more of Daddy's money and power it will take to keep you out of harm's way. Is what I'm saying getting through your thick, blonde skull, my dear?"

Cole pulled tighter and tighter as he spoke until Melody Brock's neck was bent painfully backward and the black wig that covered her thick, blonde mane, slid off her head, as fluidly as Two Hawks' body had from his horse.

Melody nodded her head as best she could under the circumstances, and Cole released her so suddenly her backside hit the ground before the captain could shout, "Walks Alone!"

Joseph and Henry had been staring in disbelief, as the events unfolded around them; immobile as if glued to the dirt under their feet like day-old molasses to a cold pot.

They both looked up when Cole said Joseph's name and walked toward them, pulling his wig off as he did.

"It's obvious you know who we are, so there's no reason to hide."

"What about the people living outside the gate? What if they come in?" Henry questioned.

"They won't. They learned what's good for them long ago. You two, on the other hand, now you pose a threat. Those people out there," he said, pointing toward the riverside dwellings, "are going to be very useful to us. When we leave, they'll see a band of Indians on horseback riding hell bent for leather away from here. As several minutes turn to an hour and they neither see nor hear anything coming from inside, they'll elect a brave soul to come in and investigate. And what will he find? One dead Indian brave, a butchered Indian school teacher and his hapless physician friend, a handful of murdered United States soldiers, and inside the stockade...tsk, tsk, tsk. What a shame that will be! My wife, dead in her cell and any others who dare to confront me dead as doornails as well. My, my! If only my men and I had been here, we might have prevented such an atrocity. But you see, we've been out since early yesterday morning investigating the previous attack. No one saw us come back last night, you see. Nor did they see us leave again.

"Only you could relate that story, Walks Alone, and if you were listening, I'm sure you realize that you won't be alive to tell it.

"Yes, this will be a very sad, sad day indeed."

Cole reached up and patted his shirt.

"Now, I'm almost ready to deal with you, but just give me a moment," he said, continuing to search for something. "I have a feeling I'll want to light up a cigar once you're gone, just a small celebration, you understand, but I don't seem to have one on me. I'll just be a moment.

"Melody, dear, be a good girl and keep an eye on these two, will you?"

Then addressing the two men, he said, "Now, remember, you've seen Melody in action, so I wouldn't turn my back on her if I were you. When I get back, we'll get down to business. Daylight is upon us."

As Cole walked past, Joseph reached into his own shirt pocket; and pulled out the two cigars he had lifted from the captain's quarters the day before.

"While we're waiting for you to get back," he said, handing one to Henry, then striking a match on the sole of his boot and lighting both with the same flame, "you won't mind if we have one final smoke, will you?"

Cole stopped and watched fascinated, as the smoke from the two cigars intertwined and rose into the air to disappear.

"Those are mine. I'd know that blend of tobacco anywhere. Where did you get them?"

"We counted coup," Henry said proudly, his cigar between his teeth as he spoke.

"Henry, you don't tell the enemy that you counted coup. If he's smart, he'll realize you've infiltrated his camp and caught him sadly off-guard."

"Oh, sorry," the older man said sheepishly.

"Infiltrated my camp? What the hell do you mean by that?"

"How can I make it clear? Your quarters, your office, your home..."

"You couldn't have possibly been in my quarters. I've locked the door myself. It's never been open."

"Well, I wouldn't say 'never'," said Joseph. "It may have come open, accidentally, of course, and we went inside, just to make sure that everything was in order."

"You were in my quarters? When? How dare you!"

"You have, or should I say, had, some very interesting items in your quarters, Cole. And they are so interesting, that I believe others will find them fascinating as well."

Sweat was beginning to form on the captain's brow.

"What are you talking about?"

"Oh, well, that painting on the wall behind your desk is a real work of art. I believe I saw the original in England. It was the subject matter that really brought it to my attention."

"You couldn't. You didn't!"

"We did. But don't worry, your documents are safe and sound. And do you know what? It was the document that was missing that most interested me. That's something I'd ask Judge Brock when he gets here, if I'm still alive that is."

"Daddy? Did he say Daddy is coming here? James, what are we going to do?"

"Shut up, Melody. He's bluffing."

Henry blew a large puff of smoke in Cole's direction. "He's telling the honest-to-God truth."

"How is Brock going to get here? You haven't had the opportunity to ride to Pierre and back."

"If you'll check your 'useful' population living along the river, you'll find that one resident is missing. I sent young Andy Riegel to bring the judge here immediately."

"How long ago was that?"

"Yesterday afternoon."

"He could be here anytime, James! We've got to get out of here!"

"He won't come. He knows the consequences of defying me."

The judge's daughter narrowed her eyes in confusion.

"What do you mean, consequences? My daddy's the most powerful man in Pierre, maybe even in the whole state. Why would he be threatened by you?"

Cole turned to the woman and snorted. "My dear, I told him that if he didn't do as I asked, I would marry you and take you so far away that he would never see you again."

"Oh, James! Married! I've been hoping but...."

"But it's not going to happen, Melody."

"But you just said...."

Cole took deep breath. "Why would I want to saddle myself with you – a vapid, self-centered, manipulative sycophant."

"Correct me if I'm wrong but isn't it redundant to call a sycophant, 'self-centered'?" Henry observed.

"I don't know what all that means, but it doesn't sound good!" Melody cried. "I thought you loved me. You gave me things... What about that silver compact that said, 'From a great admirer'? I thought you meant it, James."

"Melody, Melody. I picked that up out of the dirt after we attacked Maura and her friends. It belonged to her. Who gave it to her, I do not know – probably some sniveling fool. I gave it to you to stop your whining that you didn't have a memento from me. Does that make you happy?"

Tears streaming down her face gave those in attendance the impression that Miss Brock was not happy.

Joseph moved in.

"So it was you who attacked Maura's wagon." Then turning quickly, he said to Henry, "The blonde in Maura's photograph, must be Melody Brock. Is that possible?"

Henry nodded his assent. "Surely seems so, Joseph, but who would have thought it could be true?"

Returning his attention to Cole, Joseph asked point blank, "Did you know that Maura was in that wagon when you attacked it?"

The captain began to laugh and had a difficult time stopping.

"Did I know? Oh, my, Walks Alone, where have you been? I was beginning to believe you were too smart for me, but now, you've asked the most asinine question."

Cole collected himself and met Joseph eye to eye.

"Of course I knew. You are such a silly man, and I thought you had me all figured out. Ordinarily, I wouldn't bother, but since I'm going to kill you in a moment, I'll let you in on a thing or two.

"About 18 months ago, Coffey got word that Fort Sully was on the abandonment list. The Indian problems were pretty much taken care of and a full company of men wasn't needed anymore. I was horrified. Being an Indian yourself, you know that they're sly dogs and probably just waiting for the right moment to strike. I waited for that to happen, but when it didn't, I knew I had to do something to keep this fort here.

"I thought for a while, then this plan came to me. But I needed a victim – someone whose death would not be looked into. Then I remembered Maura. She had been the only person who ever spoke to me with anything but disdain. Though it rankled that she was younger and smarter than I was, I liked her more than anyone else at that children's home, though that's not saying much.

"I thought, what better victim could I find than an orphan? So I wrote to her with flowery words, begging her to come and marry me. I even insisted that she go through the proxy marriage because I knew it might come in handy somehow.

"I suggested places for her to stay along the trip, made arrangements for her transport; she never questioned a thing.

"I had instructed the freight driver to wait for Maura's arrival. I knew what I was looking for and the timing was perfect. A woman brutally raped and murdered by Indians on the way to her new home and adoring husband, is such an unspeakable tragedy. I knew it would pull at the heartstrings of Coffey's wife, and she would certainly put pressure on him to stay and protect other innocent women traveling through the territory.

"And I almost had them. I played the grieving husband-to-be, my wife torn from my arms before our life could even begin. So very sad, so in need of revenge. So very advantageous. But the bitch had the audacity to live! I couldn't believe it when Maura rode into the fort.

"It was all ruined when she came through that gate, and it's your fault, Walks Alone. If you hadn't stuck your nose into it, she would have died out there and everything would have been so much simpler. But no! You had to be the gallant and save the poor injured woman."

Shaking uncontrollably after what he had just heard, Joseph managed to speak.

"Please do not tell me that it was you who raped Maura? Tell me at least that it was one of these other men..."

"Yes, it was I. And that's an interesting point as well, because, now you know that Maura's son really is my son. I told you so, but you wouldn't take the hint. That's why I want him. He's flesh and bone. If it had been a girl, I wouldn't have been so covetous. But when I discovered from Melody here, that you'd been to her father's office with a white boy child – that changed my plan a bit. If her whelp had been red, I'd know she'd have lain with you, but since it was white, I was assured it was mine. No one around here would have touched her with her reputation.

"Now, I envision my son growing up under my tutelage, then going off to the military academy and when he comes back, he'll be just like me. A delightful thought, eh, Walks Alone?"

"You disgust me, Cole. That you could do that to Maura, to any woman, is absolutely diabolical."

"Yes, well, Maura is no one, Walks Alone. Kind of like you. Come to think of it, you two do make a good couple. Under other circumstances I might be offering my best wishes."

Melody piped up from behind the two men.

"James we have to get out of here. The others are already leaving."

Apparently not wishing to witness anymore, the other soldiers were making their way out of the fort and Melody began pulling on Cole's sleeve in an effort to follow.

"I can't be here like this when Daddy gets here."

Cole sneered. "Ah, yes, Daddy. We can't disappoint him, now, can we? He doesn't know his daughter is a lying back-stabber who enjoys killing people for sport.

"Which reminds me, I'll give you these two, Melody. I find I've become a bit bored with Walks Alone. And while you're dispatching them, I'll go take care of the others."

As Cole took a few steps toward the stockade, Joseph looked Miss Brock in the eyes and pointed out, "You know if he did that to Maura, he could do even worse to you, don't you? Don't let him ruin your life any more than he already has."

Cole stopped, turned and looked at the woman before him.

"Melody knows who butters her bread, don't you, my dear? Now get busy. Any other time these two would be cold by now, considering your impetuous nature."

He began moving toward the stockade, but stopped again suddenly and whirled to face Joseph. "Oh, my. I just had an intoxicating thought. I might even have Maura again before I kill her, just for old time's sake, what do you think about that, Walks Alone?"

Cole swiveled on the balls of his feet, and then continued his walk to the stockade. He was oblivious to the fact that several rifles, as well as two handguns were trained on him as he approached; ready to split his skull like an over-ripe pumpkin. The three women barricaded inside the building were not going to die willingly.

But from behind him a cry of rage split the air and the captain was struck full force in the back by Joseph's body. The two fell to the ground with Joseph the first to rise and, keeping a grip on Cole's left arm, slammed his fist solidly into the soldier's nose, feeling the bone shatter underneath.

"I think he finally got mad," Henry observed, readying himself to aid his friend.

Cole reacted by grabbing the back of Joseph's knee. He pulled and sent the Indian backward to the ground where they began wrestling for control.

"Melody, for God's sake, kill the bastard!" Cole yelled between punches.

A bullet spiraled from its warm, well-oiled chamber and entered Cole's side just below the shoulder blade. A second missed its mark when the captain wobbled sideways from the blow and turned from Joseph to look at his assailant.

"Idiot! You shot me! What have you done?"

"I'm killing the bastard, James. And that's you."

The wounded man tried to right himself, though his knees did not seem to want to support him.

"I'm a bit surprised, my dear."

"Imagine my surprise," Melody countered, "to learn that you never intended to marry me, that you were apparently using me for your own twisted game. I thought we were meant for each other. I thought we had so much in common."

"We do, Melody, we do," and suddenly it was Melody Brock who felt the searing heat of the missile Cole had set in motion from the handgun he had slipped unnoticed from its holster.

"Neither of us can be trusted."

The sentence was not the last sound the judge's daughter heard. Just before her head bounced on the ground, her ears caught the rattle of wooden wheels on packed earth and her prone body felt the pounding of hooves, before she breathed her last in the dust.

Chapter Thirty-one

The shiny black coach stopped near the base of the flagpole. The door was thrown open and out stepped Judge Brock. He looked from Joseph down to Cole, still holding the smoking gun. Tracing the line from Cole to his target, the judge gave a small cry and hurried over to the form.

"Melody! Melody!" he shouted, shaking the limp body of his daughter. When he received no response, he looked at Cole.

"You did this. The devil take you!"

The captain simply sat on the ground, holding his side, and nodded his head. "No doubt, he's on his way."

Looking to Joseph for answers, the judge continued to hold his daughter as he begged for details.

"What is...was, she doing here? She was supposed to be watching the boy in Pierre. And why is she dressed like this?"

While Henry knelt to examine Cole's wound, Joseph walked toward the judge and placed his hand on the grieving man's shoulder.

"I don't think you want to hear this story," Joseph began, but the judge looked up with tears streaming down his face and said, "I want to hear it all."

Joseph told the judge all he had known, and when he was through, he helped pick up the body of the older man's child and carried it to Cole's quarters, where he lay her on the bed.

Sunlight streamed through the window nearby, illuminating the blonde

226

head like a halo.

"It's ironic, isn't it? She has always looked so angelic, even more so now in death, but the devil has claimed her heart. I don't know what happened," Judge Brock lamented, shaking his head. "She was such a sweet child, good natured, perhaps a bit spoiled by her mother and me. Now...."

He let the sentence drift away and seemed to watch it go. When he had composed himself, he touched his daughter's hair again, smoothing some errant strands away from her face, then led Joseph outside.

Maura and her son had been waiting in the morning light and were immediately enfolded into Joseph's protective arms. They stood silently together, holding one another, and then the two adults shared a desperate kiss. When they parted, Maura would not let Joseph go, preferring to balance Ryan as she held on tightly to her husband's arm.

She explained that Cole had been taken to the infirmary next to the physician's office and that she and the other women had heard everything as it had transpired.

"I was so afraid, Joseph. Afraid more of being left without you than of being killed myself.

"I can barely believe what James had done, what that girl was capable of doing."

Joseph stopped the shiver that he felt running through her body by locking her in his arms once more.

"I want to see him." The judge's voice came from behind the couple. Joseph pointed the judge in the right direction, then gave Maura another hug before leading his family there himself.

As they entered, they could hear moans, then screams, coming from a bed at the far end of the room where several people were huddled.

Loretta and Marjorie were helping to hold Cole to the bed, as Henry poured a fluid over the hole in the captain's side.

"How is he, Henry?"

"Well, I believe this tops little Johnny Riegel's compound fracture as the most disgusting thing I've seen, but you know, this time I'm rather enjoying myself."

"How's that?"

"Well, the bullet passed right through him, so he's lucky enough there, but unfortunately," Henry said seriously, "He got some dirt in his wound, so I'm pouring alcohol over it to disinfect it. It seems to hurt him quite a bit, but I think that's a small price to pay to make sure he lives a long life behind bars. What do you think?"

Joseph grinned, as Henry returned to his task and Cole's screams filled the air.

"I think you're a very good doctor, Henry."

The older man looked up at Joseph. "Thank you, son."

Joseph turned his head as he heard others coming into the fort, but he took time to ask, "Henry?"

"Yes, Joseph?"

"Do you remember when you said you didn't have enough gumption to go face to face with Cole?"

Henry stopped what he was doing and thought a moment.

"Why yes, I do believe I do."

"I think you proved yourself wrong today."

And the older man smiled, then called for another bottle of alcohol.

Before Joseph could even make it halfway across the room, several men came through the door, preceding a familiar figure.

"Robert!"

The robust man with the full facial features and beard really didn't resemble his more famous father at all, but he was a well-known man in his own right.

"Joseph, my boy! I heard that there was some kind of trouble."

Robert Lincoln was immediately on the receiving end of a bear hug given by his foster son.

"I believe it to be over, now, Robert, but damn me if I'm not glad to see you. It's been too long. I had heard you'd come back from England."

Lincoln had not long ago finished a term as U.S. Minister to Great Britain, a post that had allowed his family, including Joseph, who had traveled overseas on a visit, to see much of Europe.

"Wait a moment. What are you doing here, Robert? How did you know there was a problem?"

Lincoln pointed to Judge Brock. "Peter here wired me in Chicago and told me you were in jeopardy. Since I frequently work with a railroad company, it wasn't hard to get here quickly."

Joseph looked intently at the man who had come from behind.

"How? Why?"

"In our dealings you had given me Robert's name as a reference." Brock clamped his hand on Lincoln's shoulder. "Robert and I have known each other for years. We attended Harvard together, and then met up again representing clients on opposite sides of a case in Chicago. We've remained in contact over the years, even while he was busy serving as Secretary of War, so I took the liberty of informing him of what was going on."

"I won't deny that we were threatened with several set-backs in our plans," and Joseph related Cole's treachery with Maura and in refusing to turn the fort over to him.

He continued, "But after what's happened here today, I've been assured by Judge Brock that everything will be straightened out personally, but perhaps you can assist in making certain that the army abandonment of the fort actually goes through."

"I still have contacts in the War Department, as you well know. I'm sure this won't be a problem. If we need new paperwork, I'll see that it gets done. I'll also get the wheels turning on Captain Cole's court martial. He could face execution for this, but even if the court is lenient, he won't be seeing the natural light of day for a very long time."

Joseph felt a warm hand touch the small of his back and turned to bring Maura and Ryan forward.

"Robert, I want you to meet my family."

The attorney smiled and looked at Joseph with a twinkle in his eye.

"My, you have been busy since we last spoke. A wife, and a child? Joseph, my boy, I always knew you were a fast worker."

Lincoln grabbed Maura's free hand and pulled her to him for a hug. "Welcome to the family, my dear."

Confusion reigned in Maura's mind and was quite evident on her face.

"Joseph, will you explain this to me?"

The Indian looked from his benefactor to his wife.

"I suppose I have neglected to relate this part of my life."

"I suppose you have," Maura agreed.

Lincoln raised his hand between the two. "He's a proud man, Maura. I hope you're prepared for that. I'm sure he wasn't trying to keep anything from you. He's just too pigheaded at times to admit his connection with me. I'm surprised that he let me help with the school, but when the opportunity arose to arrange for him to take over the fort, I thought the proximity to the reservations was too good to pass by. Knowing how some people are, I insisted he accept my help."

"But how did you meet?"

"That story begins when I was attending the Indian school," Joseph offered. "As part of the program, we were 'farmed' out to families. Most students were nothing more than slaves."

Joseph's eyes traveled from Maura to Robert.

"I was luckier, however. After I had been at the school several years, I was placed with the Lincoln family when they first arrived back in Washington. While I was expected to carry my share of the workload, it was never a burden I couldn't bear. I was treated with respect and encouraged to learn as much as I could so that I could bring the knowledge back home. I had dreamed of my own school for a long time, and ever since I told Robert about it, he has shared my dream and has helped to make it a reality."

"You really deserve the credit, though Joseph," and speaking to Maura Lincoln reported, "He's a fast learner, this one, and he's taken the tools that have been given to him and used them to make his own way. I may have pulled a few strings, but that's all I've done. With wise investments, he's made quite a little nest egg for himself and has financed all the school supplies himself. Don't sell your own role short, Joseph. You would see that this school exists with or without my help, and you know it."

Maura's eyes were brimming with unshed tears as she spoke.

"I am so glad that Joseph had someone like you, Mr. Lincoln. You are a great man, indeed."

Robert shook his head. "I don't know about that, Maura, but I've tried to remember the lessons of my father. He always treated his fellow man with compassion and respect and in doing so he gained theirs."

He looked out the window and it was several seconds before he spoke again.

"I saw pain in Joseph's eyes the first time we met, and I was determined to see it disappear. My wife and I worked very hard to make sure that Joseph felt welcome in our family; that he was a part of our family, and as far as I'm concerned he will always be family. And now you and your son will be as well."

"Maura is a teacher, too, Robert, and she will be helping with the school."

"I can see you two were made for each other. When this mess is behind you, you'd best get to work and make these stark buildings a welcoming place to bring children."

Joseph reached for Maura.

"We will. This will be a place for all of us to call 'home'."

"Yes," Maura agreed, and her husband smiled, realizing that little three-letter word meant the world to him.

Epilogue

One Year Later

Maura pressed her hand to the small of her back, as she stood in front of the blackboard. A classroom full of worried faces stared at her expectantly. She suddenly realized she had stopped speaking mid-sentence when the pain hit her back.

"This is all coming back to me now," she thought, sitting down in her chair with a thud.

"Close your books, class. You're dismissed."

Shouts of joy and the sound of running feet echoed off the classroom walls decorated with the familiar photographs of William Shakley. As her dark-haired students ran from the room to enter the bright autumn day, one little girl stopped beside the teacher and asked worriedly, "Are you all right, Mrs. Maura?"

"Yes, honey, I'm fine. Go on out and play now."

Taking a few deep breaths, Maura rose and made her way to the door. Looking around what was once an Army parade ground, Maura spied her husband playing a game with a group of children across the way. They were just some of those who now called the Long Rider School their home away from home.

A minute passed before she was able to catch Joseph's attention, and by then she was beginning to double over.

Joseph watched his wife and, reading her pain, crossed the grounds at a run.

"I think it's time," she panted.

"Really? I thought perhaps you were preparing your next science lesson by getting a closer look at that ant hill."

Maura was not in the mood for Joseph's brand of humor. Neither was she in such bad shape that she couldn't lash out with a hand, striking her husband lightly on the arm.

"Shut your smart mouth and take me home."

Joseph enfolded his wife in his supportive right arm and both moved slowly to the former commanding officer's quarters that were roomy enough for three, but might prove a bit cramped for four. In the year since the Army had left for good, Joseph had been renovating each of the buildings in the old fort, and had put the Walks Alone family quarters last on the priority list. Now he considered moving it up a notch.

Henry spied the two as they made their way and offered his assistance.

"Do you know any more about childbirth than you did the last time?" Maura asked irritably.

At Henry's sheepish grin, she said, "I didn't think so. Why don't you get your wife instead. At least she can stand the sight of blood."

"I'm already here, Maura." Loretta Pierce moved in between Joseph and his wife and took over, shoving the men out of the way, as they moved into the bedroom barking orders as she went. That included assigning them to the task of watching Ryan Walks Alone, who was by now a curious toddler interested in anything his parents were doing, as long as it centered on him.

"Momma!" he screamed, as he was dragged away from the room.

"It's all right, darlin'," Maura soothed. "Go with your father. When you come back, you'll get to see your new brother or sister."

"Henry will take you to your great-grandmother, Ryan. I am going to stay here with your mother," Joseph said, taking a seat on the bed next to his wife.

Joseph was grateful for the presence of his grandparents who had been talked into moving to the school. They were enjoying their role in helping to preserve the students' heritage by reinforcing the things the children had already learned from their families.

"No. I want you to go," Maura insisted.

"I was with you for Ryan's birth, I will be here for my second child's arrival."

"No."

"Maura, don't start this again."

"I said, no!"

"But you don't mean it, do you?"

"Yes, I..."

"That's better," he quickly interjected. "That's the word I like to hear," and an hour later, their second son greeted his father.

Printed in the United States
43270LVS00005BA/178-237